DEVIOUS MINDS

SHORT STORIES PACKED WITH SUSPENSE

VINEET VERMA

VINEET
VERMA

These stories are works of fiction. All the characters and events portrayed are fictitious. Similarities to real people, places, or events are coincidental.

Copyright 2021 Vineet Verma

Cover design by James, GoOnWrite.com

CONTENTS

THE STICK

A Detective Conley Mystery

W hen Samantha awoke, the first sensations of consciousness were unpleasant. Her mouth was dry, and her head was pounding. She opened her eyes for a split second, only to shut them tight again. The light aggravated the headache. She tried to pierce through the fog in her brain and recall the events of the previous night. There was a memory of meeting Cindy at Harry's, a bar they loved to frequent. Had she had too much to drink? Yes, that's what this felt like. Twenty-eight years old, and still repeating the same mistakes.

She realized she was naked. It could only mean one thing, and it added to her confusion. She opened her eyes again, working through the ache to keep them open this time. Her clothes were on the floor. She faintly remembered entering the apartment with someone. Kisses in the dark. Undressing. The warm embrace of a tall, ripped body. Ecstasy. Not wanting to change position and make the headache worse, she moved her left hand behind her to search the other side of the bed. It made contact with skin, and further probing confirmed it was a muscular arm. So, it was not a dream. But something felt off. Her curiosity got the better of her, and she turned over to face her mystery lover.

The scream was piercing and lasted a few seconds, ending when she fell off the bed in shock. There lay a naked body, face up. There was an addition, one that explained the reaction, and why the arm was so cold. A knife blade was sticking out of his chest. She slid back to the wall, sobbing, and sat there for a while with her knees drawn in.

Once she had calmed down, she mustered enough courage to walk over to the bed. She did not recognize the face. Or did she? What were they doing together? If only she could remember. Cindy was her best bet. Samantha called her best friend and coworker. Ten minutes later, the call ended. Things were a lot clearer now, though there were still some blank spots. But she knew what she had to do next.

Homicide Detective Paul Conley stepped out of his car and took a moment to scan the swanky apartment building in Old Town. It was his second day back at work with Wichita P.D. after a brief stint in California. Any hopes of easing into the job had been dashed, for here he was, investigating a murder, bright and early. The call had come in as he was seating himself for breakfast with Brigette. The aroma of the bacon and eggs that he had been deprived of still lingered in his nose. His stomach growled in protest.

As he approached the crime scene, he noted the impeccable job the patrol officers had done. They had taped off not only the second-floor apartment, but also the path leading up to it. The familiar face of Officer Davis greeted him at the boundary. Paul signed in and ascended the staircase.

The door to the apartment was open, with the techs dusting for prints. He stopped to examine the door without touching it. No signs of forced entry. He entered, and the first thing he noticed was the sobbing woman seated on the couch. Long blonde hair, attractive face, the beauty marred by the puffy eyes and pained expression. She had on a plain white shirt and blue jeans. Next to her sat a uniformed officer he had never seen before. Must be a rookie, he thought. He nodded to her and moved to the bedroom, where the body presented itself. This would have taken a lot of force, he mused, as he studied the knife inserted cleanly into the hefty torso.

"Morning, Paul," drawled Natalie from forensics. "Didn't know you were back."

"Wouldn't miss this for anything," he smiled back. "What do we have so far?"

"Instant death. Whoever did this knew what they were doing. Clean entry straight into the heart, no blood. Sometime between four a.m. and six a.m. We have prints on the knife. Checking for more from other parts of the apartment, but not sure if that will lead anywhere."

"Yeah, could be anybody who has been in here recently."

Paul returned to the living room and introduced himself to the officer and the witness.

"How are you doing, Samantha?"

"Okay, I guess," she replied with a sniffle.

"Can you tell me what happened?"

"I ... I don't know. I ... I woke up and there he was ... all dead."

"You were with him in bed all night?"

"I ... I guess so."

"You're not sure?"

"No. I was totally wasted. Don't remember much."

"So, you don't have any idea who did this? And when?"

"No."

"I noticed your clothes on the floor by your side of the bed. Was that what you were wearing last night?"

"Yes."

"And the clothes you have on now. Where did you get those?"

Samantha gave a confused look. "Um ... from my closet?"

"Did you touch anything else?"

"No. I called 911 as soon as I saw the body. Then I put these on and waited."

"That's good. Wouldn't want to disturb a crime scene. And what time was it you discovered it?"

"Oh. I don't remember. Around eight, I guess. When I woke up."

"Sounds about right. Dispatch received your call at eight seven a.m. What's his name?" Paul asked, indicating the bedroom.

"Alex. Alexander Khrushchev."

"And you knew him well?"

"No. Yesterday was the first time we met."

"I see. And where was this?"

"At Harry's Bar."

"Ah, Harry's. Love it. They make a mean martini. Now, tell me everything. What happened there. How the two of you got here."

"Um ... I was meeting my friend Cindy for drinks there. We were gossiping away when he walked over and started flirting with me. He was fun and so gorgeous. We hit it off right away. I don't recall much after that. Never knew when to stop drinking."

"So, you don't remember coming home with him?"

"Just very faint images. I do recall entering with him. I fumbled with the keys outside."

"I see. And did you find anything strange about the apartment?"

"Strange? Like what? I told you, I don't recall much until I woke up this morning."

"Do you remember how you got back from Harry's? It seems you weren't in a condition to drive."

"In his car. I didn't take mine since I knew I would be drinking."

"I see. So his car should still be here?"

"I guess. Should be in a visitor spot."

"Can you describe the car?"

"Red. It was red. A Honda, I think. Yes, definitely a Honda. Civic."

"We'll look for it. I assume you don't know what time you got back?"

"No."

"Do you recall getting intimate with him?"

"Kinda." Samantha's cheeks went pink as she replied. "I ... I don't usually do this kind of thing."

"Do you recognize the knife?"

"You mean if it's mine? No. Never seen it before."

"All right. We will have to keep this place sealed as a crime scene. You have someplace you can crash until then?"

"Oh. I can't stay here?"

"Nope."

"How long will you be here?"

"As long as it takes, but typically, for a case like this, I would estimate not more than a couple of days."

"I can go over to Cindy's. Just need to grab a few things first."

"Sorry, can't let you go in there or touch anything."

"But ..." She stopped on seeing Paul's unmoving face.

"Leave us your contact number and Cindy's address."

The officer noted the details. Samantha made a quick call to Cindy to notify her. And then she was off.

Paul donned his gloves and stepped back into the bedroom. He started with the walk-in closet. Chock-full of clothes. And shoes. Expensive stuff. He couldn't resist a smile. Brigette would have loved this collection.

He exited the closet and scanned the room again. Alex's discarded clothes lay on the floor – a dress shirt, blue jeans, briefs, and a leather bomber jacket. Brown Timberland boots under the bed. Paul picked up each item to confirm there was nothing else in there. He searched the pockets. No phone, no wallet. A key. Probably to his home. But no car key. Paul frowned. No way to verify the victim's identity or where he lived. Only the name Samantha had given him.

He stepped out of the apartment to canvass the neighbors. There were ten units on each floor. Forty minutes later, he had interviewed eight of the neighbors on the second floor. No one had seen or heard anything. One neighbor did not answer. He would get back to that one later. Three apartments in on the first floor, and still no luck. He knocked on the door of the one directly below Samantha's. It opened a crack to reveal a woman's questioning face. In her fifties, estimated Paul. He introduced himself and held up his badge.

"I'm Diane," she replied as she let him in.

Once settled on the couch, he explained why he was there.

"So that's what all the commotion's about," she said. "Never seen cops around here. It's a safe neighborhood. At least, it used to be." She paused for a few moments, then continued. "Last night, you say?"

"Yes."

"So it *was* her, then."

"What do you mean?"

"Well, I went to bed early last night, around nine. It was one of those exhausting days. Around two a.m., I woke up to some noise outside. It sounded like a man and a woman talking, and she was tittering away every few seconds. Drunk, I'm sure."

"Did you see who it was?"

"No. I stayed in bed. It was bad enough to be forced awake like that. I didn't have the motivation to get up."

"What happened next?"

"I tried to get back to sleep. But they just wouldn't let me. I heard them go up the stairs. Could hear her heels go clickety-clack. Then they took forever to open the door. And they slammed it shut."

"That's interesting. None of the neighbors reported hearing anything."

"You think I'm lying?" Diane narrowed her sparkling blue eyes as she said it.

"Sorry. That's not what I meant."

"No worries. I'm a light sleeper. Anyway. Thank goodness they're inside, I thought to myself. Now I might be able to sleep. But no. They just had to get some action, if you know what I mean."

"You could hear them?"

"Oh yes. The thing is, the walls between these apartments are well insulated. Can't hear much of what's going on with your next-door neighbors. But between floors, not as good."

"How long did this continue?"

"Not long, thankfully. I fell asleep after that."

"And what time was this?"

"I didn't check. Couldn't have been later than three, I'd guess."

"Anything after that?"

"I saw her this morning."

"You went to her apartment?"

"No. I was looking out the window and I saw her."

"What time was this?" asked Paul, trying to contain his excitement.

"Around seven thirty. First, she dumped a garbage bag in the community trash bin. Then she came out again with a black duffel bag and a laptop and put those in her car."

"And you're sure about this?"

Diane's eyes narrowed again. Paul threw in a question before she could protest the implied skepticism. "What color was the garbage bag?"

"Black. And it looked quite empty."

"I see. Did you see her again?"

"No."

"And how did she seem?"

"Nervous. Like she was in a hurry."

"How well do you know Samantha?"

"Not that well, actually. Other than some polite neighborly conversations. If my memory serves me right, she only moved in here a few months ago. Seems like a nice girl."

"Have you ever seen her with anyone? Any visitors?"

"No male visitors, if that's what you mean. She told me she was single. There's this woman who was here with her a couple of times. Probably a friend."

Cindy, thought Paul.

"Well, thank you, Diane. You have been most helpful. Do call me if you remember anything else," he said as he rose to leave and handed her his card.

Once outside, he wrapped up the remaining interviews. There was one neighbor who confirmed Diane's story about the late-night disturbance, but besides that, there was no new information. It was time to move on to the task he had been dreading.

Paul stood before the community dumpster, staring at it as if that would get the stench to back down. The painful memories of a previous dumpster dive were still fresh in his mind. He couldn't stand another ruined suit. Resigned, he hoisted himself up the wall of the bin and scanned the contents. To his relief, the few black bags in there stood out in a sea of white ones. And the black ones were bursting at the seams. Except for one. That would make his work easy. He carefully landed in the bin, grabbed his evidence and escaped before there was any damage done. He emptied the bag onto the ground. A wallet and a cell phone. Again, no car key. The wallet contained a twenty-dollar bill, a driver's license, and a credit card. "Alexander Dimitrovich Khrushchev" was the name on the card and the license. The phone was locked and would need some work.

He roamed the apartment complex parking lot, on the lookout for a red Civic. But there wasn't one. Had Samantha lied about this, too?

Paul spent the afternoon at his desk, writing up the case reports. He entered Harry's Bar just after 6:00 p.m., ensuring he was there before it got too crowded. Of the ten tables, only one was occupied. A man sat at the bar nursing his whiskey. Behind the bar stood the owner, Harry Belichick, breaking into a smile on seeing his regular walk in. Paul smiled back and walked up to him.

"The usual, Paul?"

"Man, I sure could use a martini, but this is a professional visit."

"Oh. What's wrong?" he asked, looking concerned.

"I have some questions about last night. New case I'm working on."

"Ask away. Anything I can do to help."

Paul held up his phone so Harry could see the picture. "Was she in here yester-day?"

"Sam? When isn't she here?" he replied with an amused expression before the concerned look returned. "Is she in some kind of trouble?"

"Perhaps. Sorry, I can't tell you much. So she was here last evening?"

"Yes. Sat there." Harry pointed to the table in the corner.

"Who was she with?"

"Her friend. Cindy. Another regular."

"No one else?"

"A man joined them a while later."

"What did he look like?"

"Tall. Caucasian. Well-built."

"Ever seen him before?"

"Nope."

"How did they seem?"

"Can't say. I wasn't watching them or anything. It was a busy night."

"What time did they leave?"

"Not sure. But Sam and the guy left first. She looked quite drunk. Cindy stayed until closing."

"And she was alone after they left?"

"Yes. I did see her making a couple of calls. But that's about it."

"I see."

"Speaking of Cindy ..." Harry's gaze moved past Paul.

Paul turned around to see a woman standing by the corner table, taking off her coat. She was about the same height as Samantha and just as attractive.

"That her?"

Harry nodded.

"Thanks, Harry. I have some questions for her."

"Sure. Say hi to Brigette."

"Will do. And I'll be back soon for that martini."

"Welcome any time, my friend."

Paul walked up to the table, introduced himself and settled into the chair across from Cindy. The hazel eyes didn't hide the fact that this intrusion was not welcome.

"Expecting someone?" he asked.

"No. Sam didn't want to come, so it's just me. She's still recovering from the shock."

"She's all alone at home?"

"You judging me? Thinking I'm some cold-hearted bitch who is out to have a good time while her friend wallows in misery?"

"That's not what I ..."

"Just so you know. I called in sick at work as soon as Sam called me this morning. Took care of her all day today. The only reason I stepped out is because she said she needed some space. Needed to be alone. Capiche?"

"That's not what I was implying, but I get it. Now, I have some questions about last night."

"Sure. Go ahead."

"I assume Samantha told you everything?"

"Yes, of course. Poor thing."

"Had you ever met Alex before?"

"No. Yesterday was the first time I knew he existed."

"For Samantha too?"

"First time for her as well. Seemed like a decent guy. Though I did warn her to call it a night."

"Warn her? Why?"

"I don't think taking a random stranger home is a good idea. For all you know, he could be a serial killer. Or a rapist. Or worse. Besides, she was drunk."

"What time did they leave?"

"I think it was around one a.m."

"And you stayed back?"

"Yes. Unlike Sam, I pace myself with the alcohol. I figured I could handle one more drink."

"Do you think she did it?"

"What? The murder? Samantha couldn't hurt a fly," Cindy replied. "Then again, one never knows these days. One minute someone's living a normal life, next minute they're shooting up people at the mall. Crazy times we live in."

"But you're close friends. Surely you know her very well?"

"We're close, yes. And we do spend a lot of time together. At work, after work. But can you really be sure you know someone's deepest, darkest secrets?"

"I guess not." For an instant, Paul considered asking her about Samantha's laptop and duffel bag but decided against it. It would be better to confront Samantha directly. "Anyway, that's all the questions I have for you. I do appreciate your talking to me. Call me if you remember anything else."

He stood up, waved goodbye to Harry, and exited the building.

The next morning, after a hearty breakfast, Paul drove over to the Oakview address on Alex's license. It was a run-down building. Alex rented a studio there. Paul used the key and entered. A whiff of pepperoni hit him, and his thoughts drifted to lunch for a few moments before returning to the scene before him. The apartment was empty except for a twin mattress on the carpeted floor. It had a navy blue fitted sheet on it. A matching comforter lay in a heap at the foot of the mattress. He scanned the small closet to the side. A couple of shirts, a pair of jeans, some socks and underwear.

He walked over to the kitchen and inspected the cabinets. Two unopened bottles of Smirnoff. A glass. Nothing else. In the sink were two dirty plates, two dirty spoons, and a glass. An empty pizza box lay next to the sink. He opened the fridge. Half a loaf of white bread and a half-full gallon jug of whole milk. Paul moved on to the bathroom. Only the basic necessities. He stepped out. This time he noticed a black adapter and cable plugged into an outlet. So Alex had a laptop. Where was it? He checked under the mattress, but there was nothing there. Disappointed, he left the studio.

Paul sat across from Lieutenant Matt Zigler, filling him in on case progress. It had been two days since the murder. They had been partners at one time, before Matt moved up the career ladder. He watched as Matt stuffed his face with one more chocolate doughnut. That was once Paul's specialty, until he had wised up and drilled himself back into shape. Yet, he felt a hint of temptation building up inside him.

"Thanks, but no duh-nuts for me," he replied as Zigler offered him one. "That stuff will kill ya."

"Duh-nuts. Funny. I get it. I must be stupid eating this stuff. You know what, bud? You only get one life. And what's life without this sweet goodness? Anyway, more for me. Now, what you got on this case?"

"The autopsy confirmed the time of death and cause of death. Now, this woman, Samantha. She's little. I didn't think she could have done it. Wouldn't have the physical strength. Plus, she was blind drunk. I verified it with folks at the bar. But the fingerprint analysis came back today. She was all over the knife."

"So, she's our man! Or woman."

"Perhaps. I also know she lied."

"How so?"

"She told me she woke up around eight a.m., saw him dead and called 911, all within minutes. But one of the neighbors I interviewed was positive she saw her up and about at seven thirty."

"Oh!"

Paul told him about the trash bag.

"Jackpot!" Matt said as he slammed his hand on the desk. "She killed him. Why else would she need to dump his stuff?"

"That's what I thought too. But why bother giving me his name? It was a one-night stand, after all. She could have claimed she didn't get his name."

"Playing it smart. Leave out too much, and it rouses suspicion. But if she cooperates a little, well, it's like she's on our side. Now, the car bit is interesting. You didn't find the key or the car. Did she just make it up?"

"That was my first thought too. But the DMV confirmed Alex had a red Civic registered. So, either the killer stole it, or Samantha is lying about coming home in it."

"My bet is, she's the killer, and she got rid of his car, just like she tried to dump his wallet and card. We need to find it."

"We've widened our search for it. Didn't find much at his apartment either." Paul related what he had discovered at the studio.

"Interesting. And his laptop was not at Samantha's?"

"No."

"Run a search on him?"

"I did. He'd been in the country two years now, and he lived alone. As far as I can tell, he has no family here. He came in on a student visa to study industrial engineering at Wichita State. But something's fishy there. He didn't attend any classes, though he's still enrolled."

"Interesting." Matt furrowed his brows to project a pensive look. "And the phone?"

"It's under analysis. There's more going on here than a simple one-night stand gone wrong. My guess is that these two had a history. I need search warrants. For Samantha's car and Cindy's apartment."

"Get an arrest warrant as well. We have sufficient probable cause."

"Our case will be stronger if I can establish without doubt that Samantha and Alex already knew each other. I should be able to verify that with their phone records."

"What about other prints in the apartment?"

"We found a couple, still working on those."

"All this could take time. Let's make the arrest. The search and phone records can happen in parallel."

"Sure, I'll get cracking on the warrants," Paul replied as he stood up to leave.

"And Paul ..."

"What?"

"I had to jump through a lot of hoops to get you back in Homicide. Don't let me down."

"You know you can count on me."

Once out of earshot, he muttered to himself, "No pressure, Paul. No pressure."

Cindy awoke to the sound of the coffee machine, surprised that Samantha was up before her. Perhaps Sam was finally feeling better. She got out of bed and walked over to the kitchen. Samantha gave a start on seeing Cindy and dropped the canister lid she was holding.

"Jesus, Cindy! You scared me. I didn't hear you coming."

"Sorry, dear. I guess that means I still got that stealthy cat-like walk," Cindy replied with a smile. "You're up early."

Samantha picked up the lid and placed it back on the canister. "Yes, I figured I should get back to work," she said as she handed a coffee mug to her friend. "I have a lot to catch up on."

"Ah, I was hoping you made some for me too." Cindy took a sip. "You sure you're ready? It's only been three days. I'm sure they wouldn't mind giving you a few more days off considering what you've been through."

"I think I'm ready. Besides, I need to work to get my mind off what happened. You know how I get when I have nothing to do."

"Yes. And what about the problem we were discussing last night? You sure you don't need my help? You'll be in big trouble if the cops find out."

"Don't worry about it. I have it under control."

"Alright. Go on then. I'll see you at the office."

Samantha stepped out of the apartment and breathed in the fresh morning air, glad to be getting back to her regular routine. She walked down the street and turned into the alley leading to her parked Porsche. A burly man approached in the distance. He seemed vaguely familiar, but she couldn't place him. Her polite smile morphed into wide-eyed horror as he grabbed her shoulders instead of walking past.

"Where is it?"

"Wh ... what?" she replied, trembling in fear.

"The stick. Where is it?"

Her heart sank as she realized what he wanted. And instantly she recalled where she had seen him before. So it hadn't been a dream. Her knees buckled with the memory of the knife in her hand.

He pushed her against the wall, his face close enough that she could feel the warmth of his breath.

"Where is it? In your bag?"

"Samantha!"

A voice rang out as the man reached for her laptop case. They turned to see who had spoken. Relief surged through her body. The man cursed and made one last attempt to wrest the bag from her before he admitted defeat and escaped. Even in that fearful state, she had maintained her iron grip.

⇉⇉ ⇇⇇

Back at Cindy's, Samantha calmed her nerves with a steaming mug of cocoa. Paul sat across from her, eagerly waiting for answers. Her friend looked on anxiously.

"What happened back there? Who was that guy?" he began once he concluded Samantha was stable.

"He was trying to rob me. Thankfully, you arrived in time, or he would have made off with my laptop."

"So, you don't know him?"

"No. Never seen him before." She took another sip. Paul wished he had some cocoa too.

"This laptop, is this the one you moved to your car before calling 911?"

Samantha's face froze, but her hands trembled just enough that the cocoa would have spilled if she hadn't steadied the mug in time.

"I ... I don't know what you mean. I told you before, I made the call immediately. Didn't go anywhere until the cops arrived."

"Then how come the laptop was in the car?"

"I left it there the previous night."

"I see. What about the duffel bag? Did you leave that in the car too?"

Cindy shifted uneasily. Samantha tightened her grip on the mug, her knuckles turning white.

"What bag? I don't know what you're talking about."

"It's the one you put in the car along with the laptop. After you dumped the trash."

This time her mouth opened in shock, but no words came out.

"I know about his phone and wallet."

"Oh!"

Paul could see this revelation had hit home. Time to turn on the pressure. "I have a warrant for your arrest. For Alex's murder. You would have been in jail by now if not for the incident this morning. So, if you want to make your case, this is your chance."

"I didn't do it. Please believe me." For the first time, there was a hint of desperation in her voice.

"What's in the bag?"

"I ... I ..."

"I find it hard to trust you about the murder, if you can't give me straight answers for the simple questions."

"Cash. Two hundred thousand in cash."

"Oh, Sam!" Cindy cut in, concern written all over her face.

Paul turned back to Samantha. "That's a lot of money. Where did you get it?"

"He ... he gave it to me."

"Who? Alex?"

"Yes."

"What for?"

"For information."

"What information?" Paul tried to keep his excitement in check. His heart would leap out of his chest at any moment, he thought. It made sense now, the expensive clothes and accessories, the Porsche. This is how she could afford it.

"I ... I work for LumioD. We handle defense contracts. Alex was a Russian agent. For the past year, I had been sharing confidential information with him for money."

So he was right. They did know each other before that night. But this espionage angle was unexpected.

"You got your money. Why kill him?" he asked in a casual tone. Perhaps she would slip up.

"I didn't kill him!"

"Then who did? You were the only one there when he died."

"I don't know," she replied as she broke into tears.

"Did you give Alex the information that night?"

"No. I was going to give it to him before he left in the morning."

"Is it on the laptop?"

"No. On a USB stick."

"And where is the stick now?"

"Oh." Samantha's eyes widened as if a thought had struck her. "I remember where I saw him."

"Saw who?"

"The man who attacked me today."

"Ah, so you remember him now? I thought you said you had never seen him before."

"I know, but it just came to me. You know how foggy my memory was that night."

"Very conveniently foggy. Anyway, go on."

"He wanted the stick. I saw him that night."

"Saw him where?"

"In my bedroom. He must have killed Alex."

"Then why were your prints on the knife?"

"Oh! I ... I ..."

"And how did he get in?"

"He must have broken in."

"No signs of a break-in anywhere."

"Oh. I must have forgotten to lock the door. I was wasted, remember?"

"Perhaps. Where's the stick now?"

"He took it."

"What else did he want from you?"

"Nothing."

"Then why was he trying to snatch your laptop?"

"I don't know."

"Don't know or don't want to tell?"

"I really don't know. It's my work laptop. Maybe he thought he could get some more data off of it."

"I see. How often did you meet Alex?"

"This was the first time."

"But you said ..."

"We did dead drops before. We would decide on a location via text. I would place the stick there and pick up the money he had left for me. It was strictly professional in the beginning. But around a month ago, the texts started getting personal. We just had to meet. So, we figured we could combine business with pleasure. I didn't know what he looked like until Harry's."

A fresh tear flowed down her face. She wiped it and glanced up at Paul. He stared back, processing what he had heard. To believe her or not to believe. That was the question.

"He was so sweet. There's no way I would kill him," she added for good measure.

"There's a lot of money involved here. How do I know you really cared for him? Perhaps you lured him into your apartment, so he would let down his guard. Then you stabbed him. You get to keep the dough and the information."

"Not true! And what about the man from this morning?"

"Yeah, what about him? What was his motive for killing Alex? He didn't take the stick. He didn't take the cash. You're making it all up."

"No, I'm not. He didn't take the stick that night, because he couldn't find it. I know he searched for it. The place was a mess."

"Didn't look messy to me."

"Because I cleaned up before placing the call. I didn't want anyone to suspect he was looking for something. At first, I panicked when I saw Alex dead. But then I realized I could get into trouble. I moved the money, the stick, and the laptop to the car. I trashed his phone and wallet to make it harder to trace him and find any prior connection to me."

"And yet you gave me his real name."

"It would be too suspicious if I gave you nothing."

"It's still suspicious. The fact is, your prints are on the murder weapon."

"Look at me. Do you seriously think I could push a knife through Alex's body like that? Besides, do I look so stupid that I wouldn't wipe the prints?"

"No, and no. But, all the evidence points in your direction. So, tell me, what time did you really wake up that morning?"

"I don't know. It was probably around seven."

"Much better. Now, you said you drove home in Alex's red Civic."

"Right. That's what I remember."

"And that it should have been in a visitor parking spot."

"Right. What are you getting at?"

"We didn't find a red Civic anywhere."

"Oh." The confusion on her face seemed genuine. Could fool anyone, thought Paul. She continued, "Then the killer must have taken it."

"And why would he ... or she do that?"

"I don't know. How else could it disappear?"

"I hope to find out soon. Now, here's what we're going to do. I'm going to take you down to the station. I have a couple of officers waiting outside. They'll come in and search this apartment and your car."

"Search the apartment? Do you have a warrant?" asked Cindy, alarmed.

"Yes, I do. And you'll have to step out while they're here."

He called his officers, briefing them once they arrived. The women protested as he arrested Samantha. A few minutes later they departed, Paul and Samantha to the station, and Cindy going no one knew where, as she grumbled about police heavy-handedness.

⇛⇛ ⇚⇚

Cindy laced up and stepped out of her apartment at 6:30 a.m., eager to squeeze a quick run into her busy schedule. She jogged a few laps through the charming streets of Old Town before entering Hyde Park. It was still early, and the usually bustling children's playground in the center of the park was deserted. There were a handful of runners like her out and about. She collapsed onto one of the benches, sweat streaming down her face. A young couple strolled past, hand in hand. Following close behind them was a hefty man. Without saying anything, he settled beside her. She casually fished out a USB stick from her pocket and placed it between them. Just as casually, he pocketed it. After a minute, he glanced at his watch and walked away. Another minute later, Cindy was relaxing against the back of the bench when a suit filled up the vacant spot next to her.

"Hello, Cindy," he said.

The voice was familiar, and she didn't need to see the face to know who it was. In an instant, she felt a sinking feeling in the pit of her stomach. She looked past him down the path and saw the first man being handcuffed.

"How did you get it, Cindy? I know Samantha didn't tell you."

"I knew it had to be in the apartment. So I searched everywhere after you took Sam away. Took me all day to find it."

"Where was it?"

"At the bottom of the sugar canister."

"How on earth did you think of looking there?"

"In all the years I've known Sam, I've never seen her use sugar. She considers it unhealthy. But when I walked into the kitchen that morning, the morning she was arrested, she was closing the canister. She gave a start when she saw me. I didn't think much of it at the time, but it got me thinking once I'd exhausted all my options."

"Funny business," Paul chuckled.

"What's so funny about it?"

"She didn't want us to search for the stick, so she told me Kurt had it. She thought she was safe with you. But when you started asking her about it, she got worried. She told me, so you wouldn't get your hands on it."

"Hmm ... wonder what aroused her suspicion. It's not like I didn't know what she had been up to. We discussed this stuff all the time."

"But never in so much detail. Never the specifics. That's where you messed up."

"If you knew where it was, why didn't you just come and get it yourself? I needn't have gone to all this trouble."

"We needed to know how much you actually knew and how deeply you were involved in this. This way we caught you in the act. With him. Besides, she didn't tell us exactly where it was hidden. Just that we needed to watch out for you."

Cindy sighed, her shoulders drooping. Paul read her the Miranda warning before cuffing her. It was all over.

Paul stepped in the front door to find Brigette looking stunning in a red cocktail dress. He feasted his eyes as he went up to her and kissed her on the lips. As he held his wife tight, he counted his blessings. Life was awesome with her back in it.

"Are we going somewhere?" he asked once he got his breath back.

"Maybe. But we begin by celebrating with a home-cooked dinner. You just wrapped up your first case after getting back."

"It's no big deal."

"Well, I think it is. Remember how we celebrated your first one in Homicide?"

"Oh yeah, can't forget that one. We went crazy, didn't we?"

"We sure did," she replied as she kissed him again.

An hour later, they lay on the floor, glowing with satisfaction. Brigette's head rested on his chest.

"So, it wasn't Samantha?" she asked, curious about the remaining details of the case she had been hearing about all week.

"No. She was telling the truth about the murder after all. Though, she'll get into plenty of trouble for espionage. We've notified Homeland Security."

"Who killed him, then?"

"It was the man who accosted her in the alley. Another spy. Kurt Woolsey. He works for the Chinese. He wanted the data she was supplying to the Russians."

"I don't get it. If he murdered the Russian, why didn't he get the data that night?"

"Couldn't find it. He tried to rouse Sam, to force her to tell him, but she was in no condition to answer. That's why he came after her in the alley."

"If this Kurt guy did it, why were her prints on the knife?"

"My wife, the detective," Paul replied with a smile.

"Living with you all these years has rubbed off on me."

"Why were her prints on the knife? Well, he wiped it clean and placed her hands on it while she was semi-conscious to implicate her. Sam told me she remembered having it in her hands. For a while, she was worried she had really done it."

"So, her friend Cindy, she didn't have anything to do with it?"

"Quite the opposite. Cindy is the one who fed Kurt with the information. You see, they both worked in the same department at LumioD, but had different levels of access. While Sam was supplying information to the Russians, Cindy supplied the Chinese. She tried to convince Sam to join her. The Chinese offered her a lot more than what the Russians were paying. But by then Sam was enchanted with Alex. She refused. Cindy was furious but didn't show it. Meeting for drinks that evening was Cindy's idea. She knew her friend was doing the drop. So she notified Kurt. She ensured Sam and Alex got drunk. Kurt followed them home to get the stick. He murdered Alex to get a rival out of the way."

"What an awful woman! Deceiving her friend like that. Didn't care if she was implicated for murder. I'm so glad you were able to figure it all out."

"Yeah. Though Samantha's no angel. She kinda deserved it."

"Yes, she did. What happens to Cindy?"

"She's in trouble with Homeland too."

"Good. What happened to the Civic?"

"Kurt drove off with it. He figured if the stick was not in the apartment, then it must be in Alex's car. He didn't want to risk a search in the parking lot. A secluded spot would work better. He burned the car once he was done to ensure there was no evidence of his presence. We found the remains out by Greenwich Elementary."

"He didn't search Samantha's car?"

"He wanted to, but it was already morning by the time he returned. Too risky."

"What about Alex's laptop?"

"It was in his car. Kurt took it home with him. We've handed it off to Homeland."

The house fell silent for a few seconds.

"Honey?" Paul broke the silence.

"Yes?"

"What's for dinner?"

"Your favorite."

"I'm starving."

"Why am I not surprised?" Brigette chuckled. Paul joined in.

"Let's eat," she said.

"Yes, let's do that."

AUTHOR'S NOTE

This is where it all started — my first short story. The basic idea had been camping in my head for a while — a woman wakes up to find a dead man next to her, with no memory of what happened. It's a common trope, but I was sure I had a compelling story to tell. At the time I was wrapping up *Barefoot in the Parking Lot*, and my mind only functioned in terms of novels. So I let it sit, like a lot of other ideas that were popping up. But I couldn't stop thinking about this one. The plot developed — there's a mystery man watching her, she's innocent, but I still didn't have anything for a full novel. It's only after I completed my novel that it occurred to me that I didn't have to limit myself to longer works. Short stories were a great alternative. It was so liberating, and soon things fell in place. I started writing, not knowing that the story would veer into spy territory. Writing the Detective Conley character in *Barefoot in the Parking Lot* was a delight, and this story allowed me to keep him going. And you finally got to meet lovely Brigette.

THE VISITOR

Can you risk letting him in?

RYAN

Three murders in as many weeks have rocked the tranquil community of Darwin. All three victims were women in their late twenties to early thirties. They were found naked in their homes, strangled with a rope. Ligature marks on their wrists and ankles indicate they had been bound for some time before they were killed. Given the similarity of the crimes, the current theory is that this is the work of a serial killer. He already has a name — The Darwin Strangler. Witnesses claim he's around six feet tall and has a beard. What's not clear is his motive. None of the women were sexually assaulted, and there were no signs of a robbery. The authorities are—

A relieved sigh escapes me when Ash turns off the TV. I've been struggling with my thriller, thanks to the background noise from the news. It's a shame, because the cold weather and howling winds create just the right atmosphere for a spine-tingling story. If it were up to me, I'd be curled up with the book in the study, but she insists we huddle together on the couch. "The couple that chills together, stays together." That's her motto.

Perhaps now that the TV's off, I'll be able to read further. They found the first body at the end of chapter three, so I'm dying to know what happens next. But Ash looks tense. I would be too if there was a serial killer on the loose and he was targeting my demographic.

"Now, now, don't get so nervous. We'll be fine as long as we're cautious."

"What makes you think I'm nervous?"

I turn my gaze to her bouncing knees. It's her nervous tic. She follows my eyes and smiles. *Ah, what a beauty!* And that smile enhances her appeal. I consider dropping the book and holding her instead, but she stands up before I can make my move.

"I'll get dinner started."

"What're you making?"

"Kale and salmon salad."

Damn! Not again! I hate kale. And I'm not into seafood either. I'd rather eat a steak or scarf down a cheeseburger, but she's been on this healthy eating journey for the past few months. I got caught in the wake. No point protesting, so I let her go and return to my book.

I'm deep into chapter eight when there's a knock on the door. Three rhythmic raps, to be precise. I wonder who it could be, for we aren't expecting company. My mind immediately jumps to the worst-case scenario. That's the downside of my obsession with thrillers. Before I can decide what to do, Ash is at the door.

"What do you think you're doing?" I ask.

"Opening the door," she replies with a puzzled look.

"What if it's him? I told you we need to be careful."

"Who?" A couple of seconds pass before she gets my drift. "The Darwin Strangler?"

"Yes. Who else?"

"You know, you worry too much."

Her hand's on the doorknob now.

"Wait!" I say as I leap off the couch and join her. "At least let's check who's out there first."

I look through the peephole, then step back.

"Damn!"

"What is it?" she asks, then peers through the peephole.

"Do you know this guy?" I ask, moving my hand on top of hers lest she open the door.

"No."

Realizing he might be able to hear us, I lower my voice to a whisper. "Then don't open it. He has a beard. Seems tall too. It must be The Strangler."

Taking my cue, she whispers back. "Or it's someone who needs our help. You know how cold it is out there. We should let him in. He looks innocent enough."

That's the problem with Ash. She's naive. Too trusting. It worries me.

"I bet that's what the other women said, too."

"What if he's genuinely in need? We can't leave him outside to suffer."

"First of all, we don't know if he needs help. Besides, he could always walk over to one of the neighbors."

"You're going to let a man in need stumble around in the cold and dark? And come to think of it, are you really going to assume every tall man with facial hair is a serial killer?"

"No, but it doesn't hurt to be careful."

"We don't even have to open the door. We can ask him what he needs from here. Then we can decide whether to let him in."

"And you think he'll tell the truth?"

"Why are you being so paranoid? It's not like anyone actually saw him do it. All the witnesses said is they saw someone tall and bearded in the vicinity around the time of the murders. That doesn't mean this guy's the killer." She's really riled up now. It's not the first time we have clashed like this, but we value our relationship enough to never let it escalate. Thankfully, she realizes she's overreacting and adopts a softer tone. "Okay, even if it is him, he wouldn't dare touch me with you around." Her hand moves to my bulging bicep, and she gazes at me with those seductive eyes. "You'll protect me, right?"

"Of course I will," I reply, my hands cradling her face, my eyes locked on hers. "Always."

She's the love of my life. I would do anything for her and she knows it. But she needs reassurance from time to time.

"Then we have nothing to fear," she says and opens the door before I can react. A frigid gust hits me hard as I brace myself for an attack, but all I see is a harmless, bearded man standing there, shivering. Unlike me, he's handsome and could easily pass for a movie star. We're around the same height, but I've got way more muscle on me. If it comes down to it, I'm confident I can tackle him. But under the circumstances, precautions are necessary. Something about this guy doesn't seem right — I can sense it.

"I'm sorry to trouble you good folk," he says as he glances at me and then at Ash. "My car broke down not far from here. I was hoping I could get some help. The weather's getting nasty as you can see."

"Sure, do come …" she starts saying but I cut in.

It's a relief he hasn't attacked us, but it doesn't mean he won't. Maybe he's just assessing the situation first. Or he's smart enough to get inside and wait for the door to close. Out here he risks being seen. I must go on the offensive. Catch him off guard. Keep him talking till he's lost in his lies and slips up.

"What do you drive?"

"Oh … uh … it's an Audi S4."

I shake my head. "If you'd just stuck with a trusty Honda. They never let you down."

"Well …"

"So you walked all the way here from your car?"

He nods.

"How far did you say?"

"About a mile."

"A mile, eh? Quite the trooper. You could have just called for help. Don't you have roadside assistance? Like AAA or something?"

"I do, but my cell's dead."

"Of course it is." I'm not buying his story. "There are three other houses around here. Why did you stop at ours?"

"Um …"

"I'll tell you why. There are no women at the Turner house — just ol' Turner. The Wades have women, but they're either too old or too young. Amanda Lee's around thirty, but I guess you only love white skin, right?"

"Ryan!" Ash is clearly unhappy with me, but I'll deal with that later. She should be thankful I haven't slammed the door in his face yet.

"I have no clue what you're talking about. I just walked up to the first house that had a light on."

"What have you got in that bag of yours?" I ask, pointing to his backpack. He can't throw me off with his innocent act.

"Just my laptop and a change of clothes."

"Ryan, why are we torturing ourselves out here in the cold? Shall we move inside?" Ash cuts in before I can interrogate him further.

He pounces on the opportunity and steps forward, extending his hand to me. "Thank you. I'm Justin."

"Ryan," I reply. My hands stay in my pockets.

"Gosling or Reynolds?" he asks with a grin.

Ash giggles.

"Neither. Just Simmons." If lame jokes could kill, this guy wouldn't need any rope.

"Ashley," she says as they shake hands.

I'm not happy with him inside my house. This is the time to call his bluff. I hand him my phone. "You can call AAA."

He hesitates for a moment before taking it and placing the call. Minutes pass.

"They're quite backed up tonight," he says once he's done. "It'll be two hours before they can get here."

"No worries. You can wait here," says Ash.

He returns my phone and we head to the couch.

"Are you from around here?" I ask once we're all seated, alert to any movement on his part.

"No. Just passing through."

"Where do you live?"

"Benton."

"That's a long way from home. Where are you headed?"

"Honey, are you going to grill him all night?" Ash again.

"I'm not grilling him, Ash. Just getting to know our new friend here. I'm sure he doesn't mind." I turn to Justin. "Do you?"

"No, no. Not at all. You've been so kind to take me in."

"See?" I say to her. She's not amused.

I turn back to him. "So, where were you headed?"

"Um ... Ridgecrest."

"Pleasure trip?"

"Yes. You could say that."

"Planning to stay there long?"

"No. Just a night."

"You pass through here often?"

"No. My first time around these parts."

His hand moves towards his jeans pocket. My body stiffens, trying to guess what kind of weapon he has there and how I should react. But all he comes out with is a white handkerchief. *Do guys even carry those anymore?* I don't. He mops his forehead with it.

"If I were to search your backpack, I wouldn't find a rope, would I?"

"Ryan!" Sometimes I wish Ash would just mind her own business.

"What? No harm asking."

"It's okay," Justin says to her with a wave of his hand. Turning back to me, he smiles. "You worried I'm The Darwin Strangler?"

Well, well, well. Interesting move.

"Ah, so you've heard of our local tale of terror," I say, pausing for effect before I continue. "Even though it's your first time here?"

He remains calm. "Yes. It's been in the news in Benton."

"Wow, I didn't know our little town's famous."

"Well, it is. This is the kind of stuff that gets people excited in little towns like ours. But you don't have to worry about me. I don't have a rope."

"Sounds exactly like something The Strangler would say."

"Oh, enough! I'm off to continue with dinner." Ash glares at me as she stands up. "Justin, you'll join us for dinner? I'm sure you must be starving."

"Yes, thank you."

"Great!"

"You know, if anything, I should be worried about you," Justin says once she's disappeared into the kitchen.

"Me? Why?"

"I see a rope back there." He's pointing to the floor near the garage door.

"Ah, that. Ash asked me to get it. Some craft project she's been working on."

"Sounds like something The Strangler would say." A sly smile appears on this face.

"You have some nerve, accusing me like that. After we've been nice enough to offer you shelter. And a meal."

"Peace out, guys. Dinner's ready," Ash says, motioning us towards the dinner table.

If it were up to me, I would throw his sorry ass to the curb right now. Certainly not in the mood to dine with this guy. But I do as she asks. It's annoying that he's sporting a hint of a smile. *Is he enjoying seeing me upset? Or is it something more sinister?* I must remain cautious. Continue to watch his every move.

"Salmon and kale salad," Ash announces as we join her.

"Ah, my favorite." Justin's face lights up.

"I wish I could say the same," I add, reaching for the wine bottle. It's the only thing that will get me through this meal. Apparently red wine has antioxidants so it's on Ash's yay list. I'm not permitted to have beer or whiskey anymore, though. But alcohol is alcohol, so I'm not complaining. Besides, I manage to down a few beers with the guys at work. What she doesn't know won't hurt her.

Justin raises his plate as Ash doles out the salad. I imagine he could smash that plate on my head. When he picks up his fork to eat, I wonder whether he'll try to stab me with it. The wine bottle is out of his reach. It would make a handy — and deadly weapon. For that matter, the wine glass too, but I can only watch as he raises it to his lips. And who knows, he may be carrying other weapons on him. Another unknown to worry about. Other than the rope, no weapons were used in any of the murders, but that's probably because he didn't face any resistance there. Tonight, he has me to deal with. Hopefully, I've intimidated him enough and he won't make a move. Maybe it's just a recon mission? To size us up before he returns to attack Ash another day?

"By the way, I wasn't accusing you of being The Strangler. It could be her, too," Justin says, pointing to her.

They laugh. Their eyes meet. Seeing those two beautiful faces, I feel like the odd one out. The ugly runt. I often wonder what she saw in me all those years ago. With her looks she could have had anybody, but she settled for me. Is she attracted to Justin? *Nah!* She adores me. Always has. In the seven years we've been together, she's been faithful to me. I doubt that's going to change now. *Why did that thought even enter my head?* It's probably the wine.

I realize now I came on too strong with Justin. Perhaps Ash is right that I'm being paranoid and this guy's just an innocent traveler. But some more thinking leaves me unconvinced. It's no surprise a seasoned killer like him handled my questions so well. My aggressiveness didn't help either, for it made him extra cautious. It's time for a different approach. Perhaps he will slip up if I get him to relax a bit.

"You think she's strong enough to strangle someone?" I ask him.

"She doesn't look it, I agree. But appearances can be deceptive, my friend."

"True. True." I pause a few seconds, weighing my options. "Do you like to read, Justin?"

"Read? No, can't say I do."

"Well, I do. I started this great thriller earlier this morning, one of those books you don't want to put down. But guess what?"

"What?"

"Ash has been after me to install a pool in the backyard. So she forced me to start digging."

"Sounds like a lot of work."

"It is."

"All done?"

"No. So far I've only got a square, six feet by six feet."

"How deep?"

"Only three feet so far."

"Good enough."

I scoff. "For a kiddie pool, perhaps. Not even close if the two of us want to splash around in there."

He shrugs. "I guess."

"But that's the kind of stuff you put up with once you're married, right?"

"I wouldn't know."

"Sorry. I assumed you were married. A girlfriend, then?"

"Yes. You could say that."

"Great! You gonna pop the question any time soon?"

He breaks into a smile. The first genuine smile I've seen on his face. I feel I'm making some headway here.

"If all goes as planned, yes."

"Wow, so exciting!" Ash says with clasped hands. Weddings are her thing. I bet she's already imagining what kind of ring Justin will buy, what the bride will wear on the special day, and at what romantic destination they will exchange their vows. As if on cue, she touches her engagement ring and admires it. It's a five-carat solitaire that she arm-twisted me into purchasing. My initial proposal with a one-carat hadn't gone down well. Ash is perfect, well almost, except for this obsession with the expensive stuff. I caved in then, but I've held firm ever since. Having grown up poor, I know what it's like to worry about money. I don't want either of us to experience that again. This is the time to secure our financial future, not the time to fritter away our riches.

The rest of the meal continues peacefully, with Ash giving Justin ideas for destination weddings. I'm not kidding when I say she probably covered every damn beach around the world. When we're done eating, she stands and picks up a couple of plates.

"Honey, can you help me clear the table?" she asks.

"Sure dear," I reply as I grab the remaining utensils and head into the kitchen after her. She glances at me as I enter, and that angelic face floors me. Dripping with lust, I pull her close and we lock lips. She tastes sweet, like the strawberry lip gloss she loves. The kiss lasts five seconds before she turns away with a naughty smile and a wink. "Later," she whispers.

I step out of the kitchen, beaming like a teenager who's just gone to first base for the first time. Something hard connects with my head, and I drop to the floor on my knees, stunned. *No! No! No! This can't be happening!* My head's swimming, but I try to focus. Now that this monster has attacked me, Ash will be next. I promised her I would protect her, and what am I if I can't keep my promises. It takes all the effort I can muster, but I lunge and yank his legs, pulling his feet off the floor. When his head hits the floor, I'm not surprised it's Justin.

"I knew it, you evil bastard," I growl as I move on top of him and grip his throat with both hands. It's a thrill, squeezing the life out of him, witnessing the terror in his eyes. But his dread fades, and before I can process the change, a sharp ache sears through my midsection. I scream in agony and look down. There's a knife sticking out of my belly. My grip slackens, and he takes the opportunity to pull the knife out and slash my throat. I collapse, weak and helpless, my life draining away.

"Ashley ... Ashley ..."

Those are the last words I utter before I black out.

ASHLEY

P anic. It surges through me when I hear the scream. My body went stiff when I heard them scuffle. But this scream is so primal, so unexpected, that it's overwhelming. I don't have the courage to step out just yet. By the time I calm down with a few deep breaths, there's an eerie silence. It's over. I'm sure of it.

My heart's leaping out of my chest as I inch out of the kitchen to witness the scene. Blood. Everywhere. Justin's sitting propped up by the wall, a bloody knife in his hands. Ryan's prone on the floor, unmoving. It's really done. I can't believe it. He always told me how naive and trusting I was. Little did he know that the same could be said about him. He had no idea that when Justin mentioned his girlfriend, he was referring to me. We practically planned our wedding in front of his eyes, and he was clueless about what was going on.

"You idiot! I told you I wanted it clean," I say.

"It ... it all happened so fast. I had to use the knife. He left me with no choice." I've known Justin almost a year now, but it's the first time I've seen him so unsettled.

"Because you were clumsy. I warned you he's strong. Warned you not to touch the wine so you'd have the edge. All you had to do was knock him out and strangle him with the rope I got you."

"I'm sorry. But you didn't tell me he was such a jerk. Grilling me from the get-go. I got nervous. You said he was a docile guy." He stands up, the knife still in his hands. "And why couldn't we keep it simple and just poison him like I suggested?"

"You know why. If they ever find the body and figure out he was poisoned, guess who they'll suspect first?"

"And you think they won't suspect you when they find him in your backyard?"

He's got a point there, but I have some great comebacks. I resist the urge to engage, for we have work to do. Instead, I respond, "Never mind. What's done is done. No point bickering about it."

Then I remember something.

"Crap!"

"What?" he asks.

"AAA. They'll be here any minute."

A devilish grin lights up his face. "You really think I'm that stupid? I called my pal, not AAA. Just faked the whole thing."

"Well, that's a relief. But you're lucky Ryan didn't check what number you dialed."

He shrugs. "Oh, well."

"Anyway, let's clean up this mess."

First we move Ryan to the hole he dug in the backyard earlier today. He had no idea he was literally digging his own grave. The next few hours are spent cleaning up inside the house. I'm exhausted by the time we're done. We shower together to wash off the blood. And in my case, the guilt.

Yes, as unbelievable as it may sound, I do feel a bit guilty. Ryan is — was — a nice guy. He genuinely cared about me. When he said he would do anything for me, he meant it. Except when it came to money matters. I never got that. Having grown up poor, too, I know what it's like to struggle for basic necessities. To crave, and not have the means to fulfill those desires. So if I have the money, I want to spend it, to get what I want and never experience that deprivation again. And what I've wanted is designer clothes, classy jewelry, luxury cars — all the good stuff. But he wouldn't let me have it. Then I met Justin, with his drop-dead looks and easygoing attitude. He has money, but nowhere near what Ryan has. I risked losing everything if I left Ryan. So what's a girl to do?

The hot droplets help me relax and purge myself of thoughts of the dead. Watching Justin so close under the water, I'm confident I can spend the rest of my life with him, in spite of all our tiffs and disagreements. He turns off the shower and we dry ourselves off, crashing into bed soon after. I want him, want his hands on me, want to feel his lips on my body, but sleep overpowers me. One goodnight kiss and I'm out like a light.

The next morning, I wake up to see Justin lying next to me. I smile. We have finally spent an entire night together, and that's something, though there was no sex. No more hurried encounters at the local motel, no more rushing to get home before Ryan. It sounds terrific, but I know it's not going to be easy. With Ryan buried in the backyard, he will be considered a missing person. Not a dead one. Which means I will have to wait to access all the money. I will have to wait for the life insurance payout. More importantly, I can't be seen with Justin right away. I wanted a cleaner approach, to dump Ryan's body where it would be found easily, but Justin considered it risky. It would require a lot more planning to pull that off, and he was impatient to get Ryan out of the way. But it's okay. Between Justin and me, we have enough money to play with for a while.

He opens his eyes. There's that irresistible smile. My lips are on his in a flash. We move on with the unfinished business from the previous night and don't stop until I'm moaning in ecstasy. He collapses by my side. We lay there for a couple of seconds, our faces glowing with satisfaction and excitement for our lives together. That's when I notice the man standing in the corner, and I let out a shriek. I cover myself and sit up in bed. Justin does the same. The man has a gun pointed at us. He's tall. He has a beard. All of a sudden, I'm cold and sweaty.

"Now, I'm sure you're smart folks, and you know I don't want to use this," he says, indicating the gun. "So, don't force me to pull the trigger."

"What ... what do you want?" I ask, but I already know by the time I complete the question. For it's only now that I notice the rope spooled over his shoulder.

"What do you think?" he asks with a grin. "First time I'm doing a twofer. I must say, I do appreciate you helping me out by shedding your clothes in advance. Oh, and thanks for the extra rope, too."

He tosses me some rope. "Tie his hands and legs."

I hesitate, but another glance at the gun convinces me I have no choice. Justin's eyes are glued to the gun as well. With Ryan he had the element of surprise. But here, there's no way he can reach the man without getting shot. Like me, he knows we are doomed. I do as ordered. Once done, I want to ask the man why he does what he does, but it's as if he read my mind.

"Sinners, all of you. Bloody sinners!" he says as he ties my hands and legs.

I have my answer, and he's probably right. I do deserve this for what I did to Ryan. But does this mean this guy's been watching me? For a moment, I'm curious what sins the other women committed. But there's no time for those thoughts, for the monster forces me to watch as he pulls the rope around Justin's neck and executes him. I want to throw up. Tears overflow my eyes and stream down my face. The bright future I saw for us earlier this morning has been extinguished. I plead with the man. Beg for my life, but he doesn't budge. He gets on top of me and strokes my head.

"Now, now, easy, easy. I'll be gentle, I promise."

He sounds so calm, as if he's just putting a baby to sleep. The rope wraps around my neck, the pressure gradually increasing. I close my eyes, accepting my fate. My only regret is I'm leaving this world the same way I entered it — without a shred of clothing on my body. What a shame, for I had always imagined I would breathe my last in a burgundy Dior dress and matching Jimmy Choos, with Cartier bling adorning my neck and wrists.

AUTHOR'S NOTE

A stranger shows up at your door asking for help. Do you trust him enough to let him in? It started with this simple idea. It's a plot I have enjoyed before — most notably in the Bollywood movie *Kaun?* Confident that I had a winner here, I started writing it in third person, but it all felt flat. Disappointed, I slept on it. The next day I got a brainwave and I rewrote the draft in first person. That brought the story to life. And adding those twists was a blast! For the title I paid homage to another great movie (though there's absolutely no relation between the plots or genres), *The Visitor*, starring the fabulous Richard Jenkins and Hiam Abbass. Do watch it if you haven't.

FOOL ME TWICE

A Detective Lansbury mystery

He's lying on the grass, motionless, his white suit contrasting with the squalid background. One would think he's sleeping, but the grotesque expression on his face and the red patch on his belly tell a different story. Amber from forensics is squatting next to the body.

"What do you make of it?" I ask her.

"He's been dead at least a day. Stabbed."

"Murder weapon?"

"None found. The wound suggests a knife."

"Any signs of a struggle?"

"Not that I can tell. He went down easy."

I lower myself to take a look, wincing as I do so.

"Still sore?" she asks.

I nod. It's the full marathon I ran on Sunday. My first one. Six months of intense training. Four hours of non-stop running. Exhilaration at the finish line. Now two days of aching legs. Thankfully, homicide detectives don't have to run much on the job.

"I'm proud of you, Arthur."

"Thanks," I reply as I admire her gorgeous face. The flaming red hair isn't visible under her protective suit, but she's still stunning. The only one who gets my heart racing since Ruth. One of these days I'll muster the courage to ask her out, but this is neither the time nor the place.

We're at the homeless camp at the intersection of Oakland Road and Highway 101. Usually it's quite dark here, especially on nights like this one where there's only a sliver of moon, but tonight it's aglow with the lights set up for the investigation. Officer Garcia has strung yellow tape all around and is managing the scene. The body's at one end of the camp. A couple of worn tents and an overflowing shopping cart are at the other. Officer Mendez is standing between the tents with a homeless man, probably the one who found the body and called it in.

I don my gloves and search the corpse. A lot of pockets, but most turn up empty. His trouser pocket has a key which seems to be for his apartment. No car key. No wallet. No cell phone. Did he lose his life trying to resist a robbery? Scanning the area around the body, I find a black notebook. There's a name and address in there. Nathan Sandler from San Jose. If it's the killer's, I'm a lucky man.

Should I hit the slots in Vegas this weekend? The notebook goes into my evidence bag. Finding nothing else of importance, I comb the rest of the camp for more clues. There's a variety of items lying in the grass, not surprising for a place like this. Mostly trash. Figuring out what's relevant to the case is anybody's guess. I spend some time perusing these treasures and trundle over to Mendez once I am done.

"Wade. Victor Wade," the man standing next to Mendez introduces himself. The words roll off his tongue like he's a famous spy, but his appearance is nothing like that. He has long hair falling to his neck and facial hair that obscures his features but blends in with the grime.

"I'm Detective Lansbury with SJPD. You found the body?"

"Yes."

"Tell me everything."

"Sure, man," he begins, with a nasal twang. "I got home earlier and decided to take a stroll. That's when I saw him. Freaked me out good, I'm telling ya. So I went over to the gas station and called 911."

"Thanks for reporting it. Now, did you touch the body or anything around it?"

"No, man. Didn't go anywhere near it. Could tell he was done for."

"How so?"

"The blood, man," he replies, placing a hand on his belly. "He wasn't movin'. Wasn't breathin'."

"Did you see anything suspicious?"

"Nah. Nuthin'."

"Where were you all evening?"

"Here and there."

"And last night?" He should have seen something if the man's been dead a day.

"I was here. Got here later than I did tonight."

"And what did you do when you got here yesterday?"

"Crashed, man. Sooo tired."

"You didn't see the body?"

"Yesterday? Nooope," he replies, stretching out the last bit. "I'd have reported it right away if I did."

"Are you sure the body wasn't there?"

"No, man. I didn't look there. Like I said, I just got here and crashed."

"And this morning?"

"I left early. Couldn't find my buddies, Barry and Justin."

"What do you mean?"

"You see, I live here with them. They didn't come home last night. I was worried when they weren't here this morning either. So I went looking for 'em."

"When was the last time you saw them?"

"Yesterday mornin'."

"Do they have any stuff here?"

"Barry travels light. But Justin, he had things, man. It's all gone."

"I assume you didn't find them?" I ask.

"No, man. I'm worried."

"You think they could have something to do with this? Quite a coincidence they went missing around the same time."

"Dunno, man. They're decent folk. Can't see them taking a life. But you never know, right?"

"Right. Let's hope they turn up soon. Call me if you see either of them."

Once done with Victor, I spend the next thirty minutes searching the tents and the cart. There's a lot of odds and ends crammed into the small space. It's as if they've been collecting whatever they can get their hands on in the hope that it will be useful someday. None of it helps my investigation. I sigh. It's going to be a long night, but it's not like I have anything to go home to. No Ruth waiting for me like the old days.

There's a gas station and a fast-food joint next to the camp. I visit the gas station convenience store first. There's only one customer in there, and the guy at the counter is busy ogling her. He turns his attention to me once I walk up. He listens intently as I explain everything, but the vic's description doesn't ring a bell. I ask for the surveillance video. By this time the object of his desire is ready to pay for the bag of Cheetos and the Häagen-Dazs. He flashes her his best smile and processes the purchase. A final gaze as she walks away. We get back to the video. A few minutes later I have a copy which I will review later.

Next stop is at the fast-food place. It's one of those twenty-four-hour business-es, so it's still open. There's a girl behind the counter, early twenties, I estimate.

She's staring vacantly into space, not surprising considering the place is empty. Her face lights up when she sees me, and she's fully engaged once she hears why I'm there. It doesn't help, though, since she doesn't recall seeing the vic either. Even worse, she's clueless about the surveillance system. I'll have to come back later.

It's too late to canvass the neighborhood. It will have to wait until morning. Which means now I have to tackle a task that I dread. I've been in the force for years, but notifying the next of kin never gets easy. First, I have to confirm the victim's identity. I do an online search for "Nathan Sandler." Too many of those out there. Refining it to "Nathan Sandler San Jose" works a lot better. This time I find a link to Sandler's Facebook page. My Sandler. The smiling face in the profile picture belongs to the man who's lying dead a few feet away from me. He's with a woman in the selfie. She's beaming too. Some more browsing confirms she's his wife. Debbie Sandler. No kids, thankfully.

I drive over to the address I found in the notebook. It's in downtown, a couple of blocks from San Jose State University. The sign outside says "Paradise Apartments," but the place doesn't live up to its name. Even in the darkness I can tell that the property is not maintained well. The vic's apartment is on the first floor. I take a deep breath and knock. No response. I knock a second time. This time I hear movement inside. Debbie opens the door, a cautious look on her face. She's just like in the selfie, except her eyes are red and puffy, and her blonde hair's a mess. Does she know why I'm here? Introducing myself, I show her my badge. Her lips quiver.

"Is this Nathan Sandler's residence?"

"Yes. But he's not here."

"And you are ...?"

"His wife, Debbie."

"May I come in?"

She nods and walks me past a tiny kitchen with dated appliances into a sparsely furnished living room with worn carpet. The area is lit with a single floor lamp, not bright enough for my liking. There's a box of Kleenex on the coffee table and a cluster of used tissues on the floor. The couch she directs me to has seen better days. She settles into the chair opposite. On the wall to my right are three framed photographs of a radiant couple. Debbie and the man in the white suit.

"Have you ... have you found him?" she asks.

Whatever I might have gleaned from her face, I did not expect this question.

"Found who?"

"Nathan. That's why you're here, right?"

Then I get it. Of course, she knows something is wrong. If the man died the previous night, she's been missing him since.

"He didn't come home last night. That's why I reported him missing." *Shucks! Should have checked up on this.*

"We did find a man. We ... we think it's Nathan."

Her hand goes up to her mouth in shock, her eyes flooded with pain.

"But we aren't sure it's him since there was no identification on the body. Is that Nathan?" I point to the pictures on the wall.

She nods. The tears are streaming down her cheeks now. I give her a few minutes to compose herself.

"Debbie. I can't imagine how hard it is for you now. But I have some questions."

She nods again.

"When did you last see him?"

"Yesterday morning. When he left for work."

"Where did he work?"

"He's a ... a salesman at Laars Cars."

"The luxury dealership in Capitol Auto Mall?"

"Yes, that's the one."

"I see. What time did you expect him home?"

"He was usually back by eight p.m. But ... but yesterday ..."

She breaks down crying, recovering before I can react.

"He was meeting someone. Told me he would be back by ten."

"Who was he meeting?"

She's silent, but I can see the wheels turning inside her head.

"Debbie. Who was he meeting? This could be important. We have to find out who did this."

"I ... I don't know. I mean ... I mean, I know why he was going, but I don't know exactly who he was meeting. But I had a bad feeling about it. And now ..." She's sobbing again.

"Please tell me whatever you can. Every detail matters."

"He was meeting this guy. Someone he worked with a long time ago. Someone who was blackmailing him."

"Blackmailing him about what?"

"I don't know. He didn't want to talk about it. Said it was about something that happened before we met. He would tell me once it was all over."

"And you were okay with that?"

"Not exactly. But I trusted him. We'd been married ten years now. Known each other for twelve. We would share everything. If he couldn't tell me, it must have been very hard for him."

"Do you know when this incident happened? The one he was being black-mailed about?"

"No."

"And how much did this blackmailer demand?"

"Hundred thousand dollars. Our life savings. We were moving to Arizona soon. That money was for our new home."

Debbie breaks down again. I know how hard it is to lose a spouse, but at least I saw it coming. This one's a nasty shock, and losing her savings too — I can only imagine how devastating that must be.

"Do you know where they were meeting?"

"The gas station by the Oakland Road exit for 101. Is that ... is that where you found him? How did he ...?"

It's odd that she hasn't asked these questions yet. But grief and shock can act in weird ways.

"Yes. He was stabbed."

This time she has her face in her hands as she cries. "My poor Nathan. Sweet Nathan. That must have hurt so much."

She looks up at me after a couple of minutes, her face coated with tears. "He was so caring. Always so thoughtful. You know, he signed up for a million-dollar life insurance policy just a month ago. He was worried how I would manage if something were to happen to him. And now ... now he's gone. I wonder if he knew ..."

Interesting. Nathan takes out a huge policy soon before his death, with Debbie as beneficiary. The timing can't be a coincidence. But if she killed him, she wouldn't tell me this, right? Unless ...

My right eyebrow goes up a notch at the thought. A mistake, I know.

"Oh, you think I did him in for the money?" she asks with a horrified expression.

"Sorry, I didn't mean that. But as a routine question, I do have to ask — where were you yesterday evening?"

"At home. I had the TV on, though my mind was totally on Nathan. All I cared about was that he return home safe."

The tears again. It breaks my heart to see it. People say it's part of the job, that I should get used to it. But I can't. I can't suppress these basic emotions that are a part of me.

"Can anyone confirm you were here?"

"No. It was just me."

"One last question. How did Nathan get to the meeting point?"

"He drove."

"We didn't find any car key on him. What car did he drive?"

"It's a white Honda Civic."

"What year?"

"Oh, I don't know. One of the old models — he had it since before we were married."

I get the license plate number from her before moving on to another delicate matter.

"Debbie, we need someone to formally identify the body. You think you can do it?"

"Yes, of course. Do I ... do I have to do it now?"

"No. Within the next day or two. I'll contact you."

"Okay."

"Is there someone who can come by ... to take care of you?"

"I'll be fine. Really. I'll ... I'll call my mom in the morning."

I hand her my card and leave. Outside, I ponder my next move. It's only 4:00 a.m. That gives me plenty of time to review the surveillance video from the gas station. I return to my desk and get to it. It's not long before I see Nathan. At 8:58 p.m. he walked through the station in his white suit, black pouch in hand. *Was the money in that pouch?* That's the last I see of him. There are no suspicious characters in the video. No leads to pursue. Who is this mystery coworker?

My first stop for the neighborhood canvass is the Comfy Motel across the street from the crime scene. There's a man at reception. He has shifty eyes and a forced smile that I don't quite trust. I scan the guest log as he tells me about the disgusting man who checked in that night. Room twenty-three, I see. *What the ...!* Nathan Sandler. That's the name he used. We hurry over to the room. A few knocks later someone stirs inside. The door opens a crack to reveal a weather-beaten face that's been freshly shaved. The hair is trimmed short. It's a bad haircut, but his overall appearance is way better than what I'd expected based on the motel manager's description. I hold up my badge.

"Detective Lansbury from SJPD. I have some questions for you."

It's as if he has seen a ghost, but the color returns to his face in an instant.

"What about?" he asks as he opens the door wide.

"Are you Nathan Sandler?"

There it is again. That fleeting panicked look.

"No. I'm Barry. Barry Jones," he replies in a calm tone.

Barry. That's one of the names Victor gave me.

"But you signed in as Nathan Sandler."

"What?"

He seems genuinely surprised.

"We checked the register from a couple of nights ago. Room twenty-three shows Nathan Sandler."

He glances at the number on the door, then looks me straight in the eye as he says, "This is room twenty-three. But there's some mistake. I'm Barry Jones and that's the name I wrote in. Anyway, why's this important?"

Oh, he's good! As smooth as they come.

"We found a man dead across the street, and we're canvassing the neighborhood. We have reason to believe his name was Nathan Sandler."

"Oh. I see."

"Mind if we continue this interview inside?"

I can tell his brain's working overtime. Beads of sweat are forming on his forehead. "Sure, come on in," he replies as he turns around to lead the way. Then he stops. Something on the TV stand catches my eye, and I hurry over for a closer inspection. Cash. Two bundles. Around twenty grand, I estimate. A knife next to it. It has a beautiful jade handle. I put on a glove and pick up the knife, turning it both ways. The blade seems clean at first glance, almost like it's never been used, but a few more seconds of scrutiny reveal a sliver of what might be dried blood near the edges.

I give him the look. The fear in his eyes tells me everything I need to know. That's when I realize I have blundered. He moves before I do and by the time I react, he's out the door. *How could I have been so stupid to leave him unguarded by the door?* The smarmy manager tries to stop him but fails. I give chase, an exercise in futility. Barry's too fast for me. *Did I say homicide detectives don't have to run much?* My legs are cramping up, courtesy of the marathon effort. The best I can do is radio his description and hope someone nabs him.

Sergeant Williams sits across from me, deep in thought. I'm in his office for the case discussion. He's as disappointed as I am. It's awful when the prime suspect slips away like that.

"Nathan was blackmailed for a hundred thousand. This guy Barry had less than twenty grand on him. The question I have is, where's the rest? He couldn't have spent it so fast. Was Nathan's wife sure he took all hundred?" he asks.

"Yes. All their life savings. But twenty is all we found. Maybe Barry stashed the rest someplace safe. We'll know for sure once we find him."

"*If* we find him. Slippery bastard. What else did you find in his room?"

"A knife. Quite sure it's the murder weapon. He'd wiped the blade clean, but there's some blood on it. I've sent it for analysis. I expect it to match Nathan's. If we're lucky, get some good prints too. Other than that, just clothes."

"Pretty stupid holing up in a motel across from the crime scene. With all that money he could ..."

My phone buzzes. Normally I wouldn't take a call from an unknown number, but it could be someone providing a tip for the case. So I answer.

"Detective Lansbury. I found him," says a familiar voice, sounding excited.

"Found who?"

"Justin. He's here for some grub. Can you come now? I'll try to hold him till you get here."

"Sure, where are you?"

"Second Harvest."

"I'll be there. And Victor — whose phone are you calling from?"

"Borrowed it from one of the volunteers, man. Get here quick!"

Justin's not as interesting anymore now that Barry's been found with the murder weapon and the cash. But he may be able to provide useful information. Williams agrees and asks me to rush over to the food bank.

❧ ⟫⟫⟫ ⟪⟪⟪ ❧

Victor's grinning when he spots me. The man next to him, however, looks confused. He's as dirty as Victor. Reeks as much too. I introduce myself, and the color drains from his face.

"I didn't ... I didn't ... do anything," he says in a panicked voice.

"Didn't do what?" I ask.

"He was already dead when I found him."

"Who?"

"White suit."

Now it makes sense. He thinks I'm here to arrest him for the murder.

"Why did you run if you didn't do it?"

"I ... I was scared. But I didn't do it."

"Victor here saw the body too. He didn't run."

There's a strange look on Justin's face, something I can't decipher. He replies before I can put more thought into it.

"I swear I didn't do it. I think Barry did it."

Ah, music to my ears. We already have evidence, but it's not enough. I'm hoping Justin's an eyewitness who can help us nail the case.

"Why do you think he did it? Did you see him do it?"

"No. But I did see him leaving. He looked scared, the way he was looking around."

"When was this?"

"Two nights ago. I was walking back to camp when I saw him. I wondered what was wrong. Then I saw the body."

"What did you do then?"

"I collected my stuff and ran. Like I told you."

"How did you know he was dead?"

"He was just laying there."

"Could've been sleeping."

"No. He had blood here," he replies, pointing to his belly.

"So you didn't touch anything?"

"No."

"Any idea where I can find Barry?"

Justin shakes his head.

"Man, if I were him, I would've hopped on a Greyhound and escaped to Mexico by now," Victor adds helpfully.

Disappointed, I return to the station.

Barry has cemented his spot as the prime suspect. Perhaps he's the former coworker Nathan was meeting. Something tells me Laars Cars is the key to solving this one. I find Laars' number and set up an appointment for later that evening. Then I begin my homework. A few online searches and before long I come across an interesting news item. Thirteen years ago, there was a murder at the dealership. Sophia Green, the beautiful young cashier, was found dead with a stab wound.

It was clear a knife had been used, but it was nowhere to be seen. I search the department records and review the case files. Nathan worked there even back then. Could he have had something to do with the murder? Is that what this blackmail was about?

I continue reading. There's no mention of any Barry in the employee list. All the employees were interviewed, including the two janitors who were on site that night. No one had seen or heard anything. Without any progress, the case had gone cold.

"You look like shit, you know," Sergeant Williams says as he looms over my desk. I didn't notice him walking up.

"Yeah, I feel like it too."

San Jose homicide rates have been dropping in recent years, but it's been a crazy few weeks. It's as if all the local killers banded together and decided to unleash their fury at once.

"When was the last time you slept?"

I stare at him as I try to remember. Seems like ages ago.

"Go home. Get some shut-eye. You won't get far like this."

I want to protest, but I realize he's right. An hour later, I'm sound asleep in my bed. Ruth appears in my dream. It's the night she died, her gaunt face declaring that the cancer had won. I take her hand and kiss it. A tear escapes my eyes. Then she fades away, gone forever.

By the time I awake it's dark outside. My phone shows 8:30 p.m., along with two missed calls and voicemails. One from an unknown number. *Damn!* The message from Laars reminds me I was supposed to meet him at eight. I leap out of bed and speed over to the dealership.

Capitol Auto Mall is a long stretch of Capitol Expressway in San Jose, packed with car dealerships. Laars Cars stands out among them as the only one offering luxury vehicles. It's been around for thirty years now. Laars is wrapping up with a customer when I get there. The famous face from the countless ads on television. My eyes soak in the lineup of Porsches and Maseratis as I wait.

"Which one are you driving off with tonight?" he asks with a smile as he extends his hand a few minutes later. He's dressed in a navy blue suit and still looks fresh, though I would assume it must have been a long work day for him.

"Whew. Quite a collection you got there. I can't make up my mind. The red Maserati, if I could afford it."

"Excellent choice," he says as he laughs and walks me over to his office, turning somber once we're seated. "Sad business about Nathan. He's ... was an awesome guy. Been with me fifteen years. My best salesman. I can only imagine what Debbie must be going through."

"So they had a good relationship?"

"Oh yeah. They were still in love after all this time. You could just feel it when you saw them together. Surely you don't think she had anything to do with it?"

"No, I don't. Do you know anyone who might want to harm him?"

"No. Everyone loved him."

"His coworkers included?"

"Yes. They respected him."

"Anyone named Barry working here?"

"No." He pauses for a few seconds, brows furrowed. "I don't think I've ever had a Barry."

"Now, Laars. Thirteen years ago a woman was murdered here."

"Oh, Sophia. Ghastly business. How can I forget? I found the body when I opened up the next morning. Why's that important now?"

"Do you think Nathan had anything to do with her death?"

"Nathan? No way. I couldn't imagine him doing anything like that. You think their deaths are connected?"

"Not sure yet. Could anyone else working here have anything to do with it?"

"No!" he replies as the color rises in his face.

"While I was researching this, I found some interesting news items. They said you had a brief affair with Sophia which ended a couple of weeks before her death."

"So?" His nostrils are flaring now.

"Why did it end?"

"It was just a fling. There was mutual attraction. We hooked up a few times before she developed a conscience. Said it wasn't right of me to cheat on my wife. And that was that."

"So you parted on good terms?"

"Yes. She continued to work here. It was like nothing happened between us. I assure you, I had nothing to do with her death."

"I'm not the first to suspect you."

"Right. All the news stories. Her friend leaked the information about our affair after Sophia died. That sparked the speculation that I killed Sophia because she dumped me."

"But you had an airtight alibi."

"Yes. I was with my wife when it happened."

"So it seems. You had already left work that evening. Don't you close up?"

"I usually do. But it was our anniversary, and I'd promised her a dinner date. I returned later to close."

"Quite convenient."

"Lucky for me, yes. I didn't do it, so I think I deserved that convenient break."

"And you didn't notice anything odd when you closed up?"

"No, nothing at all. I was in a hurry since my wife was waiting in the car, so I didn't do a complete walkthrough."

Perhaps Laars didn't murder Sophia, but he could still have something to do with Nathan's death. I can't rule him out as the coworker Nathan met that night. At least not yet.

"Where were you the night Nathan died?"

"Right here. All throughout. Keeping busy with the summer sales events. And before you ask, anyone out here can vouch for me."

"Busy time of the year, yet your best salesman left early?"

"Nathan rarely stayed late. For him, family came first."

"Did he tell you why he had to leave early?"

"No. I assumed he had something planned with Debbie."

Laars turns out to be a dead end. Disappointed at not finding a breakthrough, I drive over to work to find a couple of items waiting for me. The phone company moved faster than usual to get me Nathan's records, and Officer Mendez picked up the surveillance video from the fast-food joint. I spend the next hour studying the records. Nathan's phone seems to have died around the time he was killed. The location matches where we found the body. Out of juice, perhaps? More likely swiped by the killer and turned off, is my guess. There's nothing suspicious about the last few calls. Another dead end. I move on to the video. There's the usual traffic you would expect at a place like that, but no sign of the vic or anyone suspicious.

Mendez has some more information for me. Nathan had parked his car at the gas station. It was towed the next night since it hadn't moved in twenty-four hours. A team's on its way to retrieve it and conduct a search.

A few minutes pass in deep thought before I remember the other missed voicemail. It's from Debbie. She says she recalled Nathan mentioning the name of the man he was meeting that night. Ian. That's all she has for me. It rings a bell. In the Sophia case files, one of the janitors was Ian Rose. I return to the files and pull up his interview. The audio crackles to life as the conversation begins. My hair stands on end when I hear the voice. I recognize it. Three sentences in, there's no doubt it's the same person I think it is.

※

Fifteen minutes later, I'm back at the homeless camp with a couple of officers. Now that it's no longer a crime scene, it resembles the other camps that have sprouted all over San Jose in the last few years. Except for one difference. There's a new body. This time the neck has been slashed. A knife sits next to it, the blade coated in dark liquid. I feel helpless. Frustrated. There are questions, too. Several questions. Could I have prevented this death? Am I sure this is the same killer? As far as I can tell, he has never left the weapon at the scene of the crime before. And the most important question of all — where's the man I'm looking for? Inspiration strikes, and I remember what he said not too long ago.

I send out the alert to check all Greyhound stops, personally rushing to the one downtown. There's a bus leaving for Tijuana in ten minutes, with around twenty people seated in the waiting area. Scanning the room, I find my prey. His eyes meet mine, and the panic is evident. But he has nowhere to go. I heave a sigh of relief.

Victor's sporting a smug countenance when I enter the interrogation room. He declined a lawyer. What I would give to be able to smack him hard and wipe that grin off. Does he really think he can get away with this? Well, I must admit, he has a chance. All we have is circumstantial evidence. No one saw him do it. We have the knife, but there's nothing to tie him to it. He had the rest of the money — the eighty thousand dollars. Nathan's cell phone and wallet too. But that doesn't prove he murdered Nathan. I'm still not sure how Barry fits into it all. I push those thoughts out of my head so I can focus on the task at hand.

"Why've you got me in here, man?"

"You know why."

"Look man, I didn't have nothing to do with it. I just found the body and reported it like a responsible citizen. Besides, we both know Barry did it."

"And how do we know that?"

"You heard Justin, man. He saw Barry sneaking away that night. It had to be him."

"Not necessarily. Barry could have been just as traumatized as Justin."

"To be honest, I don't believe Justin either, man. He could've done it."

"Justin's dead. Murdered."

"Oh!" His jaw drops in surprise. For a moment I wonder whether we got the wrong guy. "Poor Justin! Know who did it? Was it Barry?"

"Tell me something, Victor. Why were you on your way to Mexico?"

"Just needed to get away from it all, man. Make a fresh start. There's no future here."

"Pretty convenient, you leaving in the middle of a murder investigation. And the same night that Justin died."

"I'm telling you, man. I didn't know he was dead."

"You know we have the knife that was used on Nathan? The blood on it matches Nathan's. And we found your prints on it."

I'm bluffing, but it's worth a shot. The prints didn't match. Not from the notebook, not from the weapon. My guess is they're Barry's. We're still waiting for the forensic results for the blood. Here's hoping my poker face is effective. At least it's got Victor thinking, for his expression has turned grim.

"Oh, well, that's probably because I touched it when I saw the body. I know I shouldn't have, but reflex action, man."

"So you're saying the knife was in him when you found him?"

"Hell, yeah!"

"But it wasn't there when we saw the body. Where did it go?"

Confusion clouds his face. "Didn't you say you have it?"

"Yes, but we found it elsewhere."

"Where?"

"Doesn't matter where. Just explain how it disappeared between the time you saw it and we showed up."

"Shit, man! I don't know how my prints got on there! I'm sure I wiped the handle after I …"

He stops, realization dawning.

"After you what?"

No response.

"After you killed Nathan?"

"Fucking Barry! He took the knife. That's where you found it, right?"

"So you confess to murdering Nathan Sandler?"

"Yes." His shoulders droop as he replies. The body language of a man who knows he has lost.

"Why did you do it?"

"Well, see — he came over with a hundred thousand dollars, and I had nothing to give him in return. He had to go."

"So you were faking it when you blackmailed him?"

"Yeah. He was always so gullible, man. I took him for twenty grand back when I knocked off Sophia. And he fell for it again this time. Fooled him twice. Funny, considering how he's this awesome salesman. They're supposed to be street smart."

Did he just confess to killing Sophia Green as well? This is turning out to be too easy.

"You lost me there. Can you explain?"

"This goes a long way back, man. I was the janitor at Laars Cars. Nathan was there too, but of course he was a salesman — making a lot more dough than I was. Now, Sophia — oh, man, she was really something. I wanted her so bad. One night I'm there cleaning, and she's in her little corner, wearing that short skirt of hers, showing off those sexy legs. I tried to feel her up. She threatened she would report me. That pissed me off."

"So you stabbed her?"

"Yeah."

"Stabbed her with what?"

"My knife. I always carry one."

"What happened next?"

"She collapsed right away. I wiped off the handle and left the room. I was shaking, man. It was the first time I'd ever done anything like that. But I continued cleaning, making everything appear normal. A few minutes later I saw Nathan go in there, so I followed. The idiot had the knife in his hand and was scared shitless. That's when I saw my chance. I acted like I thought he'd killed her. Of course, he denied it. I offered to help him out by disposing of the knife and promised not to tell anyone."

"So you just left her there to die?"

"Pretty much," he replies with a shrug. "What? It was too late, man. If I'd helped her she would've turned me in. I couldn't take that chance."

I've dealt with a ton of lowlifes in my profession, but this one still gets to me. I shake my head in disgust.

"I assume you didn't get rid of the knife?"

"Right. The cops were there the next day. Interviewed everyone. Me too. I don't know how I kept it together. Heck, I don't know how Nathan kept it together. Then I asked him for money. He was so shocked. You shoulda seen his face, man." Victor chuckles as he says it. The urge to reach out and slap him hard bubbles up again, but I hold back.

"He paid you?"

"Yeah. Twenty grand, man. I gave him the knife and my solemn oath to never tell anyone about what happened."

"So what was this last meeting about?"

A sly grin appears on his face. *Why's this guy getting under my skin?*

"That cash didn't last long. Coming into all that money ruined me, man. I got into drugs and other rotten stuff. Ended up on the streets. But I was okay with it. I figured it was just punishment for what I'd done. To Sophia, you know. Then one day I saw Nathan at the pump. And just like that I got an idea. I walked up to him and introduced myself. He couldn't believe it was me. I told him I still had the knife, and the one I gave him was a different one. This time I asked for a lot more money."

"He agreed to pay?"

"Yes. Told you, man. He was too simple."

"And he got you the money?"

"Yes. The whole hundred grand, as agreed."

"Then why kill him?"

"I don't know, man." He shrugs again. "Just felt like it, I guess."

Just felt like it. Like he's telling me why he ordered Thai for lunch, not why he destroyed an innocent life. My blood's boiling. Hand's itching.

"Where does Barry come into all this?"

"Oh, Barry. That ass! If he'd just stayed away ..."

"What happened?"

"Nathan had the money in his pouch. I'd opened it to count the dough. When I stabbed him, some money fell. Before I could pick it up I saw Barry coming. So I hid. I was so pissed when he picked up the dough and walked away like it was his."

"It wasn't yours either."

"It was, man. It was. My idea, my money. Anyway, I started to follow him, but then I saw Justin, so I hid again. By the time Justin left, Barry was nowhere to be seen."

"So Justin didn't have anything to do with the murder?"

"No, man. He's a good soul."

"Then why did you kill him?"

"He was getting dangerous, man. Wondered why I gave you a false name. I was worried he would tell you about it."

"Ah. Is that why he looked dazed when I called you Victor?"

"Yep. I realized I'd slipped up. Thankfully, he didn't mention it until you left."

"And why did you give me a false name?"

"As you know by now, my real name's Ian Rose. I figured a smart detective like yourself would find the connection between Ian and Nathan. Got to play it safe, man. So I gave you Victor Wade. Wasn't completely lying, by the way. Victor's my middle name, and Wade's my mother's maiden name."

"Why didn't you notify us about the body the same night? Why wait a day?"

"I didn't want to tell nobody. My original plan was to scram by the next Greyhound, but I had to find Barry. I couldn't leave without that dough, man. But I couldn't find him. Then I figured, if I didn't report it you guys might suspect me once it was found. So I called."

"Did you find him eventually?"

"No, man."

"Then why were you leaving?"

"Too risky to stay. Especially after I got Justin."

"One last thing. We searched your tent that night but didn't find anything. No money, no cellphone, no wallet. Where was it?"

"A magician never tells," he replies with a wry smile. "Why do you care anyway? You already got me." The smile has disappeared, replaced with a look of pure hatred.

"Just curious, that's all. But you're right. We don't need that information ... man." I smile as I add my special touch with emphasis. "Curious about one more thing, though."

"What?"

"We didn't find his car key. What did you do with it?"

"I took it, man. Thought I'd escape in his car, but then I figured it was too risky. What if the cops traced it and found me? So I dumped the key."

Taking a few moments to think things over, I conclude that I have all my answers. The interrogation is over. I depart the room, relieved to get away from this monster.

Solving a case still thrills me. I guess it's why I continue to do what I do. By the time the paperwork's done, I'm famished. The burger joint across the street beckons, and I obey its clarion call. There are three people in the queue in front of me. The last one has luxurious red hair. I know who it is, and my heart livens up. She turns and smiles, as if she sensed my presence.

Ten minutes later we're at our table, digging into the juicy burgers. I can't remember the last time I met Amber like this, outside of work. It's time, I try to convince myself. *It's too soon,* says a voice in my head. *No, it isn't. Ruth's been gone five years now,* says another.

"What're you doing Saturday night?" I ask. My voice starts out shaky, but I manage to steady it by the end. *Why the heck am I so nervous?*

"Meeting the boyfriend for dinner."

My jaw drops. She bursts out laughing. *Why did I assume she was single?* "Oh." That's all I can muster.

"Just look at your face! Sorry, I couldn't resist," she continues. "Relax. There's no boyfriend. What do you have in mind?"

It takes me some time to figure it out. I get my jaw back in place and break into a grin. *Damn, I love this woman!*

"I have a couple of tickets to the Sting concert at SAP Center. We could catch that. Grab some dinner after?"

"I'd love to." *Oh, that radiant smile!*

I'm breathing easy now. *See, that wasn't so hard, was it?* I sink my teeth into the burger, still smiling. Saturday can't come too soon.

AUTHOR'S NOTE

S ince you're reading this, I assume you completed *Fool Me Twice*. I do hope you enjoyed it. What follows is a different perspective on the story, or at least part of it. Narrated by another character, *Fate* is not a mystery, but a lighter take on the tale. Why two perspectives? Well, for that we have to go into a history lesson. I wrote *Fate* first, in response to a contest for 2000-word short stories. It was an experiment, something different from the murder mysteries I usually write. Of course, I couldn't resist including a murder, but I did succeed in giving it a different spin.

A few weeks after I wrapped it up, inspiration struck and I realized this story could be developed into a compelling murder mystery. *Fool Me Twice* was born. Detective Arthur Lansbury found a voice. But why did I present *Fool Me Twice* before *Fate*? In my opinion, reading *Fate* first may diminish the impact of the mystery. And now you can relish this next yarn as a delicious dessert after a satisfying meal. Dig in!

FATE

I return to the camp to find it desolate. The tents are empty too. Strange for this time of night. But Oakland Road is chock-full of traffic as always. I watch as the cars crawl along, entering and exiting off 101-S. The people in these vehicles have a life. Probably homes too. Unlike me. I was like them once. I had it all. Until Fate stabbed me in the back and dumped me by the wayside.

I turn my gaze back to the camp. It's quite dark, the light from the gas station and the fast food joint providing scant illumination for the place I call home. I spot something in the distance and walk over to see what it is.

Shock. That's the first sensation that hits me when I realize it's a body. He's dressed in a white suit. I would have thought he was asleep, but the sizable red stain on his torso says otherwise. The knife handle sticking out of him explains everything. In spite of my fears, I crouch by his side. He's not breathing. I search his trouser pockets but turn up empty. There's something in his coat pocket. A small black notebook. I flip through it. His name and address are on the first page. A local. Nathan Sandler. I toss the notebook. That's all he has on him. No wallet. No cell phone. I'd hoped he would have enough cash on him to buy me my first meal in two days. Disappointed, I notice now that the knife has a beautifully carved jade handle. I pull it out and wipe the blade clean on his suit. It goes in my pocket.

Now that my eyes have adapted to the darkness, I spot something next to him. Two bundles of hundred-dollar bills. Twenty thousand dollars. I check again. It's real. What a stroke of luck! I stash the dough inside my shirt and look around furtively, relieved that no one saw me. I picture steak. And caviar. A bottle of fine champagne. But first I need a roof above my head. The sign across the street catches my eye:

"$49.99 a night   TV   Air Cond".

The Comfy Motel. Many a night have I stared at that edifice, wishing I could sleep in there. Now my wish will come true. I cross the street and enter the building. The lobby is cramped. The man behind the front desk wrinkles his nose in disgust and picks up the desk phone as he sees me walk in. I know that look. It's something I'm accustomed to on the streets. But this time it stings. It tells me I'm not good enough even for this dump of a motel. It's at this moment that I resolve to be prudent with my windfall. This cash won't last long in Silicon Valley. No parties. No lavish spending. I will use it to clean up and get myself a job. Earn some more money, get a permanent roof over my head. Become respectable. As my Pa used to say, "Think big, Barry. Think long-term, Barry."

Mind made up, I stand up tall and stride over to the desk. "I'll take a room for the month," I say as I lay fifteen crisp bills before him.

His eyes light up, and he places the phone back in the cradle. He asks me to sign in the register. With all the technology available he still uses an old-school notebook. How quaint. My lips break into a wicked smile as I fill in my name. Nathan Sandler. It's not like he's checking ID. He hands me the key, and I take the stairs up to my room.

It's odd to be in these enclosed quarters. But I eye the bed in anticipation. When was the last time I lay in one? What would it feel like, to rest on that mattress, snuggle in those sheets? But before I jump in, I need a bath. Another activity I look forward to. Wash away the filth and the stink from life in the streets.

Soon I'm soaking in the tub, my head sticking out of the bubbles, enjoying the hot water as it melts away any thoughts of the corpse. When I step out, I feel renewed. Clean and smelling like roses. I spot the heap of dirty clothes on the floor. No way can I wear that again. I should burn it. But then what will I wear? *Oops.* Should've thought of that first. Luckily there's a bathrobe in the closet. Flimsy, but serviceable. I put it on, knowing I can't go out like this. But I have to, because I'm starving and there's no room service in a place like this.

I open the front door a crack and take a peek. The door to another room opens and a man steps outside with an ice bucket in his hand. The ice machine is at the end of the corridor. He props the door open and leaves. Seizing my chance, I sprint to his room as soon as he walks past. A pair of shorts and a t-shirt are conveniently lying on the bed. I grab those and dash back to safety. It's the first time I've done anything like this, and I'm not proud of myself. But sometimes you have no choice. The clothes fit me perfectly. I could complain about the lack of underwear, but I don't. I've had plenty of luck this evening.

A short while later, I'm at the fast food place across the street, wolfing down a double cheeseburger and crisscut fries. Heaven. Not the lavish feast I had imagined earlier, but still out of this world. Meal complete, I sneak back into my room, worried that Ice Man will catch me wearing his clothes. I'm so exhausted that I crash into bed. A contented smile escapes my lips. I picture my life getting back on track now that Fate is on my side again. Fate has given me a chance again. All I have to do is to grasp it with both hands. If I work hard and apply myself, soon I'll be rolling in wealth. The last thought I have is of me relaxing on a beautiful beach, puffing away on a cigar, without a care in the world. And then I drift into blissful sleep.

There's just one blip during the night when I wake up in a cold sweat. A nightmare about Mr. Sandler showing up at my door demanding his money, the knife still sticking out of him. I take a few deep breaths to calm myself down and return to sleepyland.

It's already 10:00 a.m. by the time I'm awake the next morning, feeling well rested. What a difference a good night's sleep can make, even after accounting for the unpleasant dream. I hop into the shower and enjoy the hot drops of water massaging my body. A couple of hours later I'm in Valley Fair Mall shopping for clothes. I spend the day perusing every store, catching up on what I've missed the past few years. No dirty looks from anyone. Charming smiles from the store employees. That feels wonderful. By the time I'm done, I have several bags full of garments. And some grooming supplies. To assuage my guilt, I have also purchased some outfits for Ice Man.

Back in my room, I change into my new attire. Then I place the peace offering and the clothes I stole from him outside Ice Man's room and return to my cave. It's like a huge weight has been lifted off me. In the bathroom I take a hard look at myself in the mirror. Long, unkempt mane. Unruly beard speckled with silver hair. I start hacking away with the scissors. Then I shave. I survey my face in the mirror again. It's a familiar face, a face I knew once. My eyes well up, unable to contain my emotions. I clean up and dive into bed. This time I'm asleep before any thoughts can form.

Someone's knocking on my door. Awakened from deep sleep, I squint at the clock next to my bed. 8:00 a.m. Who's here at this ungodly hour? More importantly, who could have any business with me? I drag myself out of bed reluctantly and shuffle over to the door, opening it a crack. There's a man in a tan suit. He's about my height and age. Clean-shaven. He holds up a San Jose Police Department badge.

"Detective Lansbury from SJPD. I have some questions for you."

I want to throw up. This can't be a coincidence. There can only be one reason he's here. *Shit. Shit.* Why did I have to pick a motel so close to the crime scene? But I take a deep breath and calm myself. I might be able to tackle this if I keep it together.

"What about?" I ask as I open the door wide. Behind him I see the grinch from reception. He has a gleeful grin plastered on his face. *Got you,* he seems to be thinking.

"Are you Nathan Sandler?"

Shit. Shit. Shit. Why did I have to sign in as the deceased? It's like carrying a placard saying, "Me, me! I did it!"

"No. I'm Barry. Barry Jones."

"But you signed in as Nathan Sandler."

"What?" I do my best *I don't know what you're talking about* expression.

"We checked the register from a couple of nights ago. Room twenty-three shows a Nathan Sandler."

I glance at the door, then look him in the eye. "This is room twenty-three. But there's some mistake. I'm Barry Jones and that's the name I wrote in. Anyway, why's this important?" It's my serious *important business* face this time.

"We found a man dead across the street and we're canvassing the neighborhood. We have reason to believe his name was Nathan Sandler."

"Oh. I see."

"Mind if we continue this interview inside?"

He didn't buy it. He didn't buy it! My mind's racing and my heart's trying to keep up. Will it look suspicious if I refuse? Do I need a lawyer? Pushing the thoughts aside, I reply, "Sure, come on in." It's not like I killed the man. If there's one positive virtue about life on the streets, it's the toughness it has infused into me. I feel if I was able to survive five years out there, I can easily handle this curveball too.

I turn around to lead the way in. And then I freeze. I just made my third mistake. The fatal one. I know Lansbury has seen what I have seen, for he strides up to the TV stand and studies the objects. The cash. And lying next to it, the beautiful knife. He turns his gaze to me, giving me the stare he must have unleashed on countless criminals over the years. I tremble, and for a moment I think I will pass out. *Oh, Fate! This is a cruel, cruel trick you played on me.*

The feeling passes, and I put into action the first thought that comes to me. I do a one-eighty and make a dash for it. Reception guy tries to stop me, but I shove him aside, wishing I had time to throw in a couple of punches too. When I was ten years old, I won a hundred meter race in school. That sprint is what I picture as I speed up, hoping these middle-aged legs still have some of that magic left in them.

HER LAST CHANCE

Missed opportunities can be costly

PROLOGUE

I should have let him die when I had the chance. *Hindsight is 20/20*. A phrase that's often thrown around, but I truly understand the meaning now. My body's hurting in numerous spots, each injury a reminder of the blows he rained on me last night. Yet here I am, all decked up for the lavish dinner at the Silbermans, applying the final touches of makeup on my face to hide the hideous patch of purple I received courtesy of Adam. I would rather be lying in bed, nursing my wounds, but I don't have a choice.

Speak of the devil — Adam has entered the room, stunning in his tux, his charming smile adding to the attractiveness. This is what floored me when we first met, but it disgusts me now. *Love is blind*. Another trite phrase, but oh so true. If I hadn't ignored the red flags back then, the flashes of temper, the possessiveness, if I hadn't been blinded by his brilliance and my crazy heart, I wouldn't be in this mess.

So close. A week ago we were sitting at the breakfast table, me pecking at my oatmeal, Adam scarfing down his shredded wheat cereal when one of the bite-sized biscuits lodged in his throat and he started choking. All I had to do was sit tight for a couple of minutes until he perished. But my reflexes kicked in, and I performed the Heimlich on him. I saved his life. What did I get in return? A whack on my face with the back of his hand.

"Are you trying to kill me?" he yelled. "You messed with my cereal, didn't you?" He retrieved the cereal box from the pantry and dunked it in the trash can. It was the kind of paranoid behavior that often made me consider whether he was mentally ill. Unfortunately, he shot down my suggestions to seek professional help every single time.

The next installment was delivered yesterday. Kicks, punches — the works. It's a miracle I'm still standing. I've been cursing myself since, revisiting that moment when I could have transformed my wretched life. But I don't think I have it in me to earn my freedom. This is my fate, and I must learn to live with it.

"It's time to go," he says, pulling me out of these miserable thoughts. "We don't want to be late *again*." Landing blows even with words, his accusatory glare saying it all. I nod and take one last glance in the mirror before heading out with him.

CHAPTER ONE

Someone's at the door. The doorbell's been sounding every few seconds. Still in bed, I've been trying to ignore it, hoping this person will go away, but no such luck. My head hurts, but the older injuries are doing better. Legs are sore though, the way they ache after leg day at the gym. The soles of my feet are still killing me. I crawl out of bed and trundle downstairs towards the door. When I open it, there's a man standing there. He's wearing a suit and an expression that tells me he means business.

"Mrs. Baldwin?" he asks.

"Yes."

"I'm Detective Hopper." He holds up his badge and identification.

"What's this about?"

"Is your husband home? Adam Baldwin."

"I ... I just got out of bed. Haven't seen him this morning."

"When did you see him last?"

I pause to think, though I'm confident of the answer. "Two days ago."

"He on some trip?"

"I guess."

He frowns. "You don't know?"

"It happens all the time. He takes off without telling me." It's the truth. I can't remember a time when he bothered to tell me where he was going when he left the house. Yet, I'm nervous.

He hesitates before speaking again. "Mind if we talk inside?"

"Sure." I lead the way to the living room and settle into the couch. He sits on the chair opposite.

"Any idea where he could be?"

I shake my head. "With one of his girlfriends, I guess." *Where did that come from?* Well, too late. My frankness has surprised me as much as it seems to have shocked him.

He stares at me. An awkward silence persists for a while. I get the feeling he's studying me, wondering what to make of me. Quite sure this is not what he expected when he showed up at my door.

"He was cheating on you?"

"All the time." Might as well go the distance on this one.

"And that didn't bother you?"

"It did at first, but not anymore." Adam never bothered to hide his infidelity once we were married. That's how much he disrespected me. Though I feel it was better knowing all along rather than making the shocking discovery at a later stage.

Hopper pauses to study me again. "How did you get that?" he asks, indicating something on my face. I'm not sure if he's referring to the wound on my forehead or the fading bruise around my eye.

"I ... I fell and hit my head."

"That's quite a bump. You should get it checked out."

"I will."

"What about that?" This time I'm certain he's asking about the bruise. "That looks like somebody hit you."

I place my fingers on the mark. "You sure picked the right profession, Detective. Yes, it was a gift from my dear husband."

A wry smile shapes his lips. "So, let me get this straight. He cheats on you. Repeatedly. Hits you. On multiple occasions, I'm guessing." I nod. "You must hate his guts."

"You got that right too." *The truth shall set you free.*

"You know why I am here?"

"No, you didn't tell me."

"Your husband's partner, Jonathan Gates, he came in. He was worried because he hadn't heard from your husband in two days. Phone's been going straight to voicemail. Mr. Baldwin missed some important meetings at work, which I'm told is rather unlike him."

Ah, Jonathan. The creep has called me at least a dozen times since Adam's been gone. Whether he's genuinely concerned about Adam, or he's just aching to get his filthy paws on me, I don't know. I haven't bothered answering. That's probably why he resorted to calling the cops. Which reminds me that I have to call the Silbermans. They've been trying to reach me too.

"Must be quite the girlfriend this time if Adam skipped work for her." I can't resist the quip.

"Or something happened."

"You mean, like an accident?"

"Yes."

"Oh. I hadn't thought of that."

"Or ..." He pauses, and I have a feeling I won't like what's coming next. "Or you did him in."

Did I hear him right? Yes, he really did say that. Too direct in my opinion. Clearly, he suspects I might have something to do with Adam's disappearance. I would have expected him to take a more subtle approach to coax information out of me. Maybe he thinks he can bully me into a confession. "You think I killed him?"

"Wouldn't be surprising based on what you've told me. He's a cheat, he's abusive, and you hate the guy."

He's not pulling any punches, is he? "Well, Detective, I can assure you I did no such thing. That kind of behavior calls for a divorce, not murder." Not that I ever had the guts to divorce Adam. I feared he would still find a way to make my life hell.

Hopper produces a notebook and a pen out of his coat pocket and writes something. Then his eyes return to me. "You said you last saw him two days ago. What time was this?"

"Oh, I guess around seven."

"In the morning?"

"No, evening."

"So that's when he left the house?"

"Yes. Got into his car and drove off."

"What does he drive?"

I give him the details as he continues jotting it all down in his notebook. "I'll put out a search for his car." He stops writing and looks up. "Did he take any bags?"

"I don't remember seeing any."

"That's odd, don't you think? He's going on an overnight trip, but he doesn't take any change of clothes or toiletries?"

"He must have had everything at whatever love nest he was going to."

Hopper considers the theory for a moment. "Possible. Do you know any of these girlfriends? Any names?"

"No idea. I don't keep tabs on the competition."

His lips almost break into a smile, but he opts to maintain his professional demeanor. "Can you give me his phone details? We can check the call logs and location data."

Mistakes are costly and somebody must pay. It's a quote I read a while back. Will I pay for my mistake? I give him the information, for I don't have a choice here. It's only a matter of time before he finds what he's looking for.

"Thank you, Mrs. Baldwin."

"You can call me Sarah."

"We will find him, Sarah," he says as he stands up and heads for the door.

That's an odd thing to say considering he pretty much accused me of murdering my husband a couple of minutes ago. Maybe it's just a reflex — something he's conditioned to utter to loved ones after all the missing person cases he must have worked on over his career. Or is it a threat, and what he's really saying is *I'll find him, and when I do, I'll nail you?*

I sigh in relief once he's gone, though I know this is only a temporary reprieve. There's not much I can do about it now except play the waiting game. With the imminent threat out of the way, I realize I'm starving. Out of habit, I grab the bag of oatmeal from the pantry. A box of cereal sits next to it, but it's not the shredded wheat. This one has small flakes. It was the first time I had seen Adam try a different kind. I giggle, because it was amusing to see him so spooked after the choking incident.

I place the oatmeal back on the shelf. Adam's not home. It's an opportunity to eat what I really want, not the healthy stuff he forces me to. Of all his edicts, this healthy-eating rule is the only one that actually makes sense, but I can't do it day after day, three hundred and sixty-five days a year. I need those cheat days. Out comes my secret junk stash — a bag of Flamin' Hot Cheetos and a can of Coke. I return to the couch with my goodies and turn on the TV to watch some inane talk show. The Cheetos disappear in record time, and I burp after my last sip from the can. *Sooo satisfying.*

Now I have to figure out how to enjoy the rest of the day. Unfortunately, I've lost touch with my friends over the last few years. It was difficult maintaining those relationships, with Adam brewing trouble every step of the way. This is as good a time as any to reconnect. I wipe my red fingers on my PJs and grab my phone to call Melanie. She picks up on the first ring, her voice conveying surprise. It's so soothing to hear her. After an hour of yakking away, we agree to meet for lunch. Her six-year-old's in school, and she has some time on her hands. For a moment I'm jealous, seeing how her life has moved on while I've been stuck in hell. But all that's going to change. I'm sure of it.

I go upstairs and take a long, hot shower. It doesn't turn out to be as relaxing as I had expected. There's this constant fear that Adam will show up any minute, armed with a knife that he will gleefully use to slaughter me. It's a ridiculous thought, but somehow I'm unable to shake it off. Once out of the shower, I get dressed and head downstairs. There's still time before I meet Mel for lunch, but I want to get out of the house and breathe in some fresh air. I open the front door to see Detective Hopper standing outside. This is much sooner than expected. He surveys me up and down, and if I'm reading him right, he's concerned about my lack of concern for Adam's whereabouts.

"Going somewhere?" he asks.

"I ... uh ... what do you want?"

"Can I come in?"

No! That's what I want to say. "Sure, come on in."

We saunter back inside and settle into the same seats as before.

"I've been talking to some of your neighbors." He pauses, his gaze meeting my eyes, steady.

"And?"

"The lady next door, Mrs. Lewis, she gave me some very interesting information."

Snoopy Lewis, that's what I call her. She's always spying on everyone. If there's one person who knows everything that's happening on this street, it's her. This can't be good.

"What information?"

"She says she saw you leaving in the car with Adam the night he disappeared."

He states this in a matter-of-fact way and keeps his eyes on me. I'm sure he's scrutinizing my every pore, every aspect of my body language to determine if he has caught me in a lie.

"She must have mixed up the days. He went alone."

"So you went somewhere with him the night before?"

I take my time to chew on the question, for it's important how I answer it. Hopper maintains a neutral expression. "No. It must have been the prior weekend. That was the last time we went together anywhere."

"You think she messed up by a week? I can see how it could be a day or two, but an entire week?"

"To be honest, she's kooky. I wouldn't place too much weight on what she says. I've seen her make up stories — stuff that I know for a fact is untrue."

"I figured you would say something like that. My turn to be honest — I don't think she's kooky at all. Does she like to gossip? Sure. Nothing wrong with that, but she seemed perfectly normal to me."

All of a sudden my hands are sweaty. I wipe them on my dress. He notices and smiles. *I've got you,* it screams.

"I told you earlier you picked the right profession. Now I think, maybe not." It's my feeble attempt at a comeback.

He smiles again and stands up. "You have fun wherever it is you're off to. I have a feeling we will meet again soon." He turns around and walks out the door, leaving me dizzy and unsettled.

CHAPTER TWO

The lunch with Mel was okay. It should have been more enjoyable, but the conversation with Hopper had my nerves on edge. Nevertheless, I figured I have to keep my mind occupied or I'll go crazy. So in the days since, I've been calling my old friends and meeting them one by one. Cindy, Megan, Jessica, Marissa — all of them. It has helped me some during the day, but nights are a different matter altogether. I've been having nightmares. I dream that Adam climbs into bed and smothers me with a pillow. Sometimes it's Hopper instead of Adam. I wake up in a cold sweat every single time.

But I'm excited today, for I'm meeting Nikki for brunch. We were roommates junior year at college, and she was my closest friend until Adam happened. *Laugh and grow fat.* One of my favorite proverbs, and one I always associated with her, because she was a riot. I'm pretty sure I'll be fatter today thanks to her.

She's already seated when I arrive at the café. Her lips break into a smile when she sees me, and it warms my heart. We hug. It takes me right back to those carefree days as a student. Simpler times.

"It's so good to see you," she says as we settle into the chairs.

"You too."

Her mood darkens. I wonder if she's still harboring some resentment from the last time she came over to my house. It was around three years ago. I had invited her for lunch, but when she rang the doorbell Adam wouldn't let me answer the door. She tried a few more times, then knocked, eventually resorting to calling and texting me. Adam held my phone captive. With no response, she had left. I was furious, but there wasn't much I could do. It was one of the ways he ensured I drifted apart from the people close to me. She had accepted my apology when

I called her the next day, but I dared not invite her again. I couldn't get myself to explain the situation, embarrassed to admit that I had goofed by marrying Adam.

Looking back, I wonder why I didn't confide in her. If there was anyone in the world I should have shared my deepest, darkest concerns with, it was Nikki. She would have listened. She wouldn't have judged. She might even have talked me out of my fears and baseless justifications. Most importantly, she could have helped me escape.

"Are you okay?" she asks. A part of me is relieved when I realize it's nothing to do with that day. And why would it be? After all, she has called me a few times since then, and each time I could tell she was concerned about my well-being. I convinced her I was fine every single time. Eventually the calls stopped, and we lost touch.

I don't know how to answer her question, for she's staring at the injuries on my face. Even with all the makeup they are still visible. I had run into the same issue with the others but had managed to dodge their queries. It's a lot more difficult with Nikki; she can read me like a book.

"Did he hit you?"

I don't know how to answer this one either.

"Why do you let him do this to you?" she asks when I don't respond. My eyes fill up, and a tear threatens to drip down my face. I attack it with a tissue before it can begin its downhill slide. "You can talk to me, you know."

I nod.

"It breaks my heart to see you like this. You were one of the bravest, strongest women I knew. Do you remember how you were back in college? You didn't take shit from anybody, always standing up for yourself and others. You were my role model, Sarah."

It's reassuring to hear that. To remember the woman I once was. Depressing, too. Sad to see how the mighty have fallen. This was not how I had pictured this meeting. *Where are the laughs?* Yet, it's cathartic in a way. "Thanks," is all I can muster.

"It's not your fault. He's so handsome, so charming. It seemed like he genuinely cared about you. We were all taken in by him."

But it *was* my fault. I hadn't told her about the red flags. Of course, Adam stepped up his game after we got married. But even after I had made the mistake, I could have escaped. It's not like he had me caged. But somewhere along the way I had lost my spirit, his overbearing personality eclipsing mine. I was swayed by his sob stories — he gained my sympathies by telling me about how he had lost his parents early, and how he had suffered in various orphanages. His behavior was justified, I convinced myself.

This time I let Nikki in, sharing everything about my life with Adam. Once I have unburdened myself, she soothes me, guides me. Soon we move on to other topics, digging up old anecdotes, and I end up laughing so much that my belly is aching. It's just what I had hoped for. It's exactly what I needed.

CHAPTER THREE

Nikki did a great job lifting my spirits. We've already made plans for her to visit me next weekend. The drive back home has me in a peppy mood, singing along to the tunes on the radio, my predicament a distant memory.

I'm turning into my driveway when I spot a man peeking inside the house through one of the windows. He turns, and I realize it's Hopper, bringing me crashing down to reality. My brunch wants to escape up my throat, but I get out of the car and amble up to the front door. He's sporting a smug smile. It adds to my uneasiness. Unlocking the door without saying a word, I step inside the house. He follows. We establish our regular positions in the living room.

"We got your husband's data from the phone company. His location history shows he was last at Crystal Springs."

Damn! Here it comes.

"So we searched the surrounding area. We didn't find him, but there were skid marks along one side of the reservoir leading from the road to a tree. Next to the tree we found some fragments that could be from his car based on the description you gave us. On a hunch, we had a team search the water. Guess what we found?"

"His car?" I hate rhetorical questions, I really do.

"Bingo! With him inside it."

My hand goes up to my mouth and I gasp. It's the appropriate response under the circumstances. Hopper's not impressed.

"Initial examination of the body confirmed the timeline. He was clearly in an accident. From what we have pieced together, the car skidded and hit the tree head-on. Mr. Baldwin sustained fatal injuries. How the car ended up in the water, we don't know yet. Perhaps you can enlighten me, Sarah?"

"How ... how would I know?"

"Because you were right there with him."

I'm thankful I am seated, otherwise I would have fainted and collapsed to the floor. But I do wish I could sink further into the couch and disappear.

"I told you I wasn't with him. I was here. At home. If I was in the car, how come I'm sitting here talking to you? I should be dead and under water like him."

"Tell me — that injury on your head — how did you get it? You didn't just fall and bump your head, did you?"

"I ... I fell. It's exactly like I told you."

There's that smirk again. He's amusing himself by outsmarting me. I resent him so much, I'm itching to sock him in the face.

"You know, we have your phone records too." He pauses and watches me, waiting for a reaction. I don't give him the satisfaction of seeing one, though my insides are turning to jelly. "You know what we found?"

I think I know, but I shake my head. *Game over*, no doubt.

"Your location data shows that you were with him. All the way from home to the spot where he died. The difference is, he stayed back there, but you returned. That must have been one hell of a walk."

It sure was. It took three days for the soreness in my legs to die down. The blisters on my feet took longer to heal. Ditching my heels and going barefoot had been the only option. I couldn't risk hitching a ride.

"So now why don't you tell me what happened?"

A lie may take care of the present, but it has no future. I don't think I can wriggle out of this one, so I better tell him the truth.

"It ... it was an accident. He was driving too fast, and he lost control. We slammed into the tree. I hit my head. He ... he was injured badly and died on the spot."

"You're sure he was dead?"

"Yes. I confirmed he wasn't breathing. Then I checked his pulse. There ... there was nothing."

"I see. Where were you headed?"

"To a party. Our friends, the Silbermans. They have this fancy shindig every year."

"Okay, so the car crashes. Adam's dead. How did it end up in the lake?"

"I … I panicked. I thought everyone would suspect I had something to do with it. So I moved the car and let it roll into the water."

He is disgusted by me. I can tell from the way he's glaring. But it is what it is. I did what I had to to survive.

"Let me get this straight. You just let your husband disappear without a trace? You didn't even want to grant him the dignity of a proper funeral? No concern that his loved ones would need some closure — would want to know what happened to him?"

"I … I know what I did was wrong, but I was scared. I wasn't thinking. Besides, he has no family. No one cares." I flinch at the last remark. Even a monster like Adam doesn't deserve that.

"You could have left the car there and walked back. I still don't see why you had to sink it."

"I was worried they might find evidence that I was with him when it happened. That's why I rolled down the windows as well — so that the water would wash away everything."

"If you were worried about your fingerprints or hair, you needn't have bothered. It would be perfectly normal to find your DNA in the car. You are his wife after all."

"I was more concerned about the blood. Where I hit my head."

"Makes sense, but I still don't understand something. Why did you think anyone would suspect you? It was an accident, plain and simple. Well, at least it was until you tampered with the evidence. Now there's a real reason to suspect you of foul play."

"I didn't do anything, honest. I … I just thought that anyone who knew he was cheating on me, that he was abusive, would assume I had sufficient motive to kill him. The fact that he died and I survived with only a minor injury would only add to the suspicion."

Hopper sighs. "It does, doesn't it?" he says, and then he's quiet for a long time, while I sit there fidgeting nervously, awaiting my fate. The suspense is killing me. What I would give to get inside his head and learn what he's thinking.

"You weren't the first one." He breaks the silence.

"The first what?"

"I've been looking into your husband's past. He had a lot of girlfriends before he married you. At least three of them filed abuse complaints against him. I checked the records."

"Oh. I had no idea."

"He managed to get off lightly in every case. I don't know how he pulled it off, but the thing is, I believe you. What he did to you was very wrong. What you did wasn't right either, but I don't see the point of pursuing this any further. He died in an accident, and that's that. No more women will suffer at his hands."

He stands up and turns to leave. I'm still not sure I heard him right.

"Wait," I say as I stand up. He turns around. "You aren't going to arrest me?"

"No. There's no case here. The autopsy should be complete in a couple of days. I don't expect they will find anything more than what I already told you. You can pick up his body from the morgue after that and start arranging the funeral."

I sink into the couch, relief surging through my body. "Thank you," I say. "Thank you."

I'm free. I. Am. Free. The realization is still sinking in. It's been forever since I've slept soundly, but tonight will be the night that I do. I'm sure of it.

EPILOGUE

I feel suffocated. Trapped in this car with Adam next to me, his eyes focused on the road. We're headed to the Silbermans' party. Adam's excited about it, as he always is. I would rather have stayed home in my PJs and binged on *Netflix* and a tub of Rocky Road ice cream. My body's still hurting, and not just in one spot. Everywhere. This douchebag sure knows how to dish it out. I don't know if I can take it anymore. The pain. The fear. I don't even remember who I am anymore.

A truck is speeding our way in the opposite lane. There's no divider. I can end everything right here. For him. For me. I grab the steering wheel and push to the left, leading us across the double yellow lines.

"What the ..." he says before he turns the wheel to the right furiously and gets us back on track.

Fear grips me, for I know he will punish me for this infraction. But that terror only lasts a second. He overcorrected, and now he has lost control. We're headed for a massive tree. I close my eyes, body pulsing, wondering what I was thinking. *Do I really want to die?* We crash before I have an answer.

When I come to, my head is throbbing. Slowly, I turn my head to face left. There are shards of glass everywhere. Adam's face is bloody, but he's still breathing. For how long, I wonder. He needs help. I search for my phone frantically, and pick it up off the floor with shaking hands. I dial — nine, one, my finger hovering over the keypad, ready to tap in the last digit. My hand is frozen as my mind processes the situation. Fate has presented me with another opportunity, and I'd have to be stupid to miss it. I should let him die while I still have a chance.

AUTHOR'S NOTE

The line "I should have let him die when I had the chance" was stuck in my head for a long time. I had some sense of what the story would be about — a woman suffering abuse at the hands of her lover rues her missed opportunity to get rid of him. She gets another chance and this time she doesn't let go. Eventually the story took shape in my head and it didn't take long to write (during a remarkably productive December 2022). The original title was *The Missing Husband*, but it sounded too generic. This is a story about Sarah, and the updated title reflects that. Here's hoping that she has put all this behind her and has turned into the fierce, independent woman she once was.

THE CONVERSATION

A Detective Conley mystery

Rachel stepped out to the balcony and lit a cigarette. The first puff helped, but the latest setback still weighed on her mind. Rob's voice echoed in her head. "You're fired!" he had said earlier that morning. Stinging words that left her feeling humiliated. Why her, she questioned. Perhaps he wouldn't have been so mad if she had toned it down a bit. She had to get a better handle on her emotions. Before long, her concerns turned to money. She reckoned her savings would last her a couple of months, so she'd better get cracking on that job hunt. First the breakup, now this. Her mother always said that problems came in threes. What catastrophe could she expect next?

She took another puff, letting the cool evening air envelop her. Quite a relief from the searing heat during the day. Faint strains of "Unchained Melody" reached her, indicating that the neighbors were getting frisky again. By the time she was halfway into "I've Had the Time of My Life," she heard the moans. Did they really have to rub it in? Reminding her of what she had been missing the last few weeks? If only her last boyfriend hadn't cheated on her, she would have been in his arms now. That would have cheered her up.

The moans peaked and stopped. The music died down. Fragments of conversation caressed her ears. Tender post-coital talk at first. Then back to the real world, problems discussed, advice given and taken, solutions reached. Moving on to the next issue at hand. She was unable to catch the initial part, but it was clear as the man raised his voice, and the woman followed.

"... she has got to go. The bitch! Pain in my ..."

"... take it easy ..." The woman tried to calm him down.

"I'm telling you, I'll blow her head off if I get a gun!"

Rachel shuddered. After a few minutes she stubbed out what was left of her cigarette and reentered her apartment.

Homicide Detective Paul Conley kissed Brigette goodbye and stepped out of the house, a smile plastered on his face. A hearty breakfast and conversation with his wife to start the day, what more could a man ask for? The smile disappeared when his phone buzzed and he saw who was calling. Matt Zigler this early could only mean one thing. Trouble.

Five minutes later, he was driving towards Delano district, advancing on the scene of the crime. The Arkansas River shimmered in the distance as he turned into the apartment complex. Yet another homicide inside an apartment. Had the murderers of Wichita lost their sense of adventure? Or had they moved indoors to avoid the brutal summer heat? Not that he was complaining. He preferred indoor investigations. Much easier to control the scene. He stepped out of his car and walked over to where Officer Davis stood with his sign-in sheet. First-floor unit this time. He crossed under the tape into the apartment.

She lay sprawled in the middle of the living room with a bright red entry wound on her forehead. Her plush white bathrobe contrasted with the blood-soaked carpet above her blonde head. Natalie from forensics was with her. Beyond the body was the kitchen. A tech stood there working on the wall. To the left of the body was a small dining table with four chairs around it. A plate full of salad was on the table, a fork by its side. Getting shot is one way to avoid eating salad, Paul thought. He would consider that the next time Brigette forced him to eat some.

"She never got started with dinner," said Natalie.

"Yeah, that looks untouched. My guess is the killer interrupted her."

Natalie nodded. "Fresh out of the shower. Can still smell her body wash. Fruity."

"What's her name?"

"Emma. Emma Williams. Shooter got her point-blank. Single shot. The bullet went right through her and lodged in that wall," she continued as she pointed to the tech in the kitchen.

"Do we have the weapon?"

"No. It's probably a 9mm."

"I see. Time of death?"

"Between seven and nine last night."

"Who discovered the body?"

"Her boyfriend. Clark Daniels. He came by this morning. Poor guy's in shock."

"She lived alone?"

"Yes. That's what he said."

"Where is he?"

"The apartment manager found us an empty apartment. Officer Larsen took him there."

"I'll talk to him once I'm done here. Find anything interesting?"

"The usual prints around the place. But I doubt we'll find any from the killer."

"Why is that?"

"The place was vacuumed after the deed was done. If he went to the trouble of vacuuming ..."

"Vacuumed?"

"Yes."

"Interesting. But we might still find something inside the vacuum?"

"Already checked the bag. Empty."

"But emptied where? Did anyone check the trash cans?"

"No goodies in any of the cans."

Paul shook his head and donned gloves to search for evidence. He inspected Emma's body for any other signs of trauma but didn't find any. Then he performed a thorough scan of the living room. Other than the dining table, there was a sofa, a loveseat, a coffee table, and a TV stand on which stood the massive flat-screen. Not finding anything important there, he moved on to the kitchen, peeking into the drawers and cabinets. No clues. He was about to step out when something under the refrigerator caught his eye. He bent down to pick up the object sitting on the floor, just under the edge of the appliance. It was a platinum wedding band with an inscription inside:

Happily ever after AB.FB

The initials didn't match the victim or her boyfriend. Paul bagged the evidence and peered under the refrigerator in case there were more such treasures, but he came up empty. He walked over to the only bedroom. A queen bed dominated the room, flanked on either side by a nightstand with a lamp on top. A Katy Perry poster covered the wall behind the bed. The bed was unmade, and he wondered whether she had slept in it before showering or if it had been left that way in the morning. A smile escaped his lips — an untidy bed would have earned him a lecture from Brigette. There was a closed laptop sticking out from under one of the pillows. He opened it to find it was locked. Guessing passwords was not one of his strong suits, so he decided it was best left to the cyber forensics team. He peeked under the other pillows and found what he was looking for — her cell phone. As expected, it was locked as well. He added both items to the evidence collection.

Continuing the search, he checked under the mattress. Nothing. A quick sweep under the bed didn't reveal anything either. On to the nightstand drawers. There were a few odds and ends and some paperwork which took him a while to review. Nothing that shed light on her death. There was a walk-in closet to the right of the bed. Paul entered to find the usual array of clothes and shoes. An overflowing laundry basket. He wrapped up and stepped out. Soon he was done searching the apartment.

⤜⤜⤜ ⤛⤛⤛

He went over to the vacant apartment and found the boyfriend seated on the floor with his head in his hands. Officer Larsen stood by. Clark looked up when he heard Paul enter. His eyes were swollen and screamed pain. Late twenties, Paul estimated. Around the same age as Emma. He introduced himself and expressed his sympathies.

"I know this is a difficult time, but I have to ask you some questions."

Clark nodded.

"I understand you found her?"

"Yeah. She was going to come over this morning, but she didn't show. Didn't respond to my calls or texts either. I was worried. So I came here ... and ... and ..." He broke down crying.

Paul waited till he had calmed down.

"How did you enter the apartment?"

"I ... I have a key."

"I see. When did you see her last?"

"Yesterday afternoon. She stopped by work on her way home."

"Where do you work?"

"At Easy Rent-A-Car."

"The one downtown?"

"Yeah."

"How about Emma? Did she work too?"

"Yeah. She had her own business. A gourmet cupcake store. Emma Bakes."

Paul wondered how he hadn't heard of this place. *Shucks.* Too late to check it out now.

"Why did she visit you at work? Did you two have plans?"

"No. She just wanted to say hi. Gave me a kiss. She looked stunning," Clark said, a tear flowing down his cheek.

"So she kissed you and left?"

"Yeah. It was around four o'clock when she came, and I didn't get off until six. In any case, we were going to meet today."

"And what did you do after work?"

"Went home."

"And you stayed home all evening?"

"Yeah."

"Anyone who can vouch for you?"

"What do you mean? You think I had something to do with her ..." Clark's eyes grew wide. "Why ... why would I do that? I ... I loved her so much."

"I understand. But it's a routine question. So no one can confirm your whereabouts last evening?"

"I guess."

"How long were you together?"

"Around three months now."

"And how did you meet?"

"She visited us for a rental. I served her. We got talking and next thing you know, I asked her out to dinner."

"Does she have any family?"

"Yeah. Her parents live out in Old Town."

"Do you have their contact information?"

"Yeah."

"Officer Larsen will note it down. And we need your details too. I'll notify the parents."

"Sure."

"Do you own a gun, Clark?"

"A gun? No."

"Have you ever shot one?"

"Yeah. I used to visit the shooting range with my ex."

"Any good?"

"Better than I was when I started. Sure could use some more practice."

"Well, that's all the questions I have for you. You take care."

Paul stepped out of the apartment to canvass the neighbors, hoping someone had seen or heard something that would aid the investigation. He knocked on the door of the apartment to the right of Emma's.

"I already told ya I'm not subscribing to no newspapers!" yelled the man who opened the door. He was dressed in denim shorts and a vest. Fine lines ran across his forehead, and he was graying at the temples. "Oh," he said, realizing it wasn't who he thought it was.

Paul introduced himself and entered as the man stepped back to let him in.

"Joseph. Joseph Almena. Sorry about that. Those girls come by every week to annoy me. Want me to sign up for subscriptions I don't want. Money goes to charity, they say. Bah! I don't buy that one bit. Now, what is it you want from me?"

Paul explained the situation.

"A gunshot, you say? No, sir. I heard nothing of the sort. And I know my firearms. Served in Afghanistan, you see. But she did play the TV too loud. All of a sudden. Scared the shit out of me."

"And what time was this?"

"I reckon around eight o'clock. I'd just settled in with a nice book. And boom goes the TV."

"Did you ask her to lower the volume?"

"Didn't need to. It was off a minute later. Then it was the vacuum."

"The vacuum?" *Could this have been the killer?* he wondered.

"Yeah. Vacuumed for a couple of minutes, and then it was peaceful after that. I managed to finish the book. A real page-turner that one."

"Did you see anyone enter or leave the apartment?"

"Nope. I stayed in all evening. No idea what went on outside."

"Did you notice anything odd about her, or any visitors recently?"

"Odd? You mean if someone had reason to kill her?"

"Yes."

"No. I hardly knew her. And I don't spy on my neighbors."

"I'm sure you don't. Thanks for your help, Joseph. Do call me if you remember anything, okay?" Paul said as he handed him his card.

Paul moved on to the other neighbors, but no one had seen or heard anything suspicious. It was as if the killer was invisible.

It was late when Paul eased his car into the parking spot at Easy Rent-A-Car. The conversation with Emma's parents still weighed on his mind. Notifying the next of kin was never easy, and they had been shattered on learning they had lost their only child. They couldn't fathom why anyone would want to hurt their sweet little Emma.

Paul took a few deep breaths to clear his head before stepping out. There were five counters inside the rental office, but only two were open. The last customers, a family of four, were leaving one of the counters, broad smiles on their faces. Happy to be on vacation, thought Paul. He wondered why they were in Wichita of all places. Wouldn't those kids have preferred someplace else — like Disney World in Florida, perhaps? Probably visiting family, he concluded.

The agent at the first counter smiled at him eagerly, hoping some more business was coming her way. She had beautiful, vibrant eyes, and the smile was pleasant, he noted as he introduced himself. Her momentary disappointment vanished once he mentioned Clark. She worked the same shifts as him.

"Rekha, was Clark here for the entire shift yesterday?" Paul addressed her by the name he read off her badge.

"Yes. He came in at nine a.m. and left at six. It may not look like it today, but we were super busy yesterday."

"He didn't take any long breaks?"

"No. We just took a quick twenty-minute break for lunch around one p.m."

"Did he have any visitors?"

"Oh, yes. His girlfriend stopped by sometime in the afternoon. But he wasn't gone long."

"So he didn't stay at the counter?"

"No. They stepped outside the building."

"I see. Any idea what they talked about?"

"No. But ..."

"But what?"

"I know they fought."

"They fought? How do you know that?"

"As I told you, we were very busy yesterday. The queues were building up. So I went to call him back after five minutes. They were standing further away from the entrance. I could tell they were having words."

"Do you know what they were fighting about?"

Rekha shook her head. "They were far enough that I couldn't hear them clearly."

"What happened then?"

"I came back inside. I didn't want any of that drama."

"How did he seem when he returned?"

"Upset. As you would expect."

"Did he say anything to you?"

"No. Not a word."

"Has he ever discussed his relationship before?"

"No. I've only been here a month. All I knew was that he had a girlfriend."

"And you never met her?"

"No, but I've seen her around. She visits often."

"How did they seem on previous visits?"

"Happy. They looked happy. I don't recall any fights."

"I see. Thanks, Rekha. You've been most helpful."

"If I may ask — why are you asking all these questions? Is Clark okay?"

"Yes, he is."

Paul moved on to the lady at the other counter, but it had been her day off the previous day. Once out of the building, he reviewed the latest findings. Clark had lied. He hadn't mentioned the fight. Why? If he got off work at 6:00 p.m. that gave him sufficient time to drive to Emma's and shoot her. Paul had some digging to do.

❧ ❧

Early next morning, he stood in front of Clark's apartment door, ready to knock. He had stopped at Emma Bakes on his way back from the rental office the previous evening. With the owner out of commission, he had expected it to be closed, but it had not been the case. The couple of employees in the store had been shocked to hear about Emma's demise. Shirley, the manager, had a spare set of keys to open up in Emma's absence. She had tried calling Emma a couple of times and had been worried, but business was brisk, and she hadn't found the time to follow up. Both women told him that Emma seemed to be happy with Clark. They couldn't think of anyone who would want to harm her, considering what a wonderful woman she was. She had seemed a bit upset the previous afternoon, but nothing that would concern anyone. With no new leads, Paul had departed, disciplined enough to avoid the baked goodies on display.

He knocked. Clark opened the door a few seconds later, eyes puffy and red. *Feeling remorse over what he had done? Or was it genuine grief?*

"You lied," Paul said as he followed him into the modest studio. Clark stopped and turned around.

"Lied about what?"

"You told me Emma's visit that evening was pleasant."

"Yeah, it was. She kissed me. It's as pleasant as can be at work."

"That's not what I hear. You fought."

The color drained from Clark's face.

"Oh, so you remember now?"

"Who told you?"

"Doesn't matter who told me."

"It was Rekha, wasn't it?"

"Like I said, it doesn't matter who. The point is — you lied."

"Okay, yeah, we had an argument. Big deal. Couples fight all the time."

"How often does one of them end up dead soon after?"

"You think I killed her? I'm telling you, I didn't do it!"

"Then why did you lie?"

"This is exactly why! I knew you would suspect me even though I'm innocent. Boyfriends are always top of the list in the crime shows I watch."

"I'm asking you again — what did you do after you left work?"

"I told you already. I came straight home. Ate dinner. Watched some Netflix. Then off to bed."

"I don't see a TV in here," Paul replied after scanning the room a second time.

"I watched it on my Mac, grandpa." Clark pointed to the laptop on the floor. "You know, you don't look that old, but you do realize you can stream that stuff anywhere, right?"

"Don't get snarky with me!"

"And let me set things straight here. We did fight, but we were cool later. Look at this if you don't believe me."

Clark showed Paul his phone. It had a text conversation between him and Emma around 7:00 p.m. the previous evening.

Clark: Sorry babe. Won't happen again. I love you.

Emma: Love you too hun. See you tomorrow?

Clark: Yep. Bright and early.

Emma: xoxoxoxo

Clark: xoxoxoxo

Paul had to admit this shot down his theory about Clark. But what if Clark had planted these texts? He could have driven straight to Emma's after work, got into her phone and sent these texts before killing her. He hoped Clark's phone records would shed some light.

"You kids made up quick. What did you fight about? Clearly you messed up about something."

"Well ..." Clark hesitated, his pale skin turning red.

"Go on."

"I had clicked some pictures of her when she was here a couple of weeks ago. You know ... umm ..."

"Nude pics?"

"Yeah. It was ... it was just a fun thing. She was cool with it. Said she loved them."

"So what was the problem?"

"I was stupid. I forwarded them to my bud Riley — you know how it is — just showing off what a hot chick I was banging."

"And this is your girlfriend you are talking about?"

"Sorry, I know that came off as crass. But you know what I mean."

Paul nodded.

"Riley's girlfriend found the pics and told Emma. That's what she was furious about. For what it's worth, Riley got his ass kicked too." Clark smirked before turning serious again.

With no more questions to ask, Paul left the apartment, shaking his head as he said, "Kids today."

***

"No chocolate, Paul," Sergeant Matt Zigler remarked as he chomped on another donut. "The chocolate ones are the best. But they were out. You love 'em too. Did you beat me to it?"

"You know I don't eat this stuff anymore," Paul replied, eyeing the box full of temptations. This is what made trips to Zigler's office so difficult.

"Oh, yeah. Duh-nuts. That's what you call 'em, right?" Matt brushed off the sugar from his shirt before reaching for another piece. "Anyhoo. So you think lover boy did it?"

"He lied about the fight. But that's not sufficient motive. I'm still digging."

"His phone records here yet?"

"No. Got the autopsy results, though. Confirms our findings from the scene. Ballistics confirmed a 9mm was used, but we haven't located the gun yet. Time of death is around eight p.m."

"And I guess there's no point matching Clark's prints to any found in the apartment since he was a regular there?"

"Right."

"How about her cell phone and laptop?"

"They're still trying to crack the codes. No luck yet."

"Damn security! No other leads?"

"Not yet."

"Odd that no one heard the shot. You think the TV masked it?"

"Yes. That's my theory."

"Smart fucker. I don't like these smart ones. Vacuumed the place to suck up evidence. Unbelievable. Where are those killers who leave us clear prints and hair and all the good stuff? I miss those days. Darn *CSI!*"

Paul smiled. "We just got to be smarter than them, Sarge. We'll get this one. Don't you worry."

Paul had barely reached his desk when his phone buzzed. An unknown caller. Junk call or someone with information about the case, he wondered. Betting on the latter, he answered.

Thirty minutes later he was knocking on the door of Rachel Donovan. When it opened, it was a delight for his senses. There stood before him a striking young woman, dressed in a white tank top and denim shorts. One of the reasons he loved summer was how much more skin he got to see. But that wasn't all. The aroma of cookies baking wafted through. It took some effort, but he refocused his attention on the task at hand once they were seated.

"Rachel, you said on the phone that you had important information about Emma Williams' death."

"Yes. Around ten days ago I overheard my neighbors plotting a murder. They wanted to kill a woman. With a gun. And then I see this in the news."

Here we go again, thought Paul. Another crazy tipster.

"You sure it wasn't just talk? I mean, a lot of people say things without actually meaning it."

"Oh, no. They sounded serious."

"Still, they could have been talking about anybody. How do you know they were targeting Emma?"

"Because that's the name they used."

His ears perked up. Maybe this would amount to something after all.

"You sure about that?"

The oven dinged.

"Hang on," she said as she walked over to the kitchen and opened the oven door. By now the aroma of the cookies was overwhelming. Chocolate chip, he thought as he tried not to drool.

"Would you like one?" she asked.

He controlled himself and declined, but soon regretted the decision when she returned and sank her teeth into a cookie. *Soft bake!* His favorite.

"So, where were we?"

"Are you sure they said 'Emma'?"

"Hmmhh," she nodded, her mouth too full to speak.

"What else did they talk about?"

"Nothing important. That's all I got."

"Have you ever heard them say anything like this before?"

"No, this was the first time. That's why I was so scared."

Another bite of the cookie.

"How well do you know them?"

"Not much, really. I mean, we try to be friendly neighbors. As you can tell, I love to bake. So I take over stuff for them from time to time. And he helps me fix up things. But we don't hang out much beyond that."

"So you wouldn't know how they know Emma?"

Rachel shook her head as she brushed off the crumbs.

"Thank you, Rachel. I'll talk to them. Do call me if you remember anything else."

He handed her his card and departed.

It was not long before Paul stood before a woman in her late forties, with a man, who he guessed was her husband, peering at him in the background. She had answered the door after several knocks and gazed at him inquiringly with her steely gray eyes. He introduced himself and followed her inside.

"I'm Felicia, and this is my husband, Alex," she said as they seated themselves in the tastefully decorated living room. "How can we help you?"

"Do you know a woman named Emma Williams?"

"No," they replied in unison with identical furrowed brows as they turned to each other for confirmation. "Why do you ask?" continued Alex.

"She was found dead a few days ago. Shot through the head."

"Oh, that's awful!" Felicia's face clouded with what Paul deduced was genuine concern.

"But what does this have to do with us?" asked Alex.

"Where were you the evening of the seventh?"

"The seventh? What was that — three days ago?"

"Yes."

"Is that when she ..."

Paul nodded.

"We were here at home, right Alex?" Felicia turned to her husband.

"Yes, I think so. Oh yes, of course! That was the night we ..." Alex smiled at her. She smiled back demurely, flushing.

"You were doing what?"

"Well, we were in bed all evening. You know ..." Alex replied with a hint of embarrassment.

"I see. Anyone who can verify that?"

"Of course not! Just what kind of people do you think we are? It was just the two of us," Felicia replied with a frown.

"Oh, that's not what I meant. So, no alibi?"

"Alibi? Alibi for what? Surely you don't think we had anything to do with that woman's death?"

"A few days before she died you were overheard plotting a murder. Murdering a woman, specifically."

"Utter nonsense! Who told you this?" Alex almost jumped out of his seat.

"I can't tell you that. So you deny any such discussion? Planning how to shoot a woman named Emma?"

"No way! Do we look like murderers?" He turned to Felicia. The next second he burst out laughing.

"What's so funny?" asked Paul. He figured Felicia had the same question, for she was eyeing Alex with a dazed expression.

"I think I know what this is about. Clearly a misunderstanding. You see, my ex, Claudia, is being a real bitch. I've been blowing off a lot of steam, and Felicia here has been bravely tolerating me. I think I said I wanted to blow her brains out. And gut her. And throw her off the Burj or whatever that tower's called. You get the drift. That's probably what this person heard."

"My source was sure it was Emma."

"Well, how's this source so sure? Was he — I'm assuming this was a he — was he standing right next to us?"

"No. Not that close."

"There you go. Must have misheard, then," Alex replied with a flourish.

As Alex's hand settled back in his lap, Paul noticed the tan mark on his ring finger.

"Where's your wedding band?"

"My wedding band?" Alex asked, looking confused. "Why do you care?"

"You obviously have one, which you have worn for a long time. Where's it now?"

"I don't understand ..."

"Just answer the question. Where is it?"

"Honestly, I don't know. I seem to have lost it. I remember taking it off before doing the dishes the other day. Haven't seen it since. Must have fallen and rolled off under some furniture. I'll look for it later."

"What did you say your last name was?"

"I didn't. It's Baum."

Alex Baum. Felicia Baum. AB.FB. Yes, it was possible, thought Paul.

"What kind of band was it?"

"Look, I'm not sure why you care about my wedding band. But anyway. It's a platinum band. With an inscription with our initials."

Paul's heart raced. This could not be a coincidence.

"Happily ever after?"

"Yes! But how do you ..." Alex trailed off as his excitement changed to confusion.

"It was lying two feet away from Emma's body."

If Alex had anything to do with the murder, he was hiding it well with the shocked expression. Felicia gaped at him open-mouthed.

"I ... I don't understand. How could it have ended up there? I don't know this woman. Surely you're mistaken?"

"I don't think so. Now, maybe you know this woman by some other name?" Paul replied, showing the couple a picture of Emma on his phone.

They shook their heads. "Never seen her before," Alex added for emphasis.

"Poor little thing. It's awful dying so young." Felicia's face was drawn.

"Alex, don't forget — this is a murder investigation, and we found your ring close to the body. I understand there may be reasons you don't want to disclose your relationship with this woman, but it could get you in trouble," Paul said as he stole a glance at Felicia.

"What are you trying to say, Detective? My Alex would never do anything like that!" As she said this, Felicia's face and tone reminded him of his second grade teacher when she caught him doing stuff he shouldn't have been doing.

"Do either of you own a gun?"

The familiar head shake again.

He paused to review the facts in his head. Rachel had overheard the Baums plotting to shoot a woman dead. She was sure the target was Emma. The couple had no alibi for the evening Emma died, and Alex's ring was found close to the body. The needle of suspicion pointed at Alex. Perhaps Felicia was involved too. But why would they do it? What would be the motive? It was something Paul would have to dig into. But for now, he had to search their apartment. He got cracking on the warrant and readied the search team.

It was four long hours before he had the warrant and they were able to begin. He kept busy, avoiding the glares from the Baums. Two hours later, Officer Larsen showed up holding his prize. Paul's eyes stretched wide.

"Awesome! Where did you find that?"

"In one of the flowerpots on the balcony. It was hidden well."

"What made you look in there?"

"They have a lot of pots out there. All neat and tidy. But something didn't look right about that one."

"Great work, Larsen."

Paul stared at the Beretta M9. This had to be the murder weapon. The bullet that killed Emma was from a 9mm pistol. Now if only ballistics could confirm this was the gun used. He showed it to Alex, whose jaw dropped.

"I've never seen that before," was all he could say.

"Me neither," added Felicia.

"Then what was it doing on your balcony?"

"I don't know. Someone must have put it there."

"Seriously? You expect me to buy that?"

"Well you had better, since it's the truth." Felicia was adamant.

The ballistics report came back after a week and confirmed that the gun found at the Baums' was the one used on Emma. The arrest warrant was ready a day later. Alex Baum was cooling his heels in jail by the end of that day, but Paul still didn't have a motive. Alex's cell phone records placed him at home during the murder window, as he had claimed. Of course, he could have left his phone there to mislead everyone. But something didn't seem right. Was it possible Paul was looking at the wrong Baum? What if things weren't as great as they seemed between the Baums? What if Felicia had motive to kill Emma, and decided to implicate Alex in the process? It was so easy, living in the same apartment. He would have to investigate Felicia further.

His thoughts drifted back to Clark. *Could Clark be ruled out?* Clark's phone records had arrived a couple of days ago, but Paul had ignored them. He started reviewing them. The location data placed Clark at home when Emma breathed her last. A number in the call logs caught Paul's eye. It was familiar, but he couldn't recall where he had seen it. Five calls in the last week. Tons of calls and texts in the past, then a two-month gap that ended the previous week. When he discovered whose number it was a few minutes later, it was as if someone had socked him in the gut. *Could it really be?*

Paul hastened to Clark's apartment. Faint strains of the evening news floated out. To his surprise, the door was open a crack. He raised his hand to knock, but his instincts told him not to. He eased the door open wide. A woman stood in the living room with her back to him. Even though he had only met her once, he knew who it was. The one from the call logs. Beyond her stood Clark, looking like he had seen a ghost. Clark spotted Paul. Evidently the woman noticed the glance, for she turned around. By the time Paul reached for his gun, it was too late. She was pointing her Beretta at him.

"Drop it!" she commanded.

He cursed himself and complied. *Should have pulled it out before entering,* he thought to himself. "That your favorite gun?" he asked.

She leered. "Yep. Too bad I had to sacrifice the other one. Now, get over here with my sweetheart," she said as she nudged him to move over to where Clark was standing. He took his time moving, wondering how to get out of this jam.

"Faster!"

He sped up.

"That's better. Now, Clark, sweetie, where's the remote? I want to turn up the volume."

Paul's heart skipped a beat. "So you can mask the sound when you fire?" he asked.

"You're a smart cookie, you know? I liked you the first time I laid eyes on you. Too bad you'll have to go too. But don't get any ideas. Any tricks and I'll shoot you even if the volume's low."

"Why did you kill Emma?"

A smirk this time. "Why did I kill Emma? Why don't you ask Casanova here?" She turned to Clark, who was trembling. He grew more nervous once he realized all eyes were on him.

"Clark?" Paul prodded.

"I ... I ..."

"What happened, sweetie? Cat got your tongue? Weren't trembling this way when you cheated on me with Emma. You were all macho back then when I found out. Told me to fuck off, remember?"

"You ... you dumped me. You ..."

"Because you cheated on me, you asshole! I loved you so much. Gave you everything. Yet you screwed around behind my back. And after I dumped you, you went around rubbing it in my face. That bitch was stopping by at work pretty much every day to suck your face in front of me. And when I complained about it, no one cared. *I* was the one who got fired."

"You ... you kinda had it coming. You were pissing off customers to get even with me."

"Hey! Watch what you say. Don't forget I still have the gun." Her face turned red with rage.

"So you killed Emma to get back at them?" Paul asked.

"Yeah. The bitch deserved it. And now this jerk needs to go too." She took aim at Clark.

"Clark didn't have anything to do with her death?"

"Nope. Clueless as always."

"Why did you implicate Alex, Rachel?"

She laughed. "Good question. Genius idea, wasn't it? I was worried someone might trace the murder back to me. I had a motive, after all. It would be a lot safer if the evidence led to someone else."

"Even if it meant an innocent man paid the price?"

"Yeah. Pretty much. No one gives a shit about me. Why should I care about anyone else?"

"You're clearly not worth giving a shit about," Paul replied before he realized his mistake. The gun was now pointed at him, and her expression told him she was itching to pull the trigger. This was not the model citizen who tipped him off about the killer next door. She sure had him fooled.

Keep your cool, Paul, he reminded himself. "So you made up the story about the Baums plotting the murder?" *Got to keep her talking, Paul. The more she talks, the less she shoots.*

"Not exactly. I did overhear them talking about killing someone. I just twisted the conversation to suit my needs."

"What about the evidence?"

"The gun was easy. I wiped it off once I was done. It's easy getting from my balcony to theirs. I found a time when they were not home and put it there."

"And the ring?"

"That took a little more effort. I hadn't really planned that. It just so happened that I had baked an apple pie for them the day before I shot Emma. You know I love baking, Detective, and this was my way of calming my nerves. I took it over. Felicia invited me in. Alex was doing the dishes. I noticed his ring sitting there and that got my mind working. I swiped it. Then all I had to do was drop it next to Emma once I was done."

"How did you get the guns?"

"Oh, I have my sources. I have quite a collection. Just careful to get the ones that can't be traced back to me."

"How did you get into her apartment?"

"Oh, that was the easiest part. I knocked, she opened the door. The look on her face. To die for. I'm the last person she would have expected. She knew who I was, of course. She was kinda embarrassed, actually. After all, she did steal my boyfriend from me. She was nice enough to let me in. For a moment there I considered letting her go. But then I convinced myself. She had been very naughty, and she had to be punished. The TV was on. She was just sitting down to dinner, I think. I picked up the remote and maxed out the volume. Before she could understand what was happening, I took out my gun and shot her."

"And then you cleaned up?"

"Yes, I did. The most important part, don't you think? Can't leave any evidence. I've done my CSI homework. Now, Clark dear, where's that remote?"

Rachel's eyes scanned the room. This was the opportunity Paul was waiting for. He pounced on her, grabbing her gun arm as they both went crashing to the floor. The gun went off, the bullet lodging in the ceiling. He wrested the pistol from her and pinned her to the ground. She struggled for a few seconds before realizing it was a futile effort.

"It's a shame you didn't taste my cookies."

"A shame indeed, but this will make up for it," he replied as he turned her around to cuff her and read her her rights.

Author's Note

We have all overheard conversations, some interesting, and others we wished we could shut out. But what if we misinterpreted a conversation, concluding that the speaker was going to commit a crime? That was the seed for this story. Again, it's a trope that's been used before, but it was compelling. By the time I started writing, the story developed into something different. Rachel didn't misinterpret the conversation. Instead, the conversation sparked an idea, and she used it to her advantage. When it came to the title, I wanted it simple, keeping it consistent with the first Conley story. But that didn't mean I couldn't have fun with it. Though the plots are unrelated, I paid homage to one my favorite movies, *The Conversation*, directed by Francis Ford Coppola and starring Gene Hackman. Watch it if you haven't.

WOMAN IN RED

A PSYCHOLOGICAL THRILLER

JASON

Have you ever had such a fright that you thought, this is it — this is where I bid adieu to this world? You must have, though you might not remember it. Well, I had such an experience less than a minute ago. There I was, dropping a shopping bag in the trunk of my car, when my body tingled, and I had this feeling that someone was right behind me, ready to attack. *That* was my horrifying moment. I whirled around, only to realize that my fears were unfounded. There *is* someone out there, though. Standing beside the Civic that's parked a few spots away from mine. I don't scare easily, so why am I so jumpy tonight? It's probably the environment — late at night in a mostly empty parking lot with nary a soul in sight. The stuff horror movies are made of.

The Civic's away from the streetlight, but even in the darkness I can tell it's a woman, her tall, curvy silhouette clearly visible. My heart speeds up again as she approaches, my thoughts flooded with the news story I read earlier in *The Mercury News*. It was something about attractive women accosting unwitting men around the Bay Area and robbing them. That must be the other reason I'm so skittish — that report's lodged in my subconscious, warning me to stay cautious.

"Excuse me," she says as she stops a couple of parking spots away.

By now she's directly under the streetlight and I can't help but notice that she's indeed attractive. Wavy, blonde hair complementing a sculpted face with high cheekbones. Her lips are full and painted red, matching the red dress that clings to her body. She has a good two to three inches on me, and that's after accounting for the heels she's wearing. I push my glasses up my nose with my index finger, something I find myself doing several times a day. I immediately regret the action, for it accentuates my nerdy appearance. If there was any chance she was interested in me, I'm pretty sure I've blown it. Though given my history, I figure I was never in the running. Two alternatives present themselves — either she needs help, or she's out to con me. The second option makes me shudder.

"My car broke down. I was wondering whether you could give me a ride home."

"You ... you don't have AAA?" I ask, unable to hide my nervousness.

"No, I don't."

"Well, I do. I can call and they should be able to help you out."

"Aw, that's so sweet of you, but that will take time, won't it? I have an early start tomorrow. It's a very important day for me. I was hoping I could get home and turn in early."

The young man in me wants to hold her hand and lead her into my car, but the mature adult warns me to stay away. "You could get an Uber."

Her brow creases. She bites her lip, her hands coming together. "I ... I can't afford that."

I relax a bit. Perhaps she is in genuine need. Perhaps she isn't out to get me.

"Where do you live?"

"Downtown. Shouldn't take more than fifteen minutes to get there."

It's close enough. Besides, I can't resist the chance to spend time with her. It's not every day that I am graced with the company of a beauty such as this one. *Who knows what it will lead to?*

Mature adult isn't giving up so easily, though. "Okay. But you said you had an early start tomorrow. How will you get there if your car's here?"

"Oh, I'll ask my friend to drop me."

Well, that's that. "Come on, then." I gesture to her to get in my car.

She walks up to me and extends her hand. "Thank you so much! I'm Jessica."

"Jason." I shake her hand. It's soft. And warm. I hope I'm not making a mistake.

Inside, we're so close that I want to touch her again. She smells divine. It takes quite an effort to stay away. I start the car and drive off.

"Sweet ride," she says once we're out of the lot.

"Thanks." I can't believe I'm blushing at the compliment. This car is already proving to be worth the fortune I spent on it.

"So, what do you do, Jason?"

"I'm a software engineer."

"So I guessed right." Jessica smiles as she places her hand on my arm. The gesture has an electric effect on me. *Is she flirting?* I can't tell. Reading people, especially women, is beyond me.

"How about you?" I ask.

"I'm in showbiz. I write scripts and do some acting on the side."

"Cool. Not surprised there. You look like you're a model or a movie star."

"You're too kind." This time her hand lands just above my knee. I shudder again, this time in a good way. *How pathetic is that?* I'm nearing thirty, but still behaving like I did when I was twelve.

"Anything I might have seen?"

"No, not much other than local plays and the like. I've been to a few auditions for TV shows and movies, but nothing's worked out yet."

"That's too bad. I'm sure you will land something soon."

"Fingers crossed." Both her hands go up in front of her with crossed fingers. "Most of the roles out there are meaningless dumb blonde bits, you know? Like, the audition today was for a two-minute part. A blonde who's stupid enough to get killed by this guy she just met. Do I really look that stupid?"

"I'm pretty sure you're a smart woman."

"You're so sweet." Her hand is back on my arm.

"You mentioned scripts. How's that going?"

"I've written some stuff, shopped it around, but nothing yet."

"What kind of stories?"

"Oh, all kinds of stuff. The most recent one was about this woman who hitches rides with strangers and knocks them out before taking off in their cars."

I grip the steering wheel tight with both hands. I don't like this at all, my feelings about Jessica oscillating like this. *Pretty woman in trouble, or a con artist out to get me?*

She laughs, her hand still on my arm. "Relax, I'm just kidding. Didn't mean to frighten you."

But is she really kidding? Or is she mocking me, challenging me to ward off her evil intentions? I must remain alert. Watch her every move. It's difficult, since I have to keep an eye on the road as well, but I get through the next few minutes without incident. We're in San Jose downtown now, and she directs me to stop in front of a row of rundown apartments. The street is dark, and the lights are off in most of the windows. I don't see a soul around. If she's going to attack me, this is the perfect opportunity.

"Want to come in for a drink?" she asks.

I should decline. That's the sensible thing to do, but I can't resist. No one can argue I didn't try to get out of it, though. "Don't you have an early start tomorrow?"

She flashes a charming smile. "I do, but you've been so nice to give me a ride. It's the least I can do."

Now, who can turn that down? We walk to her door together. She opens it after fumbling with the keys. My heart's been thumping throughout. Jessica turns on the light and steps inside. I follow. It's a modest studio, the compact kitchen to the right, the bed straight across, and a door to what I presume is the bathroom, on the left.

"Ah, that bed looks so inviting, doesn't it?" She's gazing at me, a grin on her face.

Is she hinting what I think she's hinting?

"I'm so exhausted I could just crash," she says as she moves past me and shuts the front door. *I guess not.*

"I can leave."

"Oh no, that's not what I meant. Please stay. What will you have? Wine okay?"

"Sure," I reply as she enters the kitchen.

Stay alert, I remind myself. She's on home turf and if she has any nefarious plans, this is where she will make her move. She pulls out a bottle and a couple of glasses from one of the cabinets and places them on the counter. It would be so easy for her to drop some poison into my glass and see my life ebb with every sip. I focus on her hands as she pours the wine into a glass and offers it to me. She watches me, her eyes urging me to take a sip. I know I shouldn't risk it. As far as I can tell, she didn't slip anything into my drink, but what if she had already put something in the bottle? I didn't see her uncork it, so it must have been open. Maybe she's always prepared for situations such as this one.

There's a sense of relief as she pours some wine into the other glass and takes a swig. I'm about to do the same, but I notice she hasn't swallowed yet. The liquid is still in her mouth. The wine might be poisoned after all.

She catches me staring and swallows. "I like to taste it. You know, discern the subtle flavors like those high-brow connoisseurs do." There's a hint of sarcasm in the way she says it, as if she's mocking said experts. It's like she read my mind.

"I can't tell one wine from another," I say, finally taking a sip. It's safe, I convince myself. I just have to ensure I don't drink too much. Perhaps the real plan is to get me drunk and vulnerable before she attacks.

I take the opportunity to scan the kitchen, to get the lay of the land. There's a refrigerator to the left. On the counter is a toaster, a microwave, and a knife rack. *Knives!* She could grab one and stab me when I'm not looking. But she takes her glass and walks over to the space behind me. There's a couch and a table there, both of which had escaped my notice earlier. She drops onto one end of the couch, crosses her legs, and smiles. I'm trying to decipher whether it's an invitation for me to join her, when I spot a copy of *The Mercury News* on the table. The news article I'd read before is face up.

"You read the papers too?"

"Yeah. Probably the last three people on the planet who still do, right?"

"Who's the third?"

"My neighbor. She's nice enough to lend it to me once she's done reading. I can't afford a subscription. You know, my dad would settle into his favorite chair and scan the papers for an hour every morning. When I read the paper I feel like he's still around somewhere."

"He doesn't live in the area?"

"He passed away a few years ago."

"I'm sorry."

She shrugs. "All part of life."

I eye the newspaper again. Next to the news item about the con woman is another one. Someone's been killing young women around the Valley over the past year. The reason they think it's the same person, most likely male, is because the word "SLUT" is scrawled in the victim's blood beside each corpse. There have been eight victims, the article says. *Nine*, I want to correct them. Of course it's not their fault they don't know about the first one, for I didn't write that word when I killed Becky. Come to think of it, it was an accident. She turned me down when I asked her out. Laughed in my face. So humiliating. I lost my temper and smashed my baseball bat on her head. A momentary loss of control, that's what it was. *You wouldn't call it murder, would you?*

I panicked at first, but then managed to calm down and take stock of the situation. No one had seen it happen. No one knew we were together. I walked away with the bat and tossed it somewhere far, far away. But fear engulfed me for weeks. They would find me for sure. Thankfully, nothing happened. When my anxiety receded, realization dawned. I had enjoyed it all — that feeling of control, of power. I wanted to — *needed* to — experience that rush again.

Soon there was a second woman. And then a third. I'm not proud of what I've done. I tell myself I will stop someday. Yes, I will stop the day I've conquered my fears and I'm able to pull this off like a pro. But as you can see, the fears still have my number. So far I have eight more victims, but unlike the first one, I left my signature with the rest. To let the world know what I think about these women. These were random women who caught my fancy. Like the one sitting before me now. It's time for number ten. *What do you say?*

For an instant I consider joining Jessica on the couch and kissing her in case she really is trying to seduce me, but I don't think I can handle any more rejection. So I walk back to the kitchen, debating whether to use the bottle or one of the knives. This is the right moment since she's seated and I'm standing. It will give me the advantage. Decision made, I clutch the bottle, ready to return to her, but she stands up and ambles towards me. Not good. I can't smash the bottle over a head that's soaring inches above mine. But then I have an idea. Clumsy me drops my glass. As expected, it smashes when it hits the floor.

"I'm sorry," I say.

She hesitates, then bends over to pick up the pieces, just as I had hoped. I raise my weapon and strike.

JESSICA

What. A. Shitty. Day. I didn't get the part, not even after all that preparation. I can't believe I blew a hundred bucks on this dress, thinking I'd nail the audition if I dressed the part. Hundred bucks that I can't afford. And then two of my scripts got turned down. Now I've walked out of Walmart empty-handed. I rang up all those items, but my card didn't work. My purse had two measly dollars in cash. *Do you realize how embarrassing that was?* The way that girl at the checkout counter stared at me, barely suppressing a smirk. The way everyone in line behind me gaped. As if that's not enough, rent's due in two days and my bank account's at zero. *Fuck! Fuck! Fuck!* Now I just hope my car starts.

I'm about to turn on the ignition when I see him walking this way, a shopping bag in one hand. He walks over to his swanky, red Maserati, parked a few spots away from me, and drops the bag in there. Way to rub it in. In spite of these riches, he looks needy. Vulnerable. The perfect prey. I step out of my ancient Civic and let the show begin.

Minutes later I'm seated next to him as he races off. Not only does this car cost six figures, it's new. I already noticed the temporary plates before I got in, and the new-car smell confirms it. He's definitely rolling in money. I imagine what it would be like, sitting at the wheel, cruising along in comfort, knowing the ride was all mine. It can't be a coincidence that the color of my dress matches the car.

I almost thought I wouldn't make it inside, but I did. He didn't stand a chance considering how he was looking me over. We get talking. He seems anxious about something. I try to flirt, touching him every now and then to get him to relax. It will be a lot easier to make my move if he's not so wound up. Unfortunately, my joke about the script falls flat, and gets him nervous all over again. It gives me pause. *Do I really want to do this?* He's kinda cute. And sweet. Maybe he doesn't deserve this. I think a part of me is falling for him, for why else would I be stupid enough to give him my home address? But I have bills to pay. Gotta keep my priorities straight.

Soon we're inside my apartment after another convincing effort from me. My comment about the bed falls flat too. *What's up with this guy?* The previous marks lapped up every word coming out of my mouth. My instincts tell me it's going to be a difficult night. On the bright side, he accepts my offer of wine, but he's not making it easy. I don't have a chance to slip in the sedative. *Is this another sign?* It gets me thinking. I've already messed up by bringing him home. How long will I keep doing these small jobs, risking my life for a little money? Isn't it better to snag a guy like him permanently? Someone who loves me and is rich enough to keep me happy. He likes me, of that I'm sure, or he wouldn't be here, weird behavior notwithstanding. If I can seduce him tonight maybe I can make him mine for life.

He hasn't started on his wine yet, so I take a sip in case he's waiting for me. It's heavenly. This was one of two bottles that I found in the previous mark's car. I walk over to the couch to enjoy it, hoping Jason joins me. Perhaps a few sips of his drink will loosen him up, and that's when the magic will happen. But he doesn't come. My disappointment softens a bit when we bond over the newspaper. Even that doesn't bring us together, for he returns to the kitchen. Something's bothering him again. Too shy to make a move? These tech nerds often are. It's all up to me now.

I get on my feet and sashay towards him. That's when I notice his eyes. For a moment there was something cold there, and now all I see is guile. Those thick glasses can't hide it. Something's wrong, horribly wrong. I can sense it, but I continue, trying to breathe evenly.

Crash! He drops his glass. Though he apologizes for his "mistake," I'm convinced it was deliberate. I pause, unsure about my next move. Might be best to do what is expected of me to avoid arousing his suspicions. I bend and extend my hand to pick up a shard, but stay alert for any movement on his part. He moves, and I instinctively charge at him, slamming my head into his core. The bottle falls from his hand as he reels backwards and slams into the wall. Unlike the glass, the bottle's still in one piece. I grab it and smash it on his head a couple of times, watching him crumple to the floor. There's blood oozing out of his head. If he's not dead yet, he soon will be. Not how I wanted the night to end, but it was either him or me.

Everything sinks in as I watch him bleed. My heart's thudding inside my trembling body. Did I just kill a man? Me, who has never squashed a bug or zapped a fly — did I just do that? No, I tell myself. He's still alive, and I can save his life. All it will take is a call to 911 to get him the help he needs. Claiming self-defense might be a way out with the cops, but with the cons I've been involved in, do I want that kind of attention? I take deep breaths to calm myself and take stock of the situation. Jason is completely still now. I'll have to move his body and scrub away any trace of him inside the apartment. His car. I must move that as well.

It's all so overwhelming, but I burst out laughing. Maybe it's the stress. Maybe I'm going crazy, but I imagine Dad's favorite movie character standing next to me going, "Well, here's another fine mess you've gotten me into."

I take another deep breath and get to work.

AUTHOR'S NOTE

This is another story that I finished very quickly during that remarkably productive December 2022. Two strangers meet, and it's not clear who's conning who. As a reader and moviegoer, I enjoy such plots and I'm pleased that I was able to write this one. At the end of the story Jessica is amused by a quote by her Dad's favorite character. Did you guess who she was referring to?

DON'T TALK TO STRANGERS

YOU NEVER KNOW WHO YOU'RE GOING TO GET

"I can kill her for you." The words rolled out of Richard Jenkins' mouth casually, as if he had just offered to walk my dog. I took my eyes off the road for a second to glance at his face, searching for a sign that he was joking about murdering my wife. He seemed serious. It was so surreal, like I had walked right into a Hitchcock movie.

"You don't really mean that," I said.

"Oh, I certainly do."

"Why?" I was curious to understand how his mind worked, this man whom I had only known a few hours.

"Umm ... because I'm a very helpful person?" My eyes were glued to the road, but I sensed his lips breaking into a smile. "To tell you the truth, I love killing people. I wouldn't pass up an opportunity like this."

My stomach took a lurch. *He was kidding, right?* Being stuck in a car with a deranged murderer was the stuff nightmares were made of.

"I ... I don't get it. What do you mean you love killing people? You have killed before?"

"Oh, several times. But see, the thing is, I can't just go around offing random people. There has to be a compelling reason, and based on what you've been telling me about your wife, the world would be a much better place without her. *You*, my friend, would be so much happier without her."

I had shot my mouth off again — an hour-long rant about why I hated Nancy. And my companion had concluded that I wanted her dead. *What was I thinking pouring my heart out to a stranger?* I stole a glance at the clock on the dash — three more hours till we reached our destination. Maybe I could shake him off there. Worst case scenario, I would have to tolerate him until we landed in San Francisco. Mine was one of several flights that had been canceled due to poor weather in Denver. I had found a flight to get back home from Albuquerque and had been lucky enough to snag a rental car to get me there. Jenkins had been sitting next to me at the gate and we had chatted a bit. When he learned about the backup flight, he had booked it too, and had asked if he could join me in the rental. I had agreed.

"Maybe I hate her. That doesn't mean I want her dead."

"You sure about that? You're telling me you never thought of wrapping your hands around her neck and squeezing, or grabbing a kitchen knife and running it across her throat? Ever fantasize about grabbing a shotgun and blowing her head off?"

It was like the guy had read my mind. I had to confess it had happened, several times — practically every time we fought — yet those were only fantasies. I would never actually do that, and I told him so.

He laughed. "That's what you think, my friend. But it's only a matter of time before those thoughts take flight and become reality. What do they say? Thoughts become words, words become actions — something like that?"

"I don't agree. Anyway, if I really wanted to kill her, I could do it myself. I don't need your help."

"Don't you?" He paused a second before continuing. "Guess who's gonna be their prime suspect when she's found murdered? You. You, my friend, because you are the husband. But what if she dies when you are somewhere far, far away? Then you have an alibi — an ironclad alibi — and you go free."

"But they would come after you. You would take that risk for me? For someone you just met?"

"Not for you, *amigo*. For me. Like I said, this is kind of a hobby of mine, and I'm really good at it. I leave no clues, and it will be hard for them to find me, because I have no connection to your wife. No connection, no motive. Think about it."

"Well, I appreciate the offer, but I'll pass."

"As you wish."

The rest of the drive passed in silence. We went our separate ways after I returned the car. At the gate, on the plane, at San Francisco Airport, we acted like we didn't know each other. Strangers before we had met, and still strangers.

Nancy was curled up on the couch when I got home, reading a thriller, judging from the cover. *My Darling Husband* — an innocuous title, but I was sure there was more to it than met the eye. Her beautiful dark hair fell to her shoulders, her skirt grazing the top of her knees, and she looked quite fetching even without makeup.

"You made it," she said, her face lighting up, something I hadn't seen in a long, long time. Absence really does make the heart grow fonder.

I kissed her on the lips. She kissed me back, and soon we were making love right there on the couch — quick and hurried, a *This is how much I missed you* kind of love. Later she took my hand and led me to bed where we went at it again, slower and sensual this time. I couldn't recall the last time we had looked at each other affectionately, let alone had sex. As we lay there, satisfied, her head resting on my chest, our breathing in sync, it seemed just like the good old days, the time when we had first met. Back then I was always giddy with excitement at the thought of seeing her. Our encounters were passionate, and I never wanted to leave her side.

Things were still heady once we got married, though the first cracks had already appeared before the wedding day. It hurt when she forced me to sign a prenup, but I let it go, for she assured me her will said I would get everything. *Till death do us part, Mr. Kirk,* she had whispered. We were still close for the first year, and then it all started going south. She turned cold, hurtful — I never understood why — and the resentment grew. This was also the time when the business was expanding, the stress building up, and she was spending longer hours at work. Perhaps that had something to do with it. There were occasional sparks of desire, like the one today, but for the most part we lived our own lives.

I held Nancy tight, caressing her soft skin, breathing in her flowery scent and savoring these pleasant moments, knowing they wouldn't last. Soon we would be arguing again, hurting each other, and there would be moments where I would want my hands to close around her neck rather than caress her back.

THREE MONTHS LATER

I slammed my glass on the bar, trying to make up my mind about another shot of bourbon. My watch flashed 8:30 p.m., which meant it was time to leave. Besides, I needed to stay sober for the drive back. The decision practically made itself. I paid my bill, including a huge tip for the bartender.

Twenty minutes later I turned onto my street. Something was wrong. There were cop cars outside my house, and paramedics too. Leaving my car curbside, I got out and raced towards the front door. A cop was setting up crime scene tape. Another one blocked my way.

"What happened?" I asked, panting. "This is my home. I live here. Is … is Nancy okay?"

He asked me to wait while he went inside. My heart was racing the entire time. Two minutes later a man appeared in the doorway. He was tall and well-built, dressed in a suit, his expression grim. Though we had just met, his demeanor gave me the impression that he hated me.

"Mr. Kirk?" he asked.

I nodded. "Yes. You can call me Aaron."

"Detective Murray with SJPD." He paused, his eyes scanning my face. "Is this your wife?" he asked, holding up a picture of Nancy and me. It was one of the photo frames that we had on display in the living room.

"Yes. That's Nancy."

His eyes softened a bit, and I sensed he wanted to say something but was hesitating. The words flowed a few moments later. "I'm afraid I have bad news. Your wife — she's dead."

"Nancy!" That's all I could muster as my knees buckled and I collapsed to the ground. I buried my face in my hands, my elbows planted on my thighs, and sobbed. A hand appeared on my shoulder.

"I'm so sorry for your loss, Mr. Kirk."

He gave me a few minutes to grieve, kneeling by my side, his hand staying on my shoulder. When my sobs died down, I turned to him. He still wore the stern look he had when I first laid eyes on him.

"I know this must be a difficult time, but do you mind if I ask you some questions?"

"Here?" I asked. The front yard was an odd place for an interrogation.

"We can go inside," he replied. He stood up and raised the crime scene tape, waiting for me to step through before placing a hand on my shoulder. "I'll go through first. You follow. Don't touch anything."

He led the way inside. The house was humming with activity. There were a few cops, some others who I assumed were crime scene technicians. We took two chairs at the dining table.

"Where ... where is she? Can I ... can I see her?" I asked.

He shook his head. "In the bedroom. I believe it's the master. Unfortunately, I can't allow you in there at this time."

"How did she ..."

"The ME is still examining the body. There will be an autopsy as well, but the initial examination indicates she was strangled."

"Oh." I rested my elbows on the table and buried my face in my hands again. "Who found her?"

"Her assistant."

I looked up. "Elaine?"

"Yes. She said your wife had asked her to stop by around six to drop off some files."

I frowned, a question forming at the tip of my tongue. Murray beat me to it. "You wondering how she got in?"

I nodded.

"She claimed the front door was open a crack. She rang the doorbell a few times without any response. That's when she got worried and decided to go inside."

"That must have been so horrible for her. Where is she now?"

"We took her statement and let her go home for the night. She wasn't looking too good. We'll get her in for questioning at the station tomorrow. Now, Aaron, can you tell me where you've been all day?"

"Work, mostly."

"And where is that?"

"Washburn Analytics. It's our business. Well, Nancy's business. That's where I work. In Palo Alto."

"I need specifics. What time did you go there? What time did you leave?"

"Let's see, I left home around eight a.m. Traffic sucked as usual, and I got there around nine. In the afternoon I left the office around four."

Murray glanced at his watch. "It's past nine p.m. now. Traffic can't have been *that* bad."

The words indicated he was making a joke, but you wouldn't be able to tell from his face. I realized he wanted to know what I had been up to in those five hours.

"It was a rough day at work, and I needed a stiff drink. So I stopped over at Sloshed downtown. Had a few drinks, ordered some food. Then I drove home."

"I see. Were you with anyone? Anyone who can confirm what you have told me?"

"No. I was alone, but I guess you can ask the bartender."

"That I will. When did you see Nancy last?"

"This morning. Before I left for work."

"You didn't see her at work?"

"She rarely goes into the office. Most of her time is spent meeting investors and key customers and partners."

"I see. And how did she seem? Worried? Concerned about anything?"

"No. She was her normal cheery self. Honestly, we didn't spend much time together in the morning. That's rush time. We're either in conference calls or getting ready for work."

"Did Nancy have enemies? Anyone who would want to harm her?"

"Not that I know of. I mean, she did head Washburn, and big businesses like ours are always in the public eye. No personal conflicts I'm aware of, but it could be someone who had something against the company."

"And how were relations between the two of you?"

"Fine. We were fine. As fine as can be after ten years of marriage. You know how it is. Sure, we had the occasional argument, but nothing to complain about." I debated whether I should go into details about the chasm between us, but I figured it wasn't worth mentioning. Most couples drift apart after a while. Life gets in the way. The novelty of the marriage wears off. They get bored with each other. Or they change enough that they don't share the same interests anymore.

"Ten years. No kids?"

"Neither of us wanted any."

Murray chewed on the answer for a few before speaking again. "That's all I have for you at this time, Aaron. Once again, sorry for your loss. Any way I can help?"

"No, thank you. I ... I think it hasn't fully sunk in yet that she's gone. I know I will miss her."

He stood up and placed a hand on my shoulder. I knew he meant well, but that gesture was getting annoying. "We're still processing the crime scene, so I'm afraid you can't stay here. Is there some place you can go for the night? It might be longer, depending on how long it takes us to get wrapped up here."

"Yes, I think I'll manage. Can I at least get my things?"

"I can't allow you in there, but if you tell me what you need I can have someone bring it down for you."

I listed out what I needed. It wasn't much — my PJs, change of clothes for two days, toiletries — the usual that would be expected in such a situation. While I waited, I considered my options. I could go over to Holly's — she was the closest friend I had, but that wouldn't be appropriate under the circumstances. I didn't want people to indulge in idle chatter about our relationship and draw incorrect connections to Nancy's death. There were my other friends, but they all had families, kids — I didn't want to burden them with my woes.

I was about to depart when something clicked in my head. "Detective," I called out. Murray turned and ambled back to me. He seemed a bit annoyed. "I remembered something."

"What is it?"

"You asked about enemies — anyone who wanted to kill her."

"And?"

"A few months ago I was in Denver. This man, Richard Jenkins, he approached me and offered to murder my wife."

Murray's eyes grew wide as saucers. "He just walked over and made his proposition?"

I narrated everything that had transpired. He listened intently, nodding every now and then. I couldn't tell whether he believed me, but it didn't matter. It was the truth, and it was important that I shared it with him.

"And you didn't report it to the police?"

"No. I didn't tell anyone about it. I figured he was some lunatic making a sick joke. I didn't think he would follow through, especially since I clearly told him I wasn't interested."

"Thanks for sharing this information, but I doubt he has anything to do with it."

"Why do you say that?"

"This incident happened around three months ago. Why would he wait this long?"

I shrugged. "I don't know. Maybe he was planning. Waiting for the right moment. I think you should look into it."

"Fair enough. Any idea where we can find this guy?"

"No. He must be somewhere in the Bay Area, but I don't know where."

"What does he look like?"

"Short. Balding, with a few strands of silver. Clean shaven. Slight paunch." I paused before adding, "Oh, and a wide nose." I tried to explain by holding my fingers some width apart. "The kind of nose that you would notice."

"Okay. I'll look into it."

Having settled that, I exited my home in search of a place to spend the night.

A short while later I entered the lobby of the Signia Hotel in downtown. It had started life as the Fairmont, but after an unfortunate bankruptcy it had a new owner and a new name. I had pleasant memories of meals at their restaurant, The Grill on the Alley. The check-in process was quick, and within minutes I was in my suite. I took a long, hot shower and crashed into bed, exhausted. Sleep didn't come at first. I still couldn't believe Nancy was gone. My mind replayed all the fond memories — the first time we met, the wonderful dates, the day I proposed to her, our wedding day, the honeymoon, that amazing first year of wedded bliss. Even some of the sporadic moments of intimacy that we enjoyed after that. It was all gone. I was alone once again. But I wasn't grieving. I missed her, yes, but that was to be expected when you have spent ten years of your life living with someone, no matter how strained the relationship. *Would I ever grieve for her?*

The sun was shining bright when I woke up the next morning. I felt refreshed, but soon I was reminded of the events of the previous day, and that had a sobering effect on me. Nevertheless, I ordered breakfast and while I waited, I pondered over how I should spend the day. Work was out of the question. I would have to call my assistant and let her know. More importantly, I would have to notify people at work about Nancy's death.

My meal had arrived by the time I completed the calls. That bad news travels fast is an established fact, especially when it comes to a prominent figure like Nancy. My phone started buzzing as I took my first bite of toast. I ignored it. The calls continued — from colleagues, from my friends, from Nancy's friends. I ignored them all. Once I had eaten, I took a quick shower. Then I made the mistake of going online.

The news of her death was spreading. Not only were there reports about the tragedy, there were articles spouting conspiracy theories, most claiming that I had murdered her to get my hands on her fortune. They cited all my past transgressions, which, thankfully, was not a complete list. There were some shenanigans they were still unaware of. Some pieces reminded people that I was penniless when I married Nancy, and that I had married her only for her money. All of it made me furious enough to slam my fist on the table.

I wondered how they had produced so much content so quickly. Was it really like the movies, where an editor demanded "three hundred words on Nancy Kirk and her deadbeat husband, pronto," and some harried hack pecked away at their keyboard to manufacture the requested text? Or did these organizations have the pieces ready, waiting for a significant event to occur before releasing the articles? *The vultures!* My phone buzzed again. It was Holly. I answered, for I desperately needed to hear a friendly voice.

"Aaron, I just heard. So sorry. How are you holding up?"

"Not too good, Holly."

"Want me to come over? Or you can come over here — I can cook up something nice for you."

It was tempting, but inappropriate. Holly was one of those transgressions no one was aware of, and I intended to keep it that way, more for her sake than mine. We had only slipped up once, and she felt awful the next morning. We promised each other it would never happen again. She wanted to confess to Nancy, but I managed to convince her otherwise. The thing is, Holly and I went way back. We had dated for a while in college and might have ended up together if I hadn't met Nancy. She was a friend I couldn't afford to lose.

"That sounds great," I replied, "but I don't think we should meet. I don't want anyone getting any ideas. There's already enough trash the media have been writing up."

"I understand. Just remember, I'm always there for you. Call me if you need anything."

"I know. Thanks, Holly."

"Do they know who did it?"

"Not yet."

"Awful way to die. So young, too."

"Yes."

After I hung up I didn't know what to do with myself. So I went for a walk. A long one. Even then, it was difficult to pass the time. I was relieved when night came and I was able to collapse into bed to sleep my troubles away.

Banging. Loud banging. That's what woke me up. It took me a few seconds to realize that someone was at the door. My phone showed it was just past 9:00 a.m. *Had I really slept that long?* I hurried over to the door to open it. The grim face of Detective Murray presented itself. My gut warned me it was bad news.

"Were you sleeping?" he asked, as if I had committed a crime.

"Yes, I was. How did you find me?"

He raised his eyebrow, and it told me it was his job to know things. He entered and surveyed the room.

"Nice digs," he said as he settled into the couch. "Must be great to be able to afford this."

I ignored the snide comment, choosing to focus on the matter at hand. "Did you find anything?"

"This Richard Jenkins, we haven't found anyone matching your description yet. Still looking, though." He paused before leaning forward. "He does exist, right?"

How dare he? It was the first thought that ran through my mind. How dare he insinuate that I was lying? I clenched my fists and replied, "Yes, he does exist. He's as real as you and me."

"Okay, okay. Just checking. Now, remind me about your movements again."

"My movements?"

"What time you left work that day and so on."

"Like I said, I left work at three. Then ..."

"Three or four?"

"Three."

"You said four the other day."

"Did I?"

"Yes."

"Sorry, I must have been mistaken."

"Mr. Kirk. Aaron. This is a murder investigation. Every little fact matters. You understand?"

I nodded.

"Please give it some more thought and be sure before you answer. *Capiche?*"

"Yes."

"Now, once again — what time did you leave work that day?"

"Three. It was three."

"You sure?"

"Positive."

"Good. Because that's what your assistant told me too. So you left work at three. Where did you go?"

"To Sloshed."

"You went straight to the bar? Didn't stop anywhere?"

"Right."

"What time did you get there?"

"I don't know. I didn't check. Traffic was bad, so I'm guessing I got there around four?"

"I see. So you didn't go home?"

"No. I didn't get home until later that night — when I met you."

"Hmm ..." Murray's brow furrowed. "That's not what your neighbor told me."

"My neighbor? Which one?"

"Doesn't matter. She said you got home at three forty-five, and you left thirty minutes later. It seemed like you were in a hurry on the way out."

"She must be mistaken, this neighbor, whoever it is." I had hoped I could keep things simple by not mentioning my detour. Alas, that plan did not work.

Murray had his piercing eyes on me, studying me again. I had a terrible feeling this was not going to end well.

"What did you argue about, Aaron?"

For fuck's sake! "Argue?"

"She told me she heard you two arguing."

"When was this?"

"When you came home, Aaron. Haven't you been paying attention?"

I didn't like where this was going. I wanted to scream, to curse him, but better sense prevailed. No point antagonizing him. It would only make matters worse.

"Can I use the restroom?" I asked. "I usually go as soon as I wake up, and I can't hold it in any longer."

He stared at me like I was a truant school kid trying to skip class. He nodded, and I hurried to the bedroom. Once inside, I took stock of the situation. The way things were headed, Murray could arrest me at any moment. He was grilling me like he thought I had killed Nancy, and he was just waiting for me to slip up. *Or was I misreading the situation and overreacting?* Nancy often complained that I was impulsive. Sure, there were times when she was right, but I convinced myself this wasn't one of those occasions. If I missed this opportunity I could be kicking myself for the rest of my life.

The clock was ticking. I had to move fast. I grabbed my wallet from the nightstand and slipped it into my pocket. My phone went on the nightstand. They would be able to track me easily with that. Unfortunately, it had to go. I considered wearing my shoes, but that would put Murray on alert. A quick session on the toilet, and I was back outside.

"Feeling better?" he asked when he saw me.

That tone. I wanted to smack him on his head, but I just nodded. Close enough to the front door, I glanced at the floor map for the location of the nearest staircase.

"As I was asking ..." Murray's question was cut short by the desk phone ringing. He turned to glare at the instrument. I pounced on the opportunity and scrammed out the front door. "Hey ..." was the last thing I heard as the door shut behind me.

I found the stairwell and raced down the stairs, hoping Murray didn't have any cops stationed downstairs. It was weird moving about barefoot, but I didn't have a choice. Thankfully I only had four flights to go. As I reached the lobby I realized I didn't have time to wait for the valet to fetch my car. Not that it mattered. Murray would put out an alert for the car, so it was better to avoid it. I sprinted out to the street and spotted a cab. *When was the last time I had noticed a cab or been so excited to see one?* Uber had spoiled us all. I hailed it and got inside. There was only one person I trusted, only one place I could go, so that's where I went.

⇢⇢⇢⇢➤ ⫷⫷⫷⫷⫸

Holly was surprised to see me at her door. Delighted, too. She always had that cheery smile on her face when she saw me. It warmed my heart every time. One glance at my feet, and her expression changed to concern. I stepped inside her condo and briefed her on the situation.

"You shouldn't have run, Aaron."

"But he would have arrested me. I'm sure of it."

"You didn't do it, right?"

"What? Of course not. Who do you think I am? You really think I would hurt Nancy?"

"No. That's not what I meant. I mean, if you are innocent then you should have let them arrest you. Let the law take its course. You would have gone free eventually. By running away you just look guilty."

"Eventually. That's a long time to rot in jail, Holly."

"And what's the plan now? Are you going to hide the rest of your life?"

"No. Only until they find the real killer."

"That's the problem, Aaron. They won't. They won't if they think you killed Nancy and they focus on finding you instead of investigating the case. There's still time. Turn yourself in."

"No. No. No way am I going back. You can't help me. Fine. I'll leave."

"That's not what I meant. You are welcome to stay as long as you like."

"Are you sure? I just realized, you'll be in trouble if anyone finds out. I shouldn't have come."

"Aaron, I'm sure. No one will find out if we're careful. Please stay."

I gazed into her eyes, glad to see someone I could trust. Hugging her tight, I was grateful for this one true friend I had been blessed with. We had a quick lunch that consisted of a buffet of leftovers from her fridge. As we cleaned up, she frowned.

"How did you get here? You didn't drive, did you?"

"No. I took a cab. I'm not stupid." I smiled. "And I had him drop me off a couple of blocks away just in case the cops get to him. I even stopped at the bank and withdrew whatever I could while I still had the chance."

"Awesome. Now we just need to get you some clothes and shoes."

"And toiletries."

"Of course. I'll go shopping."

Once Holly left I wondered how to pass the time. With nothing else to do, I switched on the TV. Bad decision. My mug stared at me from the news channel. It was official. I was the prime suspect for murdering Nancy. There was no way I could step out of this place.

My mood lifted when Holly returned. She showed me her loot from the shopping spree. At least I didn't have to worry about clothes and shoes. Not that I had anywhere to go. I could survive here in sweats and bare feet. Soon she started dinner. Spaghetti and meatballs — my favorite. We settled at the dining table with our plates and a bottle of wine. The conversation was light — we shared anecdotes, dug out long-forgotten memories — anything to keep our minds off my predicament.

In the kitchen, I washed the dishes, Holly put them away. A simple domestic activity that made me wonder what my life would be like if I hadn't met Nancy. Would I have married Holly? Would we be happy? As I turned away from the sink my hand grazed hers. Her eyes met mine. I could feel the passion rise inside me as we stood in close proximity. There was nothing wrong about this now that Nancy was gone, I told myself. I pulled Holly towards me and kissed her. She kissed me back. One thing led to another and soon we were in bed, our clothes long discarded on the floor.

I awoke to the sun streaming right into my eyes through the blinds. Holly was nowhere to be seen. Without my phone and not a clock in sight, I had no idea what time it was. I rolled out of bed and put on my discarded clothes. After a quick trip to the bathroom I peeked out the window. It was a good thing I did, for what I saw made my heart sink. There were four cop cars parked outside, and a couple of cops standing there. There could only be one reason they were here. *How did they find me? And where was Holly?* Surely she couldn't have betrayed me? Or had she concluded that I had killed Nancy, and her conscience wouldn't allow her to harbor a heinous criminal?

I pushed the thought out of my head. There was no time for that. I grabbed my wallet and the cash I had withdrawn, put on the shoes, hat and sunglasses that Holly had bought me, and raced to the front door. Opening it a crack, I checked if anyone was around. With the coast clear, I headed for the staircase. Behind me I heard the elevator doors open and I sped up. From inside the stairwell I peeked down the corridor. Two cops walked over to Holly's apartment and knocked. They were there for me, all right.

I rushed down the stairs, wondering how I would get past the cops stationed outside. It occurred to me that they might not recognize me with the hat and sunglasses. As long as I behaved normally, like any other resident, I might be able to walk by undetected. I trundled through the lobby keeping my head down. It was difficult to act casual when I was sweating profusely and my heart was jumping like a kid in a trampoline park. But I stuck to the plan and stepped outside the building. Out of the corner of my eye I saw the two cops chatting. One of them even glanced at me before turning back to the conversation. Fragments of the conversation reached me, and one part in particular deflated me completely: "... woman on the fourth floor called ..."

I continued walking, trying to get the betrayal out of my mind. The question now was, where would I go from here?

I had never hitchhiked before, but desperate times called for desperate measures. I hitched rides from a few different people and landed up in Corcoran, a little town in Kings County. Two hundred miles from home — far enough from Murray and his troops. I figured this place was small enough and so out of the way that I wouldn't bump into anyone who would recognize me. I took my time exploring the streets before I settled on Mo's Motel to spend the night. It looked deserted, had reasonable rates, and it was open to long-term stays. On the downside, it hadn't been maintained well, and I doubted the stability of the structure. I wasn't sure how long I would be staying, but I had the feeling it would be a while before life went back to normal.

There was a stout, middle-aged woman at reception. She scrutinized me from head to toe before deciding I was harmless. As expected, she had vacancies. I requested a room for the week and handed her the cash.

"Got some ID, sugar?" she asked with a smile.

I kicked myself for not anticipating this. "Do you really need one?"

"What are you running from, love?"

"Life?" I replied. It was a relief when she laughed out loud and let it slide. If she was suspicious about anything, at least I hoped that with my hat, sunglasses, and freshly grown stubble she wouldn't connect me with the mugshots dominating the news.

"No bags, huh?"

I shook my head.

"No car either?"

Another shake of my head.

"You aren't going to kill me, are you?"

I flashed my most charming smile. "Would I tell you if I was going to?"

She laughed again. "I like you, sugar. Up the stairs, last room on the left."

I heaved a sigh of relief and trudged up to my room. It wasn't a patch on my digs at Signia, but that didn't surprise me. I kicked off my shoes and collapsed onto the bed. Sleep engulfed me within minutes.

The next morning it took me a while to remember where I was. When it came to me, I was thankful that, for a change, there was no one out to get me so early. To be on the safe side I peeked out the window to confirm it. Then I opened the front door and scanned the surroundings. Only then did I visit the restroom.

I was starving by the time I was done. Mo's didn't seem like a place that served food, so I ventured about town and ate at a diner that looked presentable enough. *What was I going to do with myself?* That was the thought going through my mind as I chewed my breakfast. There was only one way out, I concluded — present a viable suspect to Murray on a platter, for he wouldn't bother looking for one. And by suspect I meant Richard Jenkins; I couldn't think of anyone else. Elaine, perhaps, since she was actually in the house that day, but no one, including me, would ever believe that a sweet lady like her could hurt anyone. Once I found Jenkins, Murray could verify that he was indeed booked on the same flight as me from Denver to San Francisco all those months ago, and also on the flight from Albuquerque to SF.

How to locate Jenkins was the next question. I didn't have anything to go on. Even if I did, I didn't have any tools for the search. No phone, no internet access. I doubted the Corcoran library would let me use their facilities without a membership, and for that I would have to share my identification. I exited the diner with a belly full of food and dejection. My mood brightened when I spotted an electronics store further down the street. Soon I walked out of there with a pay-as-you-go phone and a used MacBook, eager to return to my room and get started.

❧⟫⟫⟫⟫⟫ ⟪⟪⟪⟪⟪❧

"Wi-Fi?" Mo mulled over my request as I stood at her desk a few minutes later. For a moment I feared she might be one of those people who wasn't up-to-date on the latest technology. "You know, sugar, this isn't one of those fancy places that offer Wi-Fi."

"Oh."

"But don't worry, sugar. I told you I like you. You're welcome to use mine."

Minutes later I was back in my room after noting the details and thanking Mo profusely. The things we take for granted. Who knew I would be so excited about getting online? It was slow, kinda like my first days on the internet, struggling with dial-up. But at least I could make some progress.

Before starting my search I had to satisfy my curiosity, so I typed in "Nancy Kirk." It brought up several links related to the case. The latest gelled with what I knew. I was still the prime suspect and was on the run, having given the cops the slip. An unidentified person of interest was under questioning. I wondered whether they meant Holly.

After that detour it was time to search for Jenkins. I assumed he lived in the Bay Area. Was that even a valid assumption, I questioned myself. He could be a Denver resident just visiting for a few days. But I recalled the way he spoke about San Jose and the surrounding areas; it was like he was a local. My first searches for the name led nowhere. There were too many of those in the area. I had to narrow it down, but how?

I shut my eyes and cleared my head, focusing on the time I had spent with the man, trying to uncover any details that might help. Then it came to me. When we first got talking, he was reading a book. *Unfaithful*, I think it was. It had a San Jose Public Library sticker on it. So that confirmed he was a SJ resident. Excited, I refined my search to San Jose, but I didn't get very far. Disappointed, I slammed the laptop shut and hopped in the shower. The water was lukewarm, but I wasn't complaining.

After drying off and dressing I attacked the problem again. I closed my eyes and focused — if I could get one detail, then I could get more. Sure enough, I saw it — his bag had the initials M P on it. It didn't make sense, for I would have expected R J. Perhaps it was his wife's bag? Or had he lied to me? Was his name not Richard Jenkins at all? That would explain a lot.

I gave up for the day. There was only so much disappointment I could take. Soon I was out for a stroll. It helped clear my head, making me feel alive and not like a trapped man. I stopped at the same diner and ate another meal, though I didn't feel like it. It was important to keep my strength up.

It was dark by the time I returned to the motel. Mo was nowhere to be seen. I went up to my room, undressed and dozed off, hoping the next day would bring me better luck.

❧ ❧

Another morning, another day I was thankful no one was forcing me to make a dash for it. But I missed my home. My bed. Even Nancy, in spite of how things had ended between us. Yes, I did go home that afternoon, just as the neighbor told Murray. It had been one of those days when nothing was going my way at work, and I wanted to bury myself in the safety of my home. The argument didn't help, and I only ended up staying around thirty minutes — the neighbor was right about that as well.

Nancy was in the bedroom trying on a new outfit she had purchased. There was no smile when I entered the room, no greeting even. She just walked over to the dresser, picked up some sheets of paper and threw them at me. Dramatic, but not very effective, because the papers just floated in the air and fell to the floor a few feet away from me.

"What the fuck, Aaron? Have you seen your credit card bill?"

"What's wrong?"

"Forty thousand dollars? Forty thousand in one month? What the hell is wrong with you? Throwing money away like that."

This from a woman who was worth millions and made a few more every year. Forty thousand was pocket change. Besides, it was an anomaly. It's not like I spent that much every month. Yet, she had to get riled up about it, had to make me feel miserable. This wasn't what I wanted from a relationship. A silly argument indeed.

Putting those gloomy thoughts aside, I dragged myself out of bed to get on with the day. Soon I was chowing down on a hearty breakfast at my favorite diner. Al's Diner. That was the name. I wondered whether all service establishments in town had decided to use two-letter names. Feeling a lot better after my meal, I trundled back to the motel, confident that today would be the day I would locate Richard Jenkins, or MP, or whatever his name was.

Mo was at her desk, talking to a woman. I stopped dead in my tracks, for I knew who the woman was even before she turned to face me. A part of me wanted to run over to Holly and hug her, kiss her, bury my face in her hair, carry her to my room and make love to her in that uncomfortable bed. But she had betrayed me, I reminded myself. I couldn't trust her anymore. The fact that she had traced me here sent a shiver down my body. Were Murray and team here too, lying in wait to pounce on me as soon as I arrived? I looked around but didn't notice anything out of place.

"Aaron," Holly said, her thousand-watt smile threatening to sway me. "I'm so glad you are safe."

"How did you find me?" I knew the answer by the time I completed my question. How had I missed that? We had spent a night in Corcoran years ago, long before Nancy. An unscheduled stop on our way to Vegas. We were miserable, but I had joked then that this is where I wanted to retire. Neither of us had visited again, though it remained a running joke between us.

"You know how."

"You betrayed me, Holly."

She flinched, as if I had hurt her in some way. "No, I didn't. You have to believe me."

"I heard them say a woman on the fourth floor called them."

"It wasn't me."

"Then who was it?" It came out louder than I intended, and she flinched again.

"I don't know." Her voice was soft. At least one of us was remaining calm.

"Then where were you that morning?"

"At Starbucks. Picking up breakfast."

"You are lying."

"I'm not. Trust me, Aaron." She was pleading now, and I didn't like it one bit.

"The cops are on the way, right?"

"No one knows I'm here."

Her eyes were earnest, and I wanted to believe her, but I had been burned too many times.

"What did you do, sugar? Why are the cops after you?" Mo had gone around the desk and was standing next to Holly now.

"I ... I didn't do anything, Mo. It's all a big misunderstanding."

"I'm sorry, but you have to leave. I still like you, but I don't need trouble."

"I understand. I'm leaving anyway, now that I have been found out."

I raced up to my room, grabbed my things and hurried back downstairs. All the time I feared that the cops would show up and arrest me. But they never did. Holly was still with Mo when I returned to the lobby. I placed the room key on the desk and thanked Mo for everything.

"Let me help, Aaron," Holly said, her hand on my arm. I didn't understand what her game was. Thoughts swirled through my head, like a mob of shoppers on Black Friday. Maybe she hadn't betrayed me? For if she had, how come I hadn't been arrested already? Or were the cops on their way, but held up somewhere? Maybe this was all part of a grand plan — gain my confidence again and get my confession on tape. Concrete evidence that could be used at the trial to nail me.

"Let's assume you didn't call the cops, and it was all a surprise when you found them in your condo. They probably still questioned you."

"Yes, they did. I was so spooked when I got back and saw them there. I thought they got you. It was a relief when I realized they hadn't. I told them you had been there, but I had no idea you were on the run. I wasn't sure what you'd left behind — they would have figured you had been there — I didn't want to get caught in a lie."

"Fair enough. But I'm sorry. I still can't trust you. I need some time."

Her shoulders drooped. It was like all the fight had gone out of her. It hurt me to see her like that.

"Alright," she said feebly. Then I was on my way.

Another hitched ride later I was in Fresno. I was nervous the entire way, constantly turning back to check if we were being followed, but I didn't notice anything suspicious. It was a risk moving to a bigger city, one that had a lot more people passing through, but I missed the hustle and bustle of the Bay Area. I was tired of hiding, jaded with this nomadic life, and wasn't sure how much longer I could take it.

Why did I run? It's a question I'd been asking myself daily. Perhaps I was better off letting Murray arrest me as Holly had suggested. At least I wouldn't be in constant fear of being caught, and I would have a chance to prove my innocence.

I found a decent motel and checked in, again opting for the weekly rate. Wi-Fi was included in the stay, so that was a plus. Once in my room, I fired up the laptop. First, I searched for news on the case. As expected, there was no progress. More inane articles had cropped up. The fact that Holly had sheltered me for a day had leaked. There was speculation that we were in love, and we had planned Nancy's murder together. There were others who claimed I had nothing to do with it, but

Holly had killed Nancy in a jealous rage to have me for herself. It infuriated me. I decided to stop and focus instead on finding Jenkins.

Once again, I shut my eyes and worked my way through my encounter with him, paying attention to every detail. The book again. The SJPL label and barcode in one corner. A bookmark sticking out of the book. Not a bookmark — a boarding pass. *His* boarding pass. It had fallen on the ground one time when he had opened the book. Random text flashed before my eyes. Zone 6. Denver. 28C. And then — Matt. That was the name I remember seeing. It fit in with the initials MP.

It's funny how much junk we have sitting in the recesses of our memory, waiting to be discovered if we care to look. Every now and then we dig up some treasure along with the junk. It's like rummaging through the attic or the garage. You mostly find stuff you should have thrown away years ago, but sometimes you get lucky and find that antique vase that's now worth a fortune.

I searched for "Matt San Jose" in my browser. Several hits, but the mayoral election dominated. I refined the search to "Matt P San Jose". This was much better. Page after page I scrutinized every link, for I had the feeling this was the closest I would get to locating Jenkins. And then I hit the jackpot.

Matt Peterson was a private eye operating out of San Jose. The mug shot on his website matched the Richard Jenkins I had met. No wonder Murray had been unable to find him. My first instinct was to call Murray and tell him to talk to Peterson. That's what any sane person would do in my situation. But as Nancy had told me many times, not only was I impulsive, I was a daredevil. She got that part right. I couldn't resist the thrill of confronting Peterson and seeing the look on his face when he realized he had been found out. Perhaps I would be able to convince him to turn himself in. Wishful thinking, I knew. Not grounded in reality. But it was time to return to San Jose.

Bigger cities like Fresno offer some advantages, one of which is better travel options. This time I skipped risky hitchhiking and bought myself a Greyhound bus ticket. A three-hour ride later I was back in San Jose. I hurried over to the address listed for Matt's PI business downtown. It was just after four when I got there. *Matt Peterson, Private Investigator* said the sign on the compact storefront, one of many in a line of businesses along that block. I wondered whether he was inside or out working on a case. My first instinct was to storm into his office and confront him, but that would give him the advantage of home turf. I wouldn't appear as intimidating when he was in his comfort zone. So I decided to wait — wait for him to leave the building and surprise him when he least expected it.

Two hours later I was still standing there, with no sign of him. I couldn't put off a restroom run any longer. The Starbucks across the street beckoned, and I sprinted over, worried I would miss my prey if I was away for too long. Business taken care of, I exited the building only to see Matt stepping out of his office. I ran like my life depended on it, which it really did, but I missed him by a whisker. He had entered a bar a block away. I followed.

The bar was larger than I had expected. The lighting was dim, but the interiors were done well. I counted at least a dozen people inside. The place was buzzing with conversation. Matt sat at the far end of the bar, chatting up the cute bartender. This wasn't going to work. I had to accost him outside, so I left, resigning myself to another long wait. The street was busy, with a lot of passersby, people waiting for their turn in front of the adjacent businesses, customers stepping outside for a smoke. The occasional homeless guy passed by.

I tried not to get distracted by all the activity and kept my eyes on the door. After a while, my quarry filled the doorway before turning left and continuing on. I was sure he hadn't seen me.

"Hey, Matt," I shouted.

He turned around and looked directly at me. I had expected some uncertainty, darting eyes trying to figure out who had called him. Maybe he had spotted me earlier after all. I expected him to make a run for it at any moment. Instead, he walked towards me, a wide grin plastering his face.

"Well, well, well, if it isn't my friend Mr. Kirk. You found me. Not as dumb as I thought."

"We need to talk."

"Oh yes, we do. I've been looking all over for you."

"Have you?" *Why would he be looking for me? Was this another one of his tricks?* By now he was standing a foot away from me. "You lied to me."

"Everybody lies to everybody, my friend. Even to themselves. You of all people should know that."

I grabbed his collar and stared into his eyes, hoping I appeared as menacing as I thought I did. "If you know what's good for you, you will come with me to Detective Murray and confess."

"People are staring, *amigo*."

"I don't care."

"Don't you? You attract so much attention, someone will recognize you and call the cops."

"Let them call. I have you now."

"And what are you going to tell the cops? That we had a little talk a while back? I will deny it. Who do you think they will believe?"

It was the truth. *What was I thinking?* There was no way this man would confess to anything. No one in his situation would. On the run and bored out of my mind, I had let myself get carried away by the thrill of the chase. I released his collar and stood there, contemplating my next move.

"Let's walk over to my office. I have something to show you."

I hesitated. *Was it a trap?* That was a silly thought. He didn't need traps anymore; he could just call the cops and have me arrested. So I followed him into his cubbyhole of an office. He switched on the lights and dropped into the chair behind his desk.

"Sit down." He indicated the chair on my side of the desk as he unlocked a drawer and fished out a manila envelope. Dropping it on the desk, he said, "Take a look."

I picked it up with shaking hands. The smug look on his face told me I wouldn't like what was inside, and a feeling of dread spread through me. I opened the envelope and pulled out the contents. My head swam, my body turned cold when I saw what it was. Nobody spoke for a long time. It was as if time stood still, and I preferred it that way because the future wasn't looking bright.

"Beautiful, isn't it?" he asked.

I glanced at him, unable to speak.

"Don't worry. I would be a terrible friend if I didn't give you a chance." He leaned back in his chair, putting the tips of his fingers together in front of him, his eyes glued to my face. He was enjoying this.

"What do you want?"

"Ten percent."

"Ten percent of what?"

"With Nancy dead, you inherit everything. I want a cut of that pie."

"You've got to be kidding me. That's a lot of money."

"Tell me, *amigo*, how much is your life worth?"

I considered his offer. I didn't have much of a choice here.

"Okay, I agree. But I don't see how I'll get the money."

Matt leaned forward and rested his forearms on the desk. "You'll be happy to know that I have just the plan for you, my friend."

Matt dropped me outside prominent criminal defense attorney Jennifer Kegan's office. He had called her and explained the situation. She had been delighted to accept my case. I spent the next two hours telling her everything. Well, almost everything. She listened intently, taking copious notes as I spoke. When Matt presented the plan to me, he was confident I would go free, since all the evidence against me was circumstantial. Kegan concurred.

She drove me to the SJPD building downtown. We entered, and I asked for Detective Murray. When he arrived, it took him a few seconds to recognize me. I took off my hat and sunglasses in case he had any further doubt it was me.

"I'm turning myself in."

"About time. You ready to confess?"

"I'm innocent."

He rolled his eyes before reading me my rights and placing me under arrest. Then he walked us inside and into a depressing interrogation room. On Kegan's advice I refused to answer any questions. Murray wasn't happy. I derived some satisfaction from that.

The rest of the night was a blur as I was fingerprinted and booked into jail. This would be my home for the next few months. I just hoped I would be back to my real home after that and not in prison.

I had been rotting in jail for three months when the trial began. Everyone told me I was lucky it was happening so soon — most cases of this nature took a year or more to go to trial. I failed to see it that way. Each day I spent in confinement was a day I could have been chilling at home. During this time Kegan visited me several times as her team built the case for the defense. The only thing that kept me going were the visits from Holly. She made it a point to drop in every week. Even a glimpse of her face was enough to warm my heart. By now I was convinced she had been loyal to me and was not the one who had notified the cops. Word was that her neighbor had spotted me when I had shown up at her doorstep. When my mug flashed across the screen on the morning news, the neighbor put two and two together and called the hotline.

I was nervous about the trial. It was not surprising since I had never experienced anything like this, and my life was on the line. Kegan tried to calm me and assured me everything would be fine. It was nice, though, getting to clean up and don a natty suit — all to project the image of an innocent, model citizen for the jury.

The defense and the prosecution made their opening statements, and then began the lineup of people taking the stand. It went on for days. From the neighbor who claimed I had come home early that afternoon and had argued with Nancy — I'm still not sure how she heard us, for we weren't anywhere near the periphery of the house — to a few of Nancy's friends, none of whom I liked. The Tiresome Bitches, I used to call them. True to the moniker, they told the courtroom how much Nancy resented me, and how she felt I had only married her for the money. They spoke about all my affairs, how each one cut Nancy to the core.

"I knew he was no good for her the first time I laid eyes on him. I even warned Nancy, but she laughed it off," said bitch #1 with relish.

"He couldn't keep his eyes off me. Even tried to grab my ass one time," lied bitch #2. And so on — you get the idea.

What no one said is that I had a flourishing career when I married. Sure, I didn't have much money because of my lavish lifestyle, but I was anything but a deadbeat. I only quit my job because Nancy convinced me to help run her business — a position that was demanding, though people preferred to believe it was a cushy job. As for the affairs, I had no excuses. In my defense though, I only strayed once Nancy had started getting distant.

All this testimony worried me no end, but Kegan assured me it would not affect the verdict. I may be proven to be a cheat, a deadbeat even, but none of that proved I had killed Nancy. And that's what mattered above all else. The fact that I had argued with her that afternoon wasn't sufficient either. It was all circumstantial evidence and left enough reasonable doubt that the jury would not convict.

❧ ☙

On day twenty of the trial, Kegan and I were alone in the meeting room before going into the courtroom. She wasn't her usual self, and I wondered what was nagging her. Finally, she spoke.

"Did you know Nancy changed her will two months before she died?"

This was news to me. I didn't like the sound of that. "No," I replied.

"I take it the original will had everything going to you?"

"Yes, that's my understanding."

"In the new one, she leaves you the house and a hundred thousand dollars."

It was like I had been pushed off a cliff and was plummeting hundreds of feet to certain death. *How could she?*

"How do you know this? As far as I know, the details haven't been released yet."

"I have my sources. Pretty generous, don't you think?"

"Generous? Seriously?"

"Considering what you had been up to, she should have left you nothing."

"Wonderful. Quite a vote of confidence from my lawyer."

"My job is to get you a not guilty verdict for murder. That's it. At least you will inherit enough to cover my fees, so you don't have to worry about losing your lawyer. Now, I'm thinking how this development could help with our case."

"It looks bad, doesn't it? If she changed the will to leave me less, that's a negative."

"Not if we can prove you knew about it. It would show you didn't have much motive to kill her."

I nodded, but I was concerned. I couldn't shake the feeling that things were taking a turn for the worse.

I had hoped my fears were unfounded, but it was not to be. The next day the prosecution notified us they had new evidence and they would be presenting it in court. I learned about this when Kegan came to meet me, looking furious.

"You lied to me," she said.

"What do you mean?"

"I was crystal clear from the very start, wasn't I? I demanded the truth — all of it. I don't care if you are innocent or guilty — I'll defend you either way, but I cannot prepare a bulletproof case if I don't have the full picture."

"I don't know what you're talking about."

She dropped an envelope on the table. "Does this refresh your memory?"

I didn't have to open it to know what was inside, but I did anyway. Photographs. A photograph with my hands on Nancy's throat in her bedroom, both of us wearing the same clothes we had on the day she died. A photograph of me standing next to her lifeless body after the deed was done. These were the pictures Matt had shown me that day. Pictures that were worth millions to him. He had promised to keep them to himself, and now he had broken that promise. I understood why. With the change to the will I couldn't afford to pay him much, if anything at all, for Kegan's bills were massive. So he took the next best route and earned some credits with law enforcement. It was over. There was no way I could wriggle out of this one.

I learned a lot in the next few days. Matt had been hired by Nancy to watch me. He had provided her with evidence of my affairs. Our meeting in Denver wasn't a coincidence. He was tracking me, and that day he took it a step further and engaged me in conversation. With all the ways I had disappointed Nancy, she was already considering a change to the will, and when Matt told her what I really thought of her, she decided to proceed with the modification. Why she didn't divorce me or completely disinherit me, I do not know. Perhaps I earned some brownie points because I told Matt I didn't want her dead. Or she left it as compensation for the ten years I had stayed by her side. Not that it matters, because it's of no use to me. I'll rot in prison for the rest of my life.

With all that time for reflection, I realized there was so much I didn't know about my wife of ten years. For example, why was she still intimate with me after learning that I had cheated on her? *Did she feel she had driven me to it by staying distant?* That would be quite unlike her, for I'm sure she would have held me responsible for my actions, no matter what the trigger. *Or like me, she hoped someday we would recapture the magic of those early days, that someday one of those intimate moments would get our relationship back on track?*

One month after that Denver trip, Matt had installed spy cameras around the entire house with Nancy's authorization. He was convinced it was only a matter of time before I would turn violent. I had no idea I was being spied on, or I would have been more careful. The video from that fateful day was played in the courtroom, every scene neatly timestamped. The photographs Matt had showed me were screenshots of key moments in the feed. Kegan did her best to discredit the evidence, trying to cast doubts over the veracity of the video, but one glance at the faces on the jury and I knew my goose was cooked. They saw it all — me strangling Nancy, me throwing stuff around the room to make it look like a burglary gone wrong. They saw me running around the house in frenzied panic, my brain split in two — one half still not believing what I had done, the other half trying to figure out how to deflect suspicion from me. They even saw that final touch, when I slammed the door shut on my way out, then returned after a few seconds to open it just a crack.

Ten days later the jury delivered a guilty verdict. I would get what I deserved. It wasn't the verdict that destroyed me. It was the devastation apparent on Holly's face when she learned the truth about what I had done. I had let her down. She never visited me again, and I couldn't blame her.

I often think of that moment when I stood before Nancy, hearing her tirade, my blood boiling, my fists clenching and unclenching. It was nothing new, but I had always been able to control myself. If only I had restrained myself that day too. But I had stepped forward, placed my hands on her throat and squeezed. I still see her eyes clearly — the shock evident, for I'm sure she didn't expect that. I could have released the pressure at any moment, but I didn't. It was as if I was possessed. If only I had stopped. If only.

AUTHOR'S NOTE

It's not hard to figure out the inspiration for this one — the classic Hitchcock movie, *Strangers on a Train*, and, more recently, the book by Peter Swanson, *The Kind Worth Killing*. I enjoyed writing this one, especially the Mo character. A bit of trivia — the Signia Hotel where Aaron spends his first night — it first made an appearance in a crucial scene in *Barefoot in the Parking Lot* when it was still known as The Fairmont. I like writing about local spots, and it's interesting to see how these places change with time.

WHERE'S MARIA?

A PSYCHOLOGICAL THRILLER

JASON

Maria's gone. It hasn't sunk in yet. She was my life for the past three months. I miss her smile, her laughter. I miss waking up to see her lying next to me. It seems like only yesterday that she was in my arms, hugging me tight. Now I sit alone in my apartment — well not exactly alone, if you consider the woman seated across from me. Detective Natalie Abrams from SJPD. I'd be happy to have her here if not for the circumstances. She's a beauty. A brunette, with hair falling to her shoulders. Little sapphire studs dot her earlobes, drawing my attention to her neck. Smoldering black eyes. Clear complexion with not a line on it — probably in her early thirties. Full red lips which are begging to be kissed. I feel a stab of guilt. It's as if I'm cheating on Maria. But on second thoughts, this isn't wrong, is it?

"Mr. Williams. You still with me?"

Her piercing voice shakes me out of my reverie. "Sorry, what was that?" I ask.

"So she's been missing two days?"

"Yes."

"And you didn't consider reporting it?"

"I figured she'd be back."

"How so? Has she done this before?"

"Once. It was around a month ago. She disappeared for three days. But that time she left me a note."

"I see. So there's a note this time, too?"

"No. But I'm sure she'll be back."

"Yet I see you've been crying. Like you lost her for good."

"I miss her." My eyes well up. I must present quite a sight with my puffy red-rimmed eyes and tear-smeared face. *When was the last time I showered?* Through the fog of tears I see her face has softened.

"Did you try calling her?"

"She ... she doesn't have a cell."

Abrams raises an eyebrow. She should stop doing that. It mars her beauty.

"No cell? In this day and age?"

"Yeah. She's weird that way," I reply with a faint smile, recalling all the other weird things Maria did.

"Any idea where she could be?"

Do I know where she is? Kinda. I mean, I know where she was last. She could be anywhere by now.

"No." I shake my head.

"Do you know where she went last time?"

"She didn't tell me."

"And you didn't ask?"

"I did, but she didn't answer."

"And you were okay with that?"

"I didn't have a choice. I was just relieved she was back." I wipe a tear that's racing down my cheek. My nose is runny again. I look around, trying to remember where I left the tissue box. She points to my side. Silly me — it's right next to me. She watches as I use a tissue to clean up. When she looks away, I check her out again. That charcoal-gray suit hugs her perfectly. I can tell there's something special hiding under it.

"How did you know she was missing?" I ask. It's strange, this detective showing up asking about Maria, considering that Maria didn't know anyone. No job, no friends. Nothing.

"Her sister called. She was concerned since she hadn't heard from Maria in a few days. Maria wasn't returning her calls and texts either."

My jaw drops. "Her sister?"

"Yes. Sofia. You look surprised."

"I ... I had no idea she had a sister. In fact, she told me she didn't have any family. She was all alone in the world."

A frown appears on Abrams' face. She looks cute this way.

"How long have you known Maria?"

"Three months."

Three months that seemed like a lifetime. She transformed me in that short period. I'd given up on love, but she showered me with it. In her arms I felt like I was the king of the world, not a shy, diffident nerd. She spruced up my appearance and boosted my confidence. And the sex was fantastic.

"Did I lose you again, Mr. Williams?"

Lost in my thoughts again. *Focus, Jason, focus,* I remind myself.

"Sorry. What did I miss?"

"How did you meet?"

"Oh. Quite by accident. I was walking to my apartment late one evening when she bumped into me. She had been running, and she was terrified. When she asked for help, I couldn't refuse. So I brought her home."

Abrams' eyebrow inches up again. "You're telling me you just let a stranger into your house?"

"Well, she was in trouble. How could I not help? Besides, she looked so innocent." And beautiful. The most beautiful woman I'd ever laid my eyes on. How could I resist? I don't tell Abrams this. She'll just roll her eyes and go on a rant about men and their weakness for women. It's not something I need right now.

"What happened next?"

"She told me her name was Maria, and she was Colombian. She had sneaked into California a few months ago with the help of a gang. They had made promises about setting her up here, but they kept her captive and forced her to do things she didn't want to do. Terrible things. She had finally managed to escape."

"Did you go to the police?"

"No. I wanted to, but she told me these were powerful people with friends in high places. If they found out, it would just get her killed."

"And you believed her?"

"Yes. I did."

There's a moment of silence where she's studying my face. Then I realize she's waiting for me to continue the story.

"I got her cleaned up, got her some new clothes. She slept a lot the next two days. She was afraid to leave the apartment, worried the gang would spot her. Had all her meals indoors."

"How long did this continue?"

"What?"

"This staying indoors."

"About a month. She was still not comfortable, but I pushed her to go outdoors. How long would she go on living in fear? That's when we started going out together. For walks. For dinner at the neighborhood restaurant. A few movies at Oakridge."

"I see. So by the time she disappeared the first time, she knew her way around?"

"Yes."

"Mr. Williams ..."

"Jason. Call me Jason."

"Jason, aren't you worried that the gang found her? Perhaps she's not coming back?"

The lady has a point. But there's a reason I'm not worried. Worse — I'm devastated. It's because I know Maria's not coming back. I know who's responsible, but I dare not tell anyone, for that would get me into trouble. Massive trouble. It's better to just play along.

"Oh," I reply.

"Her sister doesn't think there's any gang. She thinks you are behind the disappearance."

"Me? Why would I do that? Maria meant the world to me."

The eyebrow goes up again. *Should I tell her to stop doing that?*

"You mean to tell me you were in love with her? A woman you only met three months ago?"

"Yes. She was that amazing. And what's more, she was in love with me. Can you imagine? An angel like that falling in love with a schlub like me?"

She nods. Follows it up with a smile. It makes my heart race. Here I thought Maria was the most beautiful woman I had ever laid eyes on. Nah. Abrams edges her out. But I have some questions of my own.

"I'm confused about something. You said Maria stopped calling and texting this sister of hers. But as I told you, she didn't have a cell phone. I don't understand how she could ever have contacted anyone."

"Maria did have a cell. And just so you know — she has been living with her sister in Reno for the last fifteen years. She did come from Colombia originally, but she immigrated legally."

"I ... I don't understand. This can't be."

"I know this must come as a shock, but this is what we've been told. Rest assured, we're looking into her sister's story as well. The cell phone. The immigration. All of it. Now, who else knew Maria was living with you?"

I take a few moments to think it over before replying. "The only one who might have known is the apartment manager, Eric. He showed up here a couple of times and may have seen her."

"I see. Did he talk to her?"

"Not that I know of, unless he came by when I wasn't home. But I had instructed Maria to not open the door to anyone."

"What does he look like, this Eric?"

"He's around fifty. Short, big belly. Skunk hair. Always chewing on a tooth-pick."

"Skunk hair?" she asks, a smile playing on her lips.

"Yeah, you know? Dark hair with a streak of white going up the middle?"

"Yes, I get the picture."

She's still smiling. If I can just come up with some more witty stuff like this she'll be smitten. If she isn't already. I can't really tell.

"Where can I find Eric?"

The question pulls me back to reality.

"He's in apartment one."

"I'll talk to him. Now, when was the last time you saw Maria?"

"On Friday morning. I had some errands to run. By the time I got back, she was gone."

Abrams pauses, deep in thought. Then she's on her feet in an instant and walks over to the window behind me. It's not the window that interests her. She bends to pick up something. When she turns to me, she's holding a fragment of my vintage Chinese vase.

"Where's this from?"

It's a good thing I'm still seated, or my knees would have buckled. My throat feels dry all of a sudden, and I struggle to get the words out. "My ... my vase." Noticing she's waiting for me to continue, I say, "I had a set of two. Just like the one you see on the mantel." Her gaze follows as I point at the vase. "There was another one at the other end. I accidentally knocked it over." I was so sure I had cleaned up, so how was this piece still around? My eyes scan the wall and the floor, checking for anything else I may have missed.

"When was this?" she asks as she places the fragment in an envelope.

"What?"

"When did the vase break?"

"Oh. A few days ago."

"I see. Before Maria disappeared?"

"Yes." It's the truth. It really is. Trust me. Definitely before she disappeared.

She studies the rest of the apartment from where she stands, then saunters around for a closer inspection before stopping in front of me.

"That's all I have for you, Jason. Hang in there. I hope she turns up. Do let me know if she does. In the meantime, we'll start a search."

Then she turns around and walks out the door.

Once Abrams leaves, I mull over what I've just learned. Who is this sister? Did Maria really have a cell phone? How did I never discover it? I spend the next hour searching the apartment, but I don't find it. Not even a charger. Was Abrams bluffing? Why would she? But if there really was a cell and it's not here, it means Maria had it on her when she—

Not a comforting thought. My thoughts drift to the sister. I open my laptop to search. But what do I search for? I don't know Maria's last name. I never bothered to ask, and she never bothered to tell. While Maria and Sofia are beautiful names, they aren't unique. I continue anyway. "Maria and Sofia" gives me a bunch of useless links. No surprises there. Adding "Reno" works better. Another hour passes as I research the results. Quite a few Marias and Sofias in Reno. None of them fit the profile. Frustrated, I slam the laptop shut.

I need to calm down, de-stress, and I know just what will help me. I head over to the closet and punch in the code on the safe. A wave of panic surges through me when it's rejected. Then I remember. I had changed it last time. The new code works like magic. Even though I know the album will be there, I'm filled with relief when I see it. My doubts are not surprising considering how close I'd come to losing the treasure. Picking it up, I settle into the lounge chair to review my collection. Twenty stamps. Rare ones. Estimated current value of two million dollars. My grandfather was the philatelist of the family and had spent a lifetime building most of the collection. My father had continued the tradition. I was lucky to inherit it. If either of them had still been around, they would have been disappointed to see I had not added to it. The fact is, I can't afford it. In these outrageously expensive times it's an achievement to live in San Jose and pay the rent on time. They didn't have any such worries.

I study the Penny Black and the Penny Red, the two stars of the collection, together worth around a million dollars. My favorite, though, is the Inverted Lenny, which is the lesser-known cousin of one of the most famous stamps, the 1918 Inverted Jenny. The Lenny's only worth fifty thousand, but something about it pulls me in every time. *Only fifty thousand.* Did I just say that? Fifty thousand is still a lot of money. For me it is. It's just that it pales in comparison to the Penny duo.

It would be easy for me to sell the collection and live off the proceeds for the rest of my life, but I can't do it. Holding it, viewing it, brings me closer to my grandfather. Realizing I miss him, I shut my eyes. My thoughts drift to the last time I viewed this collection. Mistakes, mistakes, mistakes. I open my eyes and close the album. It's no longer safe to keep it at home. Tomorrow I'll move it to my deposit box at the bank.

NATALIE

I park my car across the street from the apartment complex and step out. Walking towards his apartment, I scan my surroundings. It's quiet. Not a soul in sight. No security cameras either, like I was told. A minute later I'm standing before number ten. I'm sure the man inside is guilty, and not because the husband or boyfriend's always the prime suspect in such cases. Once again, rage bubbles up inside me. It's important that I tame it before he sees me.

I take a couple of deep breaths and knock, feeling myself calm down. The sound echoes in the silence. It's not long before the door opens and an odor hits me hard. His eyes are bloodshot, hair matted, and he has stubble that's a few days old. Probably hasn't showered in a while. Still, I can't tell whether the stink's from him or from the apartment. He's wearing a plain white t-shirt and black track pants. For a moment I doubt my judgment before reminding myself that he could have been crying out of guilt, or even fear. It doesn't have to be grief.

He gives me a questioning look. An introduction and a flash of my badge lead to a flicker of fear on his face before he lets me in. I step inside and take in my surroundings. It's a studio apartment and it's as I had expected, except that it's a lot messier. The large window on the far wall is what I see first. It offers a dull view of the next row of apartments. In the corner next to it is a red lounge chair. I picture myself curling up on it with an engrossing book. There's a bathroom to my immediate left, and beyond it is the unmade bed, resting against the left wall. A fireplace and mantel adorn the wall opposite the bed. No pictures anywhere. The kitchen is to my right. Dishes are piled up in the sink.

There are a couple of chairs and a table by the kitchen. I settle into the chair he indicates, while he takes the one opposite. Even in this state he can't help himself as he eyes me, taking in every inch of my body. What's going on in that head of his? Do I want to know? No. Well, actually I do, just not the dirty bits. I have to admit, he's cute in a nerdy way. Under different circumstances … Anyway, time to get to business.

I tell him why I'm here, and there's that fleeting glimpse of fear again before he acknowledges that Maria's missing. A few more questions follow before I get to the key one.

"Any idea where she could be?"

"No."

Liar! I resist the urge to attack him, to shake him and force a confession out of him. *How does he do it so easily?* Lying with a straight face, with not a shred of guilt. But then, who am I to judge him on that? I calm myself again, lest I overplay my hand.

His tears start flowing once more as I fire away with my questions. Either he's really hurting or he's an excellent actor. I vote for the latter as I take my eyes off him and scan the room. From the corner of my eye, I can tell he's checking me out again. *The pig!*

It's quite a delight when I see his jaw drop, and he tells me he didn't know Maria had a sister. He spent three intimate months with her and doesn't know this. What does it say about him? Okay, maybe not a lot since he said Maria told him she had no one. I'm tempted to ask him whether he's all alone in the world, too, and what it feels like. It was crushing when I lost my parents all those years ago, but at least I always had someone even after they were gone. *How do you cope when your support system disappears?* I hold back on the personal questions, but I probe him further about Maria. A while later he throws out a gem of a line.

"Well, she was in trouble. How could I not help? Besides, she looked so innocent."

Ah, what a good Samaritan, prancing around town helping innocent-looking women. *Bullshit.* It's obvious what he was looking for. Not that he would ever admit it. It's no surprise he's all alone. He deserves it.

As we continue talking, I notice something on the floor, below the window. I walk over and pick it up. This could be important. I turn to him, and if I didn't know any better, I would have thought he was having a heart attack. He spews some lies about his broken vase, but I know I'm onto something, because he's cagey now, eyes darting around the room like he's searching. Dropping the piece into an envelope, I decide I have all I need for now. Then I'm out the door, knowing I'll be back soon.

JASON

T he week has flown by. I'm ensconced in the chair by the kitchen, enjoying my morning coffee, when I realize I've been careless. I pick up my phone and add a reminder to move the album to the deposit box today. Just as I set the phone back on the table, there's a knock. Curious, I trundle over and open the door. It's Abrams. From her demeanor I steel myself for bad news. I let her in, trying not to throw up my breakfast. She waits for me to sit before speaking, her tone gentle.

"We found her."

"Wh … where?" I ask as my heart tries to hammer through my chest.

"Cottonwood Lake. In Hellyer Park."

Of course.

"Oh." That's all I can muster, though I know I should say more. She beats me to it.

"I'm sorry to tell you — she's dead."

"Oh!" My hand goes up to my face instinctively as I sink back in the chair.

She gives me a minute before continuing. "I can't imagine how hard this must be for you."

There's a tear flowing down my cheek. *Why?*

"How … how did she?" I manage to ask.

"We're still waiting on the autopsy."

Something tells me she knows but doesn't want to reveal it.

"Are you sure it's her?"

"Yes. Her sister identified the body."

The sister again.

"Jason, are you sure you don't know anything about what happened to her?"

I shake my head slowly. She walks over to the mantel and stares at the vase for a few moments before turning to me.

"Might as well tell you. We found her in the lake, but that's not how she died. Not drowned, I mean."

She waits for a reaction. Finding none, she continues.

"She had a head injury. Blunt force trauma. In spite of the water, there was still some blood sticking to her hair. Whoever did it killed her and dumped her in the lake."

I feel my body going cold. Yet, there's sweat forming on my forehead.

"How ... how did you know to look there?" I ask.

"We reviewed her phone records. It was the last location reported by her cell."

The damn phone again.

"Along with the blood we found some fragments. We analyzed those. Guess what we found?"

"What?" The word stumbles out of my mouth.

"The fragments matched the piece of vase I collected here the other day."

She's watching me intently now, her eyes scanning my face for every twitch, every little reaction. My breakfast may not stay down much longer. There's no doubt what's coming next. Based on what she has so far, it's surprising she hasn't arrested me already. I make an effort to sound normal.

"They ... they can do that?"

"Yes. Forensic science has come a long way, Jason."

"I see."

"So now, tell me the truth. You really don't know what happened to her?"

Checkmate. Game over.

The tears burst through as I drop my head in my hands, awaiting my fate. I'm spending the rest of my life in prison.

NATALIE

I t was a long week, but I'm finally back, ready for the moment of truth. As before, I park across the street and walk towards his apartment, scanning my surroundings as I do so. One knock is all it takes for him to get to the door. The air inside is breathable today. He's looking better too. His hair's not matted anymore, and the stubble seems to be only a day old. This time he's wearing a black t-shirt and gray pajamas. I can tell my arrival has rattled him, but he lets me in like he's been expecting me.

The bed is still unmade, but the kitchen sink's empty. A green coffee mug's sitting on the table next to the kitchen, with a half-eaten croissant on a plate next to it. I wait for him to sit before I deliver the news. He doesn't take it well. As we talk, I amble over to the mantel and study the surviving vase. *Does this vase miss its sibling? Is it better to be lifeless like this and not experience feelings of love and loss?* A fleeting thought which I interrupt to focus my attention on the task at hand. I move in for the kill and before long he's sweating. He's not going to last long. I feel it in my bones. Everything I say is pushing him closer to the edge. And then it's time to push him off.

"So now, tell me the truth. You really don't know what happened to her?"

Fear. Defeat. It's all reflected in his face before he buries it in his hands. *Got him!* Hopefully he will confess now. I know he did it, but I must hear it from him. A minute passes before he looks up again, tears welling up in his eyes.

"I didn't mean to do it," he says.

"Do what?" The anticipation is building inside me.

"I loved her so much. You understand that?"

I nod.

"But she ... she betrayed me." A pause. "I'm such a fool. I still love her even after all that."

"How did she betray you?"

"I have this ... this collection of rare stamps. Believe it or not, it's worth around two million dollars. A few days before she died, I showed it to her. She was mesmerized. You know, it's not something I share with anyone other than people closest to me. People I trust."

"And what does it have to do with the murder?"

"The evening of the incident I got home earlier than usual. It was a shocking sight. She was standing by the mantle with the stamp album in hand. I don't know how she got into the safe."

"She must have noted the combination when you opened it previously."

"Yes, I guess that's possible. So I asked her what she was doing with it. She pointed a gun at me. I don't know where she got it. It scared the heck out of me. She said she was leaving with the stamps. I couldn't believe it. This woman who I loved, she was betraying me like this, stealing my most precious possession."

"What happened next?"

"I told her I didn't want to lose my life over it, and she could leave. She lowered the gun and started walking past. That's when I ... when I ..."

"You picked up the vase and smashed it on her head?"

"Yes."

I picture the scene. Maria writhing on the floor in agony, blood oozing out of her head. Jason standing by, relieved that he had saved his stamps. It's a miracle I don't throw up.

"Was it quick?"

"What?"

"Did she die right away?"

"I ... I think so. She ... she just collapsed on the floor. I stood there for a while before I ... before I picked up the album and put it back in the safe."

"Did you change the combination too?"

"Yes. Yes, I did. It was the sensible thing to do."

"How so? As you said, she didn't know anyone so she would be the only other person to know the code, and she was already dead."

"I don't know. It was just a reflex action."

"I see. What did you do next?"

"I couldn't just leave the body here. So I rolled it up in a blanket and put it in my trunk. Then I drove to Hellyer Park and dumped it in the lake."

"And the album. You still have it here? In this apartment?"

"Yes. In the safe."

"I need it."

"What? Why?"

"Evidence."

"Oh." He's quiet for a few seconds, staring out into space. "I guess it doesn't matter anymore, does it? I'm going to prison for the rest of my life."

I nod.

He stands up and disappears into the closet. Two minutes later he's back, album in hand. I flip through it to confirm it's what I'm looking for. Satisfied, I place it on the mantel and pick up the vase.

"Careful with that," he says as he steps closer.

"Always," I say as I steady the vase in my hands. "This is for Maria."

It shatters into pieces as I smash it on his head. A flood of pent-up emotions gushes out of me, and I take a deep breath, knowing I need to keep it together. He drops to the floor, holding his bloody head.

"Why ... why ..."

I ignore the question and get moving, ensuring I wipe down every surface I have ever touched in here, starting with the vase. When I get back to him, he's still alive, so I return with a pillow.

"My name is Sofia. Ring a bell?"

His eyes tell me he understands. It's enough for me. I smother him with the pillow. He struggles a bit but it doesn't take long. When I take off the pillow, his lifeless eyes are staring at the ceiling. He's gone now, but the satisfaction I expected is missing. There's still a hollowness inside me. I feel unfulfilled, discontented, and I realize it's because this will not bring Maria back. She's gone forever, leaving me all alone in this world. My heart is heavy as I pick up the album. Two million dollars. All of it for me. But I don't want it all. I was supposed to split it with my little sis. My Maria. The adorable infant I cradled in my arms. The bouncy toddler who followed me around everywhere. The wide-eyed teenager I welcomed into my world of cons.

A stab of guilt hits me, squeezing my heart and leaving me weak in the knees. I should have left her out of it. She was smart, but not smart enough to excel in this line of work. Not disciplined enough. I should have pushed her out of it a long time ago. It was my responsibility as the older sister. She had already made one mistake on this con. That three-day absence could have cost us the job. All because she wanted a break after being stuck with Jason for a few weeks. But he was so enamored by her that he overlooked that blip. Why didn't I follow my gut and abort the mission right then? I could have saved Maria, kept her away from that second mistake. The fatal one — assuming he was harmless.

My eyes are brimming with tears. I pull a tissue from my pocket to subdue them. As I do so something falls to the floor. It's my fake Natalie Abrams ID. Maria came up with that name when we were planning the Rosenberg con five years ago. I would play Natalie and she would be my partner, Stacy Walter. Maria being Maria, she wanted to be Daisy Duke, but I shot down the idea. That name would draw too much attention. The memory brings a smile to my face. What I would give to have her by my side again. Natalie Abrams is a role I relished playing over several cons, but this time it was suffocating.

It's been an agonizing few days, knowing Maria's killer was right here, but I had to be patient and wait for the right time. If I hadn't been waiting outside for her that night, perhaps I would never have known what happened to her. I followed him to the park and saw him dump the body. Waiting for him to leave was excruciating. I don't remember how I kept it together as I dove into the frigid water in the darkness, desperately trying to find her body — an hour of fighting for breath and battling my own despair before I located her. It broke my heart to see her lifeless body in the moonlight. So exhausting to move it to my car. Considering the circumstances, going to the cops was not an option. So I buried her by myself the next day, resisting the temptation to join her in that grave.

I would have avenged her right away, but I wanted the stamps. Missing out on them would mean we had lost — that Maria had lost. For me to be successful, Jason had to trust that I was indeed a detective, that I was investigating Maria's disappearance. Waiting for a week was necessary to achieve that.

I scan the apartment a final time, ensuring I haven't left any evidence of my presence. For a moment I consider trashing the place a bit to make it look like a robbery gone wrong. But it doesn't matter. It will be a few days before anyone, probably Eric, finds the body — after a concerned neighbor complains of the stench. By then I'll be back in Reno, far away from this awful place.

I run through all the events of the past week in my head, confirming my tracks are covered. I was careful to always park away from the complex so none of the residents would notice my car. My visits were at times when there weren't a lot of people out and about. I'm pretty sure no one saw me come and go.

Satisfied that I have not left any loose ends, I walk towards the door, eager to drive back to Reno. Using a paper towel to work the handle, I step outside. There's a man standing a few feet away, staring at me with furrowed brows. Short, potbellied, skunk hair. There's a toothpick dangling between his lips. I freeze. The skunk hair does not make me smile this time.

Fuck!

AUTHOR'S NOTE

A loner is being grilled by detectives about a big robbery for which he's the prime suspect. He explains how he met this woman in trouble, helped her and fell in love, not knowing she was involving him in a big con. And now she's gone. The story was to be told from his point of view. This was the simple idea roosting in my head for over a year. When I finally got around to writing it, the plot morphed and I added Natalie's POV. Completing that first draft was fulfilling, but I felt something was missing. I set it aside for a while until the idea hit — what if Natalie isn't who she says she is? This plot twist made it more difficult to write from Natalie's POV, but I feel it elevated the story. Do you agree?

Fun fact — as a child, I loved collecting stamps. I had this neat stamp album where I had row after row, page after page of stamps from all over the world. Including stamps in the plot took me right back to the fun times I had building my collection (yeah, it's kinda nerdy). Too bad I have no idea where that album disappeared. It wasn't monetarily valuable like Jason's collection, but I do wish I could get my hands on it again.

THE FLING

A DETECTIVE CONLEY MYSTERY

"I'm married," Kevin said, raising his hand to show off his wedding band.

"I know," Tania replied. "Spotted it the moment you walked in."

"And it doesn't bother you?"

"No. It actually adds to the excitement." She smiled, her eyes bright. "Why do you think I'm serving your table?"

Kevin's heart raced as he realized what he was getting into. In twenty years of marriage his eyes had strayed many times, but *he* had never strayed. He had been faithful to Emma throughout. So what was it about this girl — for he could only think of her as a girl; she was probably born around the time he was married — that was forcing him to cross the line? She was gorgeous, of course. Smart, too. But was that all? She had made quite an impact on him in the thirty minutes he had known her, and things had escalated quickly.

A sensation of guilt engulfed him, and he stole furtive glances around the café to gauge who had witnessed him stoop so low. At the next table sat a couple who were staring into each other's eyes dreamily, kind of like how he and Emma used to, all those years ago. He figured they didn't care about what he had been up to. His gaze moved to the only other customer in the café, an old woman seated at a corner table. Her hands were wrapped around her coffee mug, her eyes transfixed on it, but he got the feeling she had been staring at him earlier.

"What're you thinking?" Tania asked. "Don't want to cheat on your wife?"

The blunt question caught him off guard. He waited a few seconds before answering, trying to shake off his paranoia. "What time do you get off work?"

"That's more like it! I get off at six."

He set down his coffee cup and placed enough cash on the table to cover the bill and an enormous tip for her. Standing up, he said, "I'll be waiting for you. Rustic Inn. Room seven."

He was grinning as he left the café, a spring in his step. *When was the last time he felt this alive?* Excitement and nervousness pulsed through him. His thoughts were so occupied by the fabulous evening that lay before him that he was oblivious to the pair of legs that followed him out.

There was a knock on his door at seven p.m. He was there in a flash, and he stood staring at Tania standing outside. She had changed out of her work clothes and was wrapped in a red dress which accentuated her figure. A touch of makeup made her look even prettier than when he had seen her last. He welcomed her in and started to ask her if she wanted anything to drink, but he never finished, for her lips found his right away. The next hour was a blur as they wrestled in bed without a care in the world. Later they lay side by side, satisfied, until Tania got up and picked up her clothes.

"You leaving already?" he asked.

"No. Do you want me to?"

"Of course not. I want you to spend the night. If you can, that is."

"Sure. It's just that I can't sleep without clothes. Feels weird."

A mischievous grin spread across his face. "Who said anything about sleep?"

"Sorry, I have an early start tomorrow."

She got back in bed and lay down, closing her eyes. Soon all he could hear was her rhythmic breathing. His hopes of more action dashed, he rolled out of bed and hopped into the shower. As the first drops of water pricked his body, guilt and shame surged through him. It had actually happened. He had cheated on Emma. How would he face her now? As he battled his feelings, another thought struck him like a punch in the gut. What did this girl see in him? What was that attractive twenty-something doing with this washed-up middle-aged man? Was she really attracted to him? Or was it something more sinister? He had heard of women entrapping men in this manner, threatening to tell their wives if their demands were not met. Was that what she was after? She said she had noticed his ring as soon as he had entered the café. She must have noticed his expensive clothes and shoes as well. Hadn't he caught her eyeing his Rolex a few times? He was the perfect target. Married and rich. *What would he do if she blackmailed him?*

⤙⟫⟩⟩   ⟨⟨⟨⟨⤚

It was just past 9:30 a.m. when Detective Paul Conley stood by the bushes in one corner of the Rustic Inn compound, staring at the dead woman lying on a floral bedspread and a white bedsheet. She had on a red dress, and her neck and the items were covered in blood. Natalie from forensics was crouched next to the body.

"Throat slashed. I estimate sometime last night," she said.

"Do we know who she is?"

"Nope."

"Who found the body?"

"One of the cleaners."

"Larsen," Paul called out to the cop standing at the perimeter. "Can you get someone, perhaps the desk clerk, to identify her? She's probably a guest."

"Sure," Officer Larsen replied as he dashed off.

Paul pulled on his gloves and bent down to survey the body. There were some marks where her neck met her shoulder. He pointed them out to Natalie.

"Look like hickeys to me. She might have had a wild evening. The ME will examine her for any signs of intercourse," she said.

"I guess we have to find her lover."

He continued looking her over, but didn't find any other injuries or defensive wounds. No keys. No purse. No cell phone. *Did the killer dump those somewhere else?* His thoughts were interrupted when he heard his name.

"Paul, I have the manager here."

He turned to see Larsen and a short man who appeared to be in his fifties, wearing a t-shirt with the Rustic Inn logo on it. The man was pale and was trying to look away from the body.

"Ivan. Ivan Mendes," he said. "I'm ... I'm the manager."

"Ivan, I know this won't be easy, but we need your help. Can you look at the body and tell us whether she's one of your guests?"

"Sure. Sure," Ivan replied with some hesitation.

He glanced at the body, then turned away. For a moment Paul thought Ivan was going to throw up, but it was a false alarm. The manager turned to the body again, stepping closer this time. He spent a full minute observing the face, his own face contorting in various ways as he did so.

"No, she's not a guest. You know, she looks a lot like one of the servers at Bluelight Café."

"You sure about that?" asked Paul.

"It's difficult to tell. I've only ever seen her in the café uniform, not dressed up like this. But quite sure it's her."

"What's her name?"

"I don't know."

"Bluelight Café. Is that the one a couple of blocks down the street?"

"Yes. That's the one."

"Hmm. Wonder what she was doing here."

"Can I go now?" asked Ivan, looking eager to escape the scene.

"One more thing. The bedspread around her — is that from your hotel?"

"Yes. It's the same design we've been using for the last couple of years."

"So that means this would be from one of your rooms. We need to find out which room is missing a bedspread and sheets. Can you help with that?"

"Sure thing. I'll get on it right away." Ivan departed.

"Larsen, where's the cleaner who found the body?"

"Davis is with her in room one. She was in quite a state."

"Not surprising. I'll go see her now."

Officer Davis opened the door to room one promptly when Paul knocked. Paul stepped in to see a slim woman seated at the writing desk, with her head resting on it. She looked up on hearing him enter, the rims of her eyes swollen.

"Brenda, this is Detective Conley. He has some questions for you," said Davis.

She nodded her head.

"What's your full name?"

"Brenda Cortez."

"Tell me what happened, Brenda."

"I ... I already told Officer Davis."

"I know, but can you tell me again?"

"I guess," she replied, looking alternately at Davis and Conley.

"Go on."

"I got here at seven a.m. as usual. Changed to my work clothes, got my cleaning stuff, and started my rounds around the compound. That's when I ... I saw her."

Brenda paused as she began sobbing. Davis pushed the tissue box towards her. She dabbed her eyes and placed the tissue on the desk.

"Sorry."

"It's alright. You've had quite a shock," Paul assured her. "What did you see?"

"There was a bundle. I ... I could tell it was our bedspread. I wondered what it was doing there, so I tried to open it up. There was ... there was a bedsheet inside, and I could see the ... the blood. It smelled awful. I thought maybe someone tossed a soiled sheet, so I opened it more."

The sobbing resumed, and she used a fresh tissue.

"Then I saw her. I saw her and I knew. I ... I screamed. I ran back inside the building. Mr. Mendes helped me call 911."

"Did you recognize the woman?"

"I didn't get a good look at her face, but I don't think I've seen her before."

"Thank you, Brenda. You have been most helpful. You can leave now."

Paul stepped out of the room to find Ivan standing there with a portly woman.

"The cop told me I could find you here," Ivan said.

"What is it?"

"This is Juanita. She was on housekeeping for all the rooms today. She says room seven was missing the bedspread and some sheets."

"Awesome! Who's in room seven?"

"That's the strange thing. There was a Kevin Barlowe in there. He was booked through the weekend. But he checked out late last night. So there's no one in the room today."

"You mean he checked out earlier than expected?"

"Yes. In fact, that's why she was cleaning up in there so early. The occupied rooms are cleaned up later in the morning."

"I need his contact information. Right away."

"Sure."

"We will also have to seal room seven for investigation. It's a secondary crime scene now."

Ivan frowned. "For how long?"

"Can't say yet. Depends on what we find. A few hours at least."

"I hope it's not going to be more than that. I can't afford to have vacancies."

"We'll do our best to get out of your way quickly, Ivan, but I can't promise anything."

"Okay. I'll be back with Kevin Barlowe's details," Ivan said as he departed.

Paul turned to Davis, who had been standing beside him since Brenda had left. "Kevin Barlowe. Isn't he an author?"

"Never heard of him."

"I'll talk to him once Ivan gets me his info. But right now I have to interview Juanita. How many guys have you got out here?"

"Only Larsen and me."

"You may want to call for help. There's a lot we need to do. Someone has to manage room seven. We also need someone to go to Bluelight Café and ask about our vic. And we'll need bodies to canvass the hotel guests."

"Sure, I'll take care of it."

Once Davis had left, Paul took Juanita into room one. She was trembling.

"You look worried," he said once she was seated on the chair.

"Trouble?"

"No. No trouble. I just need to ask you some questions."

"Woman ... *muerta*?"

"You know about that?"

"Everyone talk about it."

"Did you see her?"

"No. I clean rooms."

"Did you already clean room seven?"

"*Siete? Sí.*" Juanita nodded.

"Even though the bedspread was missing? Even though there must have been blood in there?"

"Blood?"

"*La sangre.*"

"*Sí*. My job clean. I clean."

"There goes my crime scene," Paul muttered to himself. "Tell me what you saw in room seven. Before you cleaned."

"I go in there. All look okay. But bed not have sheets."

"What else did you see?"

Juanita shook her head. "*Nada*."

"No blood? What about a knife?"

"Knife?"

Not remembering the Spanish word for knife, Paul mimed a cutting action.

"Ah, *cuchillo*? No *cuchillo*."

"What about the blood? *Sangre?*"

"Some blood on bed," she said as she pointed to the headboard of the bed in their room. "I clean."

"Did you find anything else? Like keys or a purse or a cell phone?" he asked, miming actions for each item.

"*Nada*."

"*Gracias*, Juanita. That's all I have for you."

She flashed a broad smile, brimming with relief as she fled the room. Paul stepped out to see Ivan standing there, holding out a piece of paper.

"Kevin Barlowe's contact information," he said.

Paul took the paper and read it. "He's local?"

"Yes."

"What did he need a room for?"

"Maybe he had a fight with his wife," Ivan replied with a grin.

Or he needed some place to meet his girlfriend, thought Paul.

"Tell me about last evening. When did Kevin come and go? What time did the victim arrive?"

"I don't know. My shift started at midnight. Susan, my wife, was here last evening. She should be able to answer your questions. She'll be here soon for her shift."

"Your wife works here too?"

"Yes. We own the place. I do the a.m. shifts, and she does the p.m. shifts."

"Twelve-hour shifts? Sounds exhausting. When do you get time to see each other?"

The grin reappeared on Ivan's face. "Only when we switch over."

"Wow. How does that work?"

"Perfect, if you ask me. After thirty years of marriage it's the only way."

"Well, whatever works for you. Let me know when Susan gets here. I'll be in room seven."

"Sure."

Paul donned his gloves again and entered the room. He took a quick tour and found it spick-and-span, as would be expected after a visit from housekeeping. The bed was inviting, with fresh sheets and the same kind of floral bedspread laid crisply on it. He inspected the headboard and the area around the bed but didn't see anything unusual. Then he crouched on the floor and shone a light under the bed. A smile broke out on his lips as his heart raced.

"Oh Juanita, you missed a spot," he said to himself.

He reached for the object that lay a few feet away. It was a knife. The handle was clean, but the blade was coated in what looked like dried blood. Paul fished out an evidence bag from his pocket and dropped the knife into it. Then he peeked under the bed once more and got up once he was convinced there was nothing else to find.

He stepped out of the room to find two officers standing there with crime scene tape. After instructing them, he walked over to the front desk. It was situated close to the breakfast bar. The place smelled of coffee and muffins, bacon and eggs. His mouth watered and his stomach grumbled, even though Brigette had fed him well earlier. Ivan was at the desk, talking to a woman. She looked about the same age as Ivan and had a stern demeanor, reminding Paul of a strict school principal.

"Detective, this is my wife, Susan."

Paul introduced himself. As he did so, he pictured Ivan as a truant schoolboy, and it made sense why Ivan was happy to stay away from her. He smiled.

"Can I leave now, Detective?" Ivan asked.

"You *can* certainly leave, Ivan. The question is whether you *may* leave," Susan said. "It's not about whether you have the ability to walk away, it's about whether you are permitted to."

Ivan rolled his eyes. "*May* I leave now, Detective?"

"Sure," replied Paul. Then he turned to Susan. "Grammar Nazi?"

She smiled wryly. "Retired English teacher."

"Ah, figures. I guess I'll have to watch what I say."

"Don't worry. I only harass *him* about it."

"Why's that?"

"Because I would have still been molding little minds if not for his crazy ideas."

"What crazy ideas?"

"Running this dump. He inherited it from some old uncle of his a couple of years ago. I wanted him to sell the place and bank the money, but for him this was a chance to live his dream. So, here we are, slogging away, only to lose money year after year. I thought life as a teacher was tough, but this is worse."

"Oh, well. Hopefully he'll come around soon."

"Yes, hopefully. Are you here to talk about the dead girl?"

"Yes. Susan, I have some questions for you."

"Okay. Ivan was just telling me about the tragedy."

"Were you at the desk last evening?"

"Yes."

"And you checked out the guest in room seven? Kevin Barlowe."

"Yes. It was a surprise since he was booked through the weekend."

"Did he give you any reason for checking out early?"

"No. He looked frazzled. As if he was in a rush to get out of here."

"What time was this?"

"Around ten-thirty."

"I see. Was he in his room all day?"

"No. He left the building soon after I started my shift yesterday, and he didn't get back until around five p.m. I didn't see him again until he checked out."

"What about the victim? Did you see her going to his room?"

"I haven't seen the body, so I don't know what she looks like."

Paul showed her the picture he had clicked on his phone.

Her hand went up to her mouth. "Oh, the poor little thing."

"You know her?"

"She works at the café down the street."

"You know her name?"

"No. I'm afraid not."

"Did you see her yesterday?"

"I did. She walked through here around seven p.m. I didn't recognize her at first. I'm so used to seeing her in her work clothes."

"What was she wearing?"

A faint smile appeared on Susan's face. "A beautiful red dress. She looked stunning."

"And do you recall if she was carrying anything?"

"Carrying something? What, like a box?"

"No. A purse, or keys."

"I ... I didn't notice."

"Okay. So she walked through here around seven. Do you know where she went?"

"She went that way." Susan pointed the way.

"So, towards room seven?"

"Yes, room seven is that way, but there are other rooms too."

Paul nodded. "Understood. Did you see her again?"

"No. This is so sad. To think I was just there two mornings ago. She served me coffee with that winsome smile." Susan's eyes teared up.

He paused for a few seconds before continuing. "Did you see anyone else enter or leave?"

"A few of the guests here and there. Nothing unusual." Susan wiped her eyes with a tissue. "Oh, I completely forgot. Kevin Barlowe's wife came by around four-thirty and asked for the room key."

"Anything wrong with that?"

"She hadn't checked in with him and wasn't staying here. She said it was a surprise."

"And you gave her the key?"

"Yes. She took it and went towards the room."

"What time did she return?"

"That's the strange thing. She didn't."

"Oh. Could she have exited the building through some other door?"

"Certainly. We have additional exits at either end of the building for easier access to the parking lot."

"Okay. So she could have left that way?"

"Yes."

"Anything else you remember?"

"No."

"Thank you, Susan. You have been most helpful. Do call if anything else comes to mind."

"I sure will."

Paul turned to see Officer Davis walking towards him.

"I spoke to a couple of people at the café. Showed them her picture. They identified her as Tania Lawrence. Moved into town six months ago and has been working at the café since. Lives close to work. Got off at six last evening."

"How about next of kin?"

"No one local as far as they know. Her parents are in Tennessee. Nashville."

"I'll contact the local PD there so they can deliver the news. Anything else?"

"Yes. I found author Kevin Barlowe's picture online. Showed it at the café. They said he was in there yesterday afternoon, and she served him. They had a friendly chat."

"Interesting. Maybe that's what it was then? A bit of flirting. He invites her over. Something goes wrong, and she ends up dead. Good work, Davis."

"Thanks, Paul."

"I'm off to interview the Barlowes. Care to join me?"

"Sure. You said the Barlowes. Interviewing the wife too?"

"Yes. Apparently she was here yesterday, late afternoon."

"Hmm. Maybe they did this together."

"Or it was the wife. She found out about the affair and killed her rival in a fit of rage."

Thirty minutes later Paul and Davis stood outside Kevin and Emma Barlowe's front door. Banging and drilling sounds emanated from within. Paul's knock was answered by a man with dark hair, around the same height as him. Dark circles kissed his eyes. Kevin Barlowe. The color drained from Kevin's face when he noticed Davis's uniform. When Paul held up his badge and introduced himself, Kevin tightened his grip on the door, as if to steady himself. A woman walked up behind him. She had dark hair too, and a chiseled face with high cheekbones. *Stunning,* thought Paul.

"Honey, who are these people?" she asked. Her eyes widened when she saw the uniform. "Oh!"

"The ... the police," he answered.

Her brows furrowed as she turned to Paul and Davis. "Is ... is something wrong? What do you want?"

Emma's reaction to their presence was quite normal. If she was guilty, she hid it well. "We are investigating the murder of a Tania Lawrence," Paul replied.

"What does that have to do with us?" she asked. Turning to Kevin, she said, "We don't know a Tania, do we?"

"No," he replied.

"Is she one of the neighbors?" Emma asked Paul.

"No. She's a waitress at Bluelight Café. Her body was found at the Rustic Inn."

Emma's hand went up to her mouth. "Oh no, honey. Isn't that where you were?" Her eyes widened again as realization dawned. "Oh, is that why you're here? You want to know if Kevin saw something?"

"Actually, we have questions for both of you."

"For me? Why?" she asked.

"Because you were there too," Paul replied.

"You were at the Rustic?" Kevin asked her, sounding surprised.

"What? No, I wasn't. I've never been there. Why do you say I was there?" she asked Paul. He noticed the banging had stopped.

"We can sort things out at the station."

"Wait a minute. Are we under arrest?" Kevin asked.

"No. Just need to ask you some questions."

"Don't you need a warrant or something?" His right eyebrow went up a notch.

"Not for an interview."

"Should I call my lawyer?"

"You are certainly within your rights to do so."

"I see. And what if we refuse to go with you?" *Was that a dare on Kevin's face?* Paul could tell Emma didn't approve of this approach.

"I can interview you here."

Kevin and Emma glanced at each other.

"Let's talk here then," Kevin said after a few seconds, as he stepped aside to allow Paul and Davis to enter.

The banging started again as they made their way through the house. It was a kitchen remodel from the looks of it. Plastic curtains surrounded the kitchen, and Paul saw a couple of men busy working in there.

"Is there some place quiet we can talk?" he asked, raising his voice to be heard above the noise.

"I can't promise quiet, but my office is our best bet," Kevin replied.

"Okay, let's go there. I'll start with you first, Kevin." Turning to Emma he said, "Officer Davis will keep you company out here."

"Oh. You're not going to interview us together?" she asked.

"No. It must be separate."

Kevin led the way to his office. It was spacious, and the furnishings exuded elegance. He sank into the chair behind an enormous desk. Paul settled into the plush leather chair on the other side. Kevin may have been trying to play it cool, but the beads of sweat building up on his forehead gave him away. His hands were shaking so much that he had to place them flat on the desk to steady them.

"Kevin, what were you doing at the Rustic? You have a decent home here."

"You hear that noise? I had to get away. Can't get any writing done with that cacophony. So I decided to spend a week away to wrap up edits on my latest novel."

"You got done early then?"

"What? No. Editing is painful work. Sadly, I still have a long way to go."

"Then why did you check out earlier than planned?"

Kevin stared at Paul for a few seconds before reaching for a tissue and wiping his forehead.

"I ... I was unwell."

"You were unwell?"

"Yes."

"Shouldn't you have rested in your room? Why risk a drive home in that condition?"

Kevin chewed on the question for a few beats before answering. "Actually it was Emma. She was unwell."

"I see. So she will confirm this if I ask her?"

He shifted in his chair. Scratched his eyebrow with his index finger. "Okay. It was me. I was unwell."

"You sure?"

"Positive."

"So, not Emma?"

"Right. Emma was fine. I was unwell."

"So, back to my original question. Why didn't you rest in your room instead of driving here?"

"I was just restless. I figured the inn wasn't working out for me, and I was missing home."

"You've never stayed there before?"

"No. It was the only place that was available for a week at such short notice. I decided to give it a shot."

"I see. So you were feeling unwell, and you decided to check out and come home."

"Right."

"Where was Tania when you left?"

"Who?"

"The woman who was murdered. You knew her, right?"

"Oh, right. Like Emma and I told you earlier, we don't know any Tania."

"Let me refresh your memory."

Paul pulled up Tania's pic on his phone and showed it to Kevin. It was as if Kevin had stopped breathing. He swallowed hard.

"This is Tania?"

Paul nodded.

"Never seen her before."

"I have witnesses who would disagree. You were at Bluelight Café yesterday afternoon, and Tania here served you. You two had quite the friendly chat."

Kevin's hand was shaking more than before when he reached for a second tissue and wiped his forehead.

"Can you ... can you show me that picture again?"

"Sure." Paul held up his phone.

Kevin squinted at it, then looked at him.

"Oh yes, I remember now. She served me coffee. Sorry, I just blanked out back there."

"What did you talk about?"

"Not much. She ... she asked me if I was from around there, since she had never seen me before. She said she hadn't been in town long. I asked her where she was from. So, just general chitchat."

"No plans to meet up later?"

"No. No. Why would we?"

"Why not? You get precious time away from your wife. Meet this beautiful young thing who's into you. You figure, this is your chance."

"How ... how dare you? There was no such thing. I've always been faithful to Emma."

"Tania left work at six. An hour later she shows up at the inn, dressed up as if on a date. You telling me she wasn't there to see you?"

"She could have been there to meet anyone. I'm sure she meets a lot of people daily in her line of work. And it's not like ... it's not like I was the only guy staying there."

"Fair enough. Let's assume she was there to meet someone else. Can you explain how she ended up dead, wrapped in the bedspread and sheets from your room?"

Kevin reached for the glass of water that sat beside the tissue box. He downed it in a couple of gulps and wiped his mouth with the back of his hand.

"I ... I don't know. Maybe someone went in there after I checked out and stole the stuff."

"And how did the murder weapon end up under your bed?"

Kevin's eyes went wide. "It was under my bed?"

"Yes."

"Well, maybe that same person planted it there."

Paul was quiet for a few seconds. Everything that Kevin had said sounded reasonable. It could have happened the way he had described it. But he was nervous, and he had flip-flopped on who was unwell. *Why was he nervous if he had nothing to hide?* It was time to step on the gas and get him to spill the truth.

"We found your DNA on her. *In* her. How do you explain that?"

Kevin went pale. Paul's bluff seemed to have worked. The author spoke after a long pause.

"Wait, what? How did you know it was my DNA? You don't have my samples."

Smart fucker, thought Paul.

"We do have your DNA. From your room. You won't believe how much hair the average human sheds in a day."

There was another pause before Kevin spoke again. "So you matched the hair against the semen. But how do you know it was my hair? It's a motel room, after all. Anyone could have been in there."

Paul sighed internally. The bluff wasn't working as well as he had hoped. "Fair point. But it's only a matter of time before we get your samples and confirm it."

Kevin planted his elbows on the desk and his face in his hands. Sobs followed moments later. When he was done heaving, he looked up at Paul.

"I'm ... I'm sorry. I lied, but I ... I was worried you would think I did it."

"Tell me what happened."

"So, yes, we flirted a bit at the café. She ... she was coming onto me. I resisted at first. Then I thought — what the heck. I've been faithful for twenty long years. One time's not going to hurt, especially if Emma doesn't know. She's been a bit distant lately anyway. So I invited the girl ... um ... Tania to my room. We fucked. Yes, I cheated on Emma. Please don't tell her any of this."

"There's no reason to tell her anything," Paul lied, knowing he might have to share some details when he interviewed Emma later. "What happened next?"

"Tania — so, I didn't know her name until you told me. We had not exchanged names. It was more fun that way. She slept. I hopped into the shower. When I got out she was still in bed. But ... but, she was dead."

Kevin broke down again.

"Oh, come on. You expect me to buy that? You were the only one in the room with her. You killed her."

"No! I didn't. You must believe me."

"Who did it then? How did anyone get in?"

"I don't know. I wish I did."

Kevin sounded convincing, Paul had to admit. Emma. Emma had taken the room key. Was this the surprise she had for her husband?

"What happened next?"

"I panicked. I didn't know what to do. Everyone would assume I killed her. So I decided to dump the body. You know the rest."

"But you missed the knife."

"The knife ... oh yes, the knife. You found it under my bed, you say? I didn't know it was there. I just saw the body."

"I see. What about her stuff? We didn't find anything on her. No purse, no keys, no cell phone. Any idea where we can find those?"

"She didn't have a purse. She told me she lived real close, so she had walked over. I guess that's why she didn't have a car key either."

"What about a key to her apartment? Surely she should have had that?"

Kevin gave it some thought before replying. "She did have a key in her hand when she came in. I remember she put it on the nightstand."

"Any idea where it is now?"

He shook his head.

"Hopefully not tossed by housekeeping. I'll have to check if anything was turned in at the front desk. What about a cell phone?"

"Don't remember seeing one."

"Weird, considering how people are glued to their phones these days. Anyway, you do realize what you have done is so, so wrong on so many levels? You should have called 911 as soon as you found the body. Now you've destroyed crucial evidence. I could arrest you right now for interfering with law enforcement."

"I'm ... I'm sorry. I wasn't thinking straight."

"That's all I have for you for now. I'll talk to your wife next. Please send her in."

Relief flooded Kevin's face. He didn't waste any time exiting the room. A minute later Emma entered. She looked calm and composed as she settled into the chair her husband had vacated, her eyes trained on Paul, as if she had nothing to hide.

"What were you doing at the inn, Emma?"

"I wasn't there. I don't understand where you got that idea."

"The desk clerk confirmed that you came in around four-thirty and asked for the room key. She gave it to you. I assume you must have gone to the room."

"Well, she's lying. I'm telling you, I've never been there."

"Where were you yesterday around that time?"

"I was here all afternoon and evening."

"Anyone who can confirm that?"

"You think I killed the girl?"

"I just want to know where you were. No one's accusing anyone of anything. Yet."

"So you need an alibi?"

"Yes."

"My friend Cybil was with me."

"Can you give me her contact information?"

Paul noted down the details. He would talk to Cybil next, though friends seldom made for reliable sources. She could just be covering for Emma.

"I noticed you're having work done in your kitchen. What about the contractors? Can they confirm you were here?"

"Unfortunately not. They were out yesterday. One of the guys was sick, and they were also waiting for some parts."

"I see. And have you ever met the girl?"

"Who? The one who died?"

"Yes."

"I don't know what she looks like."

Paul showed her the picture. She studied it intently before replying.

"No. Never seen her before. She looks so young. Poor thing."

"I see. Thank you, Emma. That's all the questions I have for you at this time."

Davis joined him outside and they got into the car.

"I'll drop you at the inn," Paul said. "You can manage the scene. I have to confirm Emma's alibi."

"You think she did it?" asked Davis.

"It could be her. Could be the husband. My bets are on him. He was there in the room with the girl. Emma claims she was at home."

"So he was having an affair?"

"More like a fling."

"That gives her sufficient motive."

"Yep. What we need is evidence. Good, hard evidence."

"I have another theory."

"Do share."

"Maybe they killed her together."

"Why? It doesn't make any sense."

"Hear me out. So he goes out and snags these women, uses them physically. Then she kills the women. Some couples get off on that kind of stuff, you know."

"Davis, I think you've been reading too many domestic thrillers."

"Not as many as I would like."

Paul shook his head as he drove off.

⁕⁕⁕⁕⁕ ⁕⁕⁕⁕⁕

An hour later Paul was outside Cybil Ford's apartment, having dropped Officer Davis off at the Rustic Inn on the way. The apartment was a few blocks from his own home, and he had been tempted to drop in to kiss Brigette hello, but he remembered she was working late. He knocked twice and was rewarded with an open door within seconds.

The woman who stood there was a bit taller than Emma but with none of her grace and beauty. Her furrowed brows didn't help with her appearance. Paul held up his badge and introduced himself, but the brows didn't budge. He explained further the reason for his visit.

"Oh." That was all she could muster as she led him into the apartment.

The walls of the passageway were adorned with multiple photographs of a woman, which all seemed to be taken from stage performances and T.V. shows. Paul noticed a striking resemblance to his host.

"In case you're wondering — yes, that's me," Cybil said from the living room when she saw he was still in the passageway.

"You're an actress?" he asked as he joined her in the living room. There were cabinets along one wall, all stocked with a variety of trophies. Awards for acting, he noted. From organizations he had never heard of.

"Yes. Mostly local plays and bit parts in some T.V. shows."

"Anything I might have seen?"

Cybil gave a wry smile. "I don't know what you've seen. Clearly not, since you don't remember."

"Oh, I …"

"It's okay. I never made it to Hollywood. You know why?"

"Why?"

"Because they don't give a damn about talent. It's all about looks … and glamor."

"But you look great in those pictures," he replied, his gaffe registering too late.

Cybil shook her head. "So I only look good with all those layers of makeup? Not in person?"

"I didn't mean that."

"People think acting is easy. But it's not. A great actor makes it look easy. It takes a lot of effort to inhabit a character, learn their every move and convince the audience they are watching the character, not the actor. Anyway, you're here on a professional visit. Let's get on with it."

"Right. Where were you yesterday afternoon and evening?"

"Here till around two p.m. Then I went over to Emma's."

"What time did you get there?"

"It's around a fifteen-minute drive. So I would say I was there by two thirty."

"And what time did you leave?"

"Hmm … it was late. Say, around nine?"

"So you left before Kevin got home?"

"Yes." She smiled, as if amused. "That was so funny, him rushing back early. What was he even thinking, staying at that dump of an inn?"

"So you heard about that?"

"Of course. Emma told me this morning."

"You two are close?"

"Oh yeah. We're the best of friends. We've known each other since high school."

"You must have quite a bond then."

"Yes. Though she can be annoying at times."

"Annoying how?"

"Well, it's just that … I'm sure you noticed how attractive she is. Especially compared to me."

Paul was tempted to agree, but decided it was safer to stay silent. It prompted a smile from Cybil.

"Not taking your chances this time, I see. Anyway, so the thing is, she doesn't lose an opportunity to remind me of it."

"And she's still your best friend?"

"She makes up for it in other ways. I don't think there's any perfect friendship. They all have their flaws — this is the flaw in ours."

"You two are so close, I guess you would do anything for each other."

Cybil raised an eyebrow. "Anything?"

"Like faking an alibi."

She swallowed hard. "You think I'm lying about being with Emma? To save her?"

"It's a thought."

"Well, I'm not."

"Okay. Now coming back to Kevin's early return. Why do you find it funny? He said he was sick."

Cybil chuckled. "If he says so."

"You don't believe him?"

"Well, maybe it's true, maybe it's not. What do I know, right?"

"I guess. That inn's not too bad. Just needs some work. A fresh paint job on the outside, for a start."

"Yeah, and did you see the hideous bedspreads? And those awful curtains."

"I did. Couldn't miss that. I take it you have stayed there before?"

"Nope. Wouldn't step foot in there unless absolutely necessary."

Paul chuckled. "Can't blame you there. Anything else you want to tell me, Cybil?"

"No."

"Well, thank you for your time."

Paul departed. If Emma had been home with Cybil, who was the woman impersonating her at the inn? That was the question at the top of his mind as he walked back to his car. He had a feeling that if he answered that question he would have his killer.

⤞⤞⤞ ⤝⤝⤝

Paul entered Lieutenant Matt Zigler's office and waited for him to wrap up whatever he was doing on his computer. It was a couple of minutes before Matt turned to him.

"All right, bud. What's up? You look like you have questions."

They had been partners until Zigler's career took off, but they were still close friends.

"Where's the box?" Paul asked, pointing to the spot where Zigler usually had his donut stash.

"Oh, I quit."

"Seriously?"

Zigler patted his tummy. "The Mrs. thinks I'm growing in the wrong direction."

"Well, I think Angie's right."

"Hey, you're supposed to be on my side."

"I *am* on your side. When did this happen? I swear I saw a couple of chocolate donuts the last time I was in here."

"Today is day two. I'm going crazy. But I'm proud of myself. This is two days longer than I thought I would last."

"I'm proud of you too, Zigs. Just keep it going," Paul said, relieved that he wouldn't be crossing paths with those sweet temptations anymore.

"So, about this Rustic Inn case. What's the latest?"

"Got the autopsy report this morning. The knife's what got her, as expected. Time of death was late in the evening, in line with the initial estimate."

"Get anything from the knife?"

"The blood matches the vic."

"Any prints?"

"Two sets of prints. First set is confirmed to be Tania's."

"Interesting. So she handled the knife."

"Yes. For the second set we will try to match against our suspects."

"Sounds like a plan. What else?"

"I searched her apartment. Kevin was right. It was close to the Rustic. She could have walked over."

"Find anything interesting?"

"Tiny dump of a studio. Makes the Rustic look like the Ritz."

"That bad, huh?"

Paul nodded. "She didn't have much in there, though I did find her purse. Had a couple of bucks, driver's license and one credit card."

"Car keys?"

"No car key. Apparently she didn't own a car. Work was within walking distance. Some of the others at the café told me she was saving up and would hitch a ride with them when she had to go far."

"I see. Cell phone?"

"No. I have a feeling the killer disposed of it."

"You think the writer did it?"

"He definitely had the opportunity. Was super nervous too, but that would be expected if you were to believe his story."

"Yeah, I would be shit-scared too if I found a dead woman in my bed. Especially if I'd been seeing her behind my wife's back. How about the wife then? If she had the room key she could have gone in and done it."

"Yes. That's what I thought, too. But the thing is, she claims she was at home when it happened. Her friend backs it up, though she could be lying."

"Right. If she's telling the truth, who's this mystery woman who showed up at the inn?"

"That's what we have to find out," Paul replied.

There was silence for a few seconds. Zigler chuckled. "How stupid does one have to be to wrap the body in his own bedspread?"

"He was panicked and not thinking straight." Paul froze as a thought struck him. "The bedspread ..."

"What?"

"The bedspread. Why didn't I see that before?" He rushed to the door and turned around. "Gotta go, Zigs. I think I know what happened."

When Paul left Zigler's office, he knew his final destination. By the time he got to his car, he knew he would have to make a few pit stops to make his visit more effective. Three hours later he was standing before Cybil Ford's door once again. He had to knock a few times before she showed up.

"You missing me already, Detective?" she said with a smile.

"You lied."

The smile disappeared, but she attempted a light tone. "Someone's in a hurry. Won't you come inside?"

Paul followed her to the living room. He repeated, once they were seated, "You lied."

"About what?"

"You didn't go to Emma's that day."

"I don't know what you're talking about. I told you I went over."

"No, you didn't, and I have proof."

The color drained from Cybil's face. "I ... okay. I didn't want to lie, but Emma insisted."

"You're lying again."

"No!"

"You were the one who asked Emma for an alibi." That's what Emma had claimed when Paul had confronted her at his first pit stop. Something about a practical joke which Cybil hadn't shared details about.

"Who told you that? Emma? She's lying."

"Why would she?"

"For obvious reasons. She went to the inn and killed that girl. Now she's worried she will be caught."

"Cybil, what car do you drive?"

Cybil wrinkled her brows. "What car I drive? It's … it's a red Corvette."

"And I assume that's how you get around town?"

"Yes."

"So, here's the deal. Emma didn't leave her house that day. I confirmed it with her neighbors. And you weren't there either." Paul had interviewed the neighbors after leaving Emma's. Nina, a recluse who lived directly opposite and spent most days by the window, had been particularly helpful in confirming that Emma had not left the house during the period in question. She hadn't seen Cybil's red Corvette either.

"But the lady at the inn …"

"The lady at the inn said someone claiming to be Emma showed up. It wasn't Emma, though. And if it wasn't Emma, and you asked Emma for an alibi, it's obvious who was at the inn."

Cybil laughed. "You think it was me?"

"Yes. You said yourself what a terrific actress you are. How you can inhabit a character. And you know Emma so well. It would have been so easy for you to disguise yourself as her, carry yourself as her, and do what you did."

"That's quite a fantastic story you have there, Detective. But the lady must have asked for ID. She wouldn't hand over the key unless she was sure the woman was who she claimed to be."

"Yes. She did ask for ID, and she got Emma Barlowe's driver's license."

"There you have it."

"But it was you who presented the license. You see, Emma lost her license a few months ago. My guess is, it wasn't lost. You swiped it."

"So now you're accusing me of being a thief, too? Why would I take it?"

"So that you could test your disguise."

"In case you haven't noticed, Emma and I don't look much alike. My ugly mug could never compete with her beauty."

"I'm sure a little makeup and prosthetics can do wonders. I stopped by the inn on my way here. The desk clerk said the woman was wearing large sunglasses.

She didn't get a good look at the face. I bet I'll find the license if I search your apartment, and your phone records will show you were there that afternoon."

There was silence for the next few seconds, the only sound being the ticking from the wall clock. Paul waited patiently and watched Cybil, sure that her mind was churning, trying to pick the best response.

"Okay, yes. I swiped her license. I enjoyed playing the Emma character. It was fun walking up to people who knew her and seeing them believe I was her. I decided to kick it up a notch. I tried her license at a few places, and it worked. Nothing illegal, mind you. Just harmless fun. It was my way of getting back at her."

"Getting back at her? For what?"

"For everything. For stealing Kevin. Ever since high school, wherever Emma and I went together, all eyes were on her. She was the center of attention. I was like her poor bridesmaid. It was so humiliating. Then I met Kevin. I adored him, and I could tell he liked me. All that changed once I introduced him to her. He was floored at first sight. Before I knew it, they were dating. I was out of the picture. I have resented her for it. Resented him, too."

"Yet you've been friends."

"Pathetic, isn't it?"

"I'm more interested in what happened the night Tania died."

"Okay. When Kevin and Emma married, they were crazy about each other. It was like that the first few years. So annoying. But lately I noticed they were growing distant. I thought — here's my chance. I tried to get Kevin's attention, but he wasn't interested. So I thought, perhaps he was seeing someone else. I started following him around, but there was no one. Despite the distance, he was still faithful to Emma. It was hard to believe, but at least it made me feel better about myself. He wasn't rejecting me — he was just not into other women."

"You followed him and he didn't notice?"

"Well, I always used my old-lady disguise."

"Ah, I see."

"When she told me Kevin was spending a week at a motel by himself, I had this feeling. Like something was going to happen. So I followed him there too. When I saw him flirting with that girl, I knew I was right. I was so jealous. So that's what he wanted all along. Someone young and pretty. I wanted to destroy him. So I put on my Emma disguise and got the room key."

"You went all the way home and back to disguise yourself?"

"Didn't have to. I had everything I needed in my bag. Just slipped into the restroom to make the switch."

"What happened next?"

"I entered his room and hid in the closet. He returned after a while, and she arrived later. I heard everything that went on. Oh, how I wanted to kill them both as they made love. All I had to do was grab his knife ..."

Cybil paused, her face red with rage.

"Kevin had a knife?"

"Yes. It was a gift from me on his last birthday. He always carried it with him." Her face softened, almost beaming with pride. "At least, that's what he told me. Anyway, better sense prevailed. I figured it would be difficult for me to get them both. So I waited for my chance. Sure enough, he got up to take a shower."

"And that's when you killed her?"

"No, no! I wanted to, yes, but before I could muster enough courage, she was up and about."

"When did you kill her, then?"

"I didn't. Believe me, I didn't. But I know who did."

Kevin dried himself off and stepped out of the shower. As he wiped the fog off the mirror, he saw a ray of hope. Perhaps he had dreamed it all. Perhaps she had already left, never to enter his life again. Or she was still sleeping blissfully in his bed, basking in the glow of their encounter with no evil intentions.

The bed was empty when he got out of the bathroom. Relief flooded through him for a moment until he saw her standing by his bag, rifling through it. She turned to him with a start.

"Ah, there you are," she said.

"What are you doing?"

"Getting to know you better. I know — I should have done that before jumping into bed with you, but it's too late for that."

"Going through my things? We could have just talked."

"Yeah, but I wouldn't know whether you were telling the truth."

"Listen ..."

"So, you're a rich guy, huh?"

"I'm doing well, yes. Listen — this was a mistake."

"Washed off the guilt in the shower? Regretting it now?"

She walked towards him as she spoke. He knew she had something in her hand, but he couldn't tell what it was.

"I've never done anything like this. Cheated on my wife, I mean. I don't know what got into me. I got carried away."

She continued towards him. "So you want me to leave? This was just a one-night fling?"

"Yes. I'm sorry."

"Oh, don't be sorry. It actually makes things simpler for me."

She was right next to him now, and she placed something on the counter.

"What're you doing with this?"

Kevin looked at the object.

"It's ... it's my knife," he said.

"Yes, I see that. But why do you have one?"

"It's ... it's a gift. From a close friend. I like having it with me."

"Makes you feel macho?"

"I guess."

"Anyway, getting back to business. I thought I got myself a sugar daddy. But you shot that dream down."

Kevin's heart raced. It was as he had feared.

"You want money?"

"Duh, yeah. Why else would I be interested in you? So, no ongoing stream of money. That means you make a one-time payment."

"For what?"

"So I don't tell your wife, silly."

Kevin felt sick. This ... was ... not ... happening.

"How ... how much do you want?"

"A million dollars should be good."

He held onto the counter for support. It's not that he couldn't afford it, but he had expected her to start lower.

"What ... what makes you think I have that much?"

"Oh, come on, I'm sure you do. I get it — maybe you don't have it all handy. I know you rich folk have money tied up in your investments, but I know you'll be good for it."

"I'll need some time."

"I can wait. But not for long. I'm sick of slogging away at the coffee shop for minimum wage. Plastering on a fake smile while catering to whiny customers."

She sashayed back to the bed and plopped into it. Looking up at him, she said, "So, how soon can you get it?"

"A couple of weeks, maybe."

"I like the sound of that."

A smile escaped her lips, and she buried herself in her phone. By now Kevin was bursting with rage. Rage at her for using him like this. Rage at himself for being so stupid and allowing himself to be used. He could pay her, sure, but would she stop there? He didn't think so. The demands would continue until she had depleted him.

He picked up the knife. Tania didn't notice as he approached with trembling hands. By the time she saw him it was too late. The blade was at her neck, and a second later the damage was done.

The knife dropped from Kevin's hand. He collapsed to the floor, shocked at what he had done. But it was necessary. After a few panicked minutes he got up, realizing he had to do something about the body. He grabbed the knife and placed it on her. Then he wrapped her up in the bedspread and sheet. He heard a clunk as something fell to the floor. Her cell phone. He picked it up and turned it off, wondering what to do with it. That's when he noticed her apartment key on the nightstand. Playing it safe, he tossed both in the trash bin, and threw some tissues on top.

He was about to move the body when it occurred to him that the knife had his fingerprints. He took it out and tossed it on the floor. It could be dealt with after he had moved the body. He dragged the body to the door, opened the door and took a peek. It was past 10:00 p.m., the time of night where things would be winding down.

He was about to move the body when he heard a sound. Peeking outside, he saw a man wobble down the corridor, hanging onto a woman. Probably had one drink too many, thought Kevin. They stopped at one of the doors on the opposite side, and the woman turned to unlock the door as the man nuzzled her face.

"Hold your horses, Eric! Let's get inside first."

The door opened and they disappeared inside. The last sounds Kevin heard were of the man chuckling and the door slamming shut. He waited another five minutes before he was convinced the coast was clear. Then he dragged the body out towards the side exit. It was laborious work, and he was sweating by the time he was out of the building. He left the corpse by the bushes a few feet away and returned to his room, relieved that no one had seen him. As he entered, he stopped short. The knife was gone.

The arrest warrant didn't take long. Ten minutes after it arrived, Paul and Davis were on their way. Three hours later Kevin Barlowe was seated in an interrogation room, nervously drumming his fingers on the table and sweating like he had sprung a leak. His fingers stopped when Paul entered and sat across from him. The detective didn't say anything, preferring to stare at his prime suspect. Kevin blinked first.

"I ... I don't know why you brought me here. I told you ... told you I didn't do anything."

"You know exactly why you are here. You know what you did. Let's make things easy. Confess now."

Kevin clasped his hands together and sighed. His eyes dropped, now focusing on his hands.

"We have a witness, Kevin. Someone who saw you kill Tania Lawrence."

"You're bluffing. How's ... how's that possible? We were alone in the room."

"You think you were alone, but you weren't."

Kevin's brows furrowed. "Emma. So she really was there?"

"No. It wasn't her. She didn't leave the house that day."

"So who, then?"

"I can't tell you. But this witness told me everything. How Tania and you made love. How you wanted her to stay the night. That you did go take a shower. Until that point all of it tallies with what you told me. But there's one big difference. Tania was alive when you stepped out after your shower."

"No, she wasn't! I told you, she was already dead. Probably murdered by this … by this witness of yours. And now this witness is trying to pin it on me."

"The witness told me Tania asked you about your knife. Do you recognize this?" Paul showed Kevin the evidence bag with the murder weapon.

Kevin gulped. "It does look like my knife."

"This is what you used to kill Tania when she blackmailed you."

"I told you, I didn't kill her! And yes, this looks like mine, but that doesn't prove anything. Anyone could have a similar knife."

"Don't forget, we collected your fingerprints. Someone is trying to match them against the prints we found on the knife as we speak. Even if this is not yours, you're toast if we have your prints on the murder weapon."

Kevin swallowed hard.

"Didn't you wonder where the knife disappeared after you dumped the body?"

There was silence for a few seconds as he processed the question.

"I want my lawyer."

"Sure. It's your right," Paul replied, staring into Kevin's eyes.

Once again, Kevin blinked first.

"I … I didn't want to do it. You understand?"

Paul nodded.

"It … it was just supposed to be a fun night. And before you judge me — this was the first time I had ever done anything like this. But when she threatened to tell Emma, I … I just couldn't take that chance."

"It's still murder."

"Yes, it is," replied Kevin as his head dropped into his hands. "I looked for that knife everywhere. I'm pretty sure I looked under the bed as well. How did I miss it? How did I miss it? I'm such an idiot!"

By the time Kevin raised his head, Paul was standing, a satisfied expression on his face. Another case closed, another killer on his way to justice. He couldn't wait to get home to Brigette and the comfort of her arms.

AUTHOR'S NOTE

A married writer, vacationing alone, flirts with the waitress at a cafe. She turns up dead later. That's where this one started in my head. As I chewed on it, the plot developed quickly. While Kevin was guilty of adultery, I was confident he didn't kill Tania. It was either Emma or Cybil. But Kevin had other plans once I started writing, and Kevin can be very persuasive. I enjoyed writing Cybil — an average actress with delusions of grandeur. Though a minor character, Susan was another fun one. What did you enjoy the most about this story?

PAL DETECTIVE AGENCY

A PI Ankit Pal mystery

PROLOGUE

When it comes to ransom, what's the right number? The figure hunched at the desk grappled with this question. If you ask for too much, chances are you will be disappointed. Demand too little, and you're leaving money on the table. The sheet of paper on the desk was filled with doodles interspersed with some crossed-out numbers. Seeing it all laid out in tangible form aided the thought process. Who knew kidnapping was such hard work? All the preparation and planning, the stress, the doubts, all of it. But the opportunity had presented itself, and it would be a shame to waste it.

Eventually, pen met paper once again, and a fresh set of digits made its appearance. It elicited a smile, for it was a number that would ensure a comfortable life for a while. The smile dampened the next instant with the realization that this amount would have to be split. It was a two-person job, after all. The figure sighed and crossed out the digits before writing a new set. This would have to work.

CHAPTER ONE

*L*os Altos Man Still Missing, screamed the headline in *The Mercury News*. It was the kind of news that evoked concern and sympathy. One could only imagine what the family and friends of that man would be going through. I, for one, was always affected by such stories, and this one cut deeper because I knew the missing man well. Jared Foley was my manager and mentor back in the day, when I was starting out as a techie. It was my good fortune to have worked under his guidance as I navigated my career as a software engineer. And it was Jared who always encouraged me to follow my dreams.

Three days without a trace meant things were bad. Pushing the negative thoughts out of my head, I took another sip of tea from the steaming hot mug and sighed with satisfaction. It was real *chai*, nothing like the dishwater sold at most places under the ridiculous name of chai-tea. I had brewed the beverage to perfection, with a dash of cardamom and ginger, just like my parents enjoyed it. Each sip brought me closer to them, though they were thousands of miles away in their home in Mumbai, and here I was gazing out the window of my eighteenth-floor condo in downtown San Jose. I could see the entire city and beyond. The view was one of the key selling points when I purchased the place a few years ago. I pictured Ma and Pa seated on the couch, with Ma dunking a cookie in her teacup and taking a bite before the cookie collapsed, and Pa regaling us with anecdotes, trying to sneak an extra spoonful of sugar into his tea when Ma was not looking.

I drained the last of my tea and rinsed the mug. Thirty minutes later, showered and energized, I headed out the door. In another ten, I was at the entrance to my office after a brisk walk. The Indian restaurant next door hadn't opened yet, so instead of the enticing aroma of curry I was treated to the disgusting odors from the alley on the other side of my office. Ignoring that, my chest swelled with pride as it always did when I saw the lettering on the door saying "Pal Detective Agency." Following my childhood dream, I had quit my tech job around a year ago to found the agency and work as a private investigator. Ma and Pa blamed this on the popular detective show *Karamchand* which beamed across televisions once a week in 1980s India. The brilliant, carrot-chomping lead character was beloved by all as he went about his business, solving mysteries with ease. I hoped one day I would be just as successful and would have an assistant who would say, "Sir, you are a genius" every time I nailed a culprit.

Alas, life as a private eye wasn't easy. I'd only had three cases since I had opened shop, and two of them had me searching for missing cats. Whatever happened to crowdsourcing the effort by plastering the neighborhood with "Missing cat — answers to Tabby" flyers? Anyway, I was successful in locating the pets, but it was neither satisfying nor did it pay much.

My third client was a woman who suspected her husband was cheating on her, and she wanted me to confirm it. Now, that sounded a lot more exciting until I discovered that the man was innocent. The poor sod had been busy planning a surprise birthday party for his wife. Contrary to my expectation, my client was disappointed with my report. On the bright side, the sneaky husband netted me a lot more money than the adventurous cats.

I estimated it was another three months before I would burn through my savings and be forced to camp out in front of a computer screen again. Reflection complete, I opened the office door and entered.

It was a compact room, with just enough space for a desk, a couple of chairs, a bookshelf, and a chest of drawers. I had given it my nerdy touches, paying homage to my inspirations. A smoking pipe and magnifying glass lay on the desk, à la Sherlock Holmes, alongside dark sunglasses and a fake carrot stick that were characteristic of Karamchand. Of course, Karamchand munched on real carrots, but a real carrot wouldn't last long, so I had opted for the next best thing. That wasn't all. A Hercule Poirot caricature hung on the wall, the famous mustache dominating the frame. On the coat hanger by the entrance was a deerstalker hat — Sherlock again, and a black leather jacket, the kind Karamchand preferred. I wondered whether I should start dressing in a suit and hat like Sam Spade for some of his success to rub off. Maybe even snag an office in San Francisco, but I was quite sure the steep rent would be a no-go. Better still, I could stop comparing myself to fictional detectives and carve my own path. Settling into my chair, I closed my eyes to clear my mind before starting the workday.

I must have dozed off at some point, for I was jolted awake when a sound broke the silence. The sound wasn't a familiar one, and I looked around to confirm I had heard right. At last, I convinced myself that someone had indeed knocked on the door. When was the last time that had happened? Now that someone had shown up, who could it be? My guesses were all over the map. Had I forgotten to pay the rent, thus prompting my landlord to come over to evict me? No, I was pretty sure I had been diligent about paying on time. A delivery, perhaps? No. I always had things delivered to my home address, where the concierge could keep the packages safe until I retrieved them. My train of thought was interrupted by another knock — multiple knocks, in fact. Impatient knocks.

"Come in," I said, not wishing to aggravate my visitor any further.

The door opened to reveal an attractive blonde woman. I got the feeling I had seen her before, but I couldn't recall where. Her hair was nicely done, and she was dressed in clothes that screamed money. She carried herself like someone who had it all and knew it. But there was one flaw in her appearance — her eyes were rimmed red. A damsel in distress, I thought. Except, I realized, this woman was old enough to be a damsel's mother. Not that I was any knight, nor did I own any armor, shining or not. But if she was here, she needed my help. Good news at last?

"Pal? Ankit Pal?" she asked before I had a chance to speak.

"Yes." I stood up.

She stepped forward and extended her hand. "Irene Foley," she said as we shook hands.

Foley? A coincidence?

"How may I help you?"

I motioned her to sit. She obliged. The chair let out a creak, reminding me that I had yet to fix it. It had been two months since the last time I had heard that sound. At the time I had made a mental note to fix it as soon as my client left. I made another note as I settled into my chair with nary a creak.

"My husband. He's missing."

"When did he go missing?"

"Three days ago." She wrinkled her nose, and I realized she was trying to hold back her tears. *Where was a tissue box when I needed one?*

"Did you contact the police?"

"Yes."

I waited for a few seconds before realizing she was done. "And?"

"They have been looking for him."

"But they haven't found him yet?"

"Right."

"And that's why you are here? You need my help to find him?"

Irene nodded.

A *real* case! Not a missing pet. Not a shady husband. A real live missing person! I was excited at first. Then fearful. After all, I had never done anything like this. And if the cops hadn't been able to locate him, what chance did I have? But I reminded myself why I had gotten into this line of work. I would rise to the challenge.

"What's his name?"

"Jared. Jared Foley."

My jaw dropped. So it really was Jared she was here for.

"I read about that in the papers. I knew ... know him."

"I know," Irene replied. "That's why I came to you. He talks about you all the time — tells me what a brilliant engineer you are, and how he enjoyed working with you. How you followed your calling and started your own detective agency. So when I needed help, you were the first person who came to mind."

"But the cops are already looking for him. I'm sure they are doing their best."

"Yes. And that's what I fear. That their best isn't good enough. It's been two days since I reported him missing, and they have no clues. I can't take any chances when it comes to Jared."

"I understand. When did you see him last?"

"Three mornings ago. He left very early for Yosemite. Wanted to spend the day hiking before returning the same night. He had been doing that quite a bit ever since he retired. But he didn't return this time."

I felt a twinge of regret. Three years ago Jared had quit the company we worked for and joined a hot tech startup. Not long after, he had invited me to come onboard, but I had declined, already burned out by the techie life and not wanting to endure the startup squeeze. Besides, I had already started working towards obtaining my PI license. The startup had been bought out last year for a ridiculous price, creating millionaires out of pretty much every employee. With enough money socked away, Jared had opted for early retirement. If I had accepted his offer, I might have had a million or two of my own in the bank. Perhaps I wouldn't be counting the last of my savings now.

"To Yosemite and back in a day? Sounds exhausting."

"It is. But you know Jared. Always pushing himself. He left at six a.m., hoping to beat the traffic and get there by ten. The plan was to get back home in time to kiss me goodnight." A wistful smile escaped Irene's lips.

"I see. Did you try calling him?" I asked.

"Yes. But he isn't answering. It's going straight to voicemail."

"Any idea whether he reached Yosemite?"

"No. Actually that's what worried me first. That he didn't call after he got there. But I figured he was so stoked about hiking that he forgot."

"What about his car? Has it been found?"

"No. They're still looking."

"Have they traced his cell? They can get his location."

"I don't know. I assume they're checking on that. But now that you're on the case, you can find out what they know, right?"

"I'm afraid not. I will have to work independently."

"I don't understand."

"It's not like in the movies and T.V. shows. The cops don't work with private detectives."

"Oh. But I'm sure you will find him."

"I'll do my best." I grabbed a notepad and pen. "I need details." Soon Irene had given me a lot of information, including details about Jared's car.

"Did he have any enemies? Anyone who would want to harm him?"

There was an uncomfortable silence as she hesitated before answering. "No, no enemies. He's an awesome guy — you know that. But there's something I should tell you. I just don't know how to say it."

I leaned forward. "You can share with me, Irene. I promise whatever you tell me will stay confidential. Every detail is important if we are to locate him."

"You see, I think he was having an affair."

I frowned. This was not the Jared I knew. But then, it had been a while since we had last spoken. People changed, especially when they came into a lot of money. And one thing I had learned from experience was that you never knew anyone completely. Everyone had a side that was secret, a side that no one else knew about.

"Why do you say that?" I asked.

"I grew suspicious after he started returning home late quite often. I began following him and found he was visiting some girl at SJSU."

"And you think she might have something to do with his disappearance?"

"It's possible."

"Can you give me her details?"

"Will you talk to her?"

"Yes. I certainly will."

Irene shared the information. With nothing else to discuss, she rose to leave and headed for the door before turning to me. "Oh, silly me. Your fees?"

I waved my hand. "Don't worry about it. I want to find Jared as much as you do. He was a great mentor."

"Oh no. I must pay you a retainer."

She pulled out her checkbook and a pen from her purse, scribbling something in it before tearing out the check and handing it to me. My eyes popped as I read the figure — five thousand dollars. Not a fortune, but it would get me through another month. I wasn't in a position to turn it down.

"Thank you," I replied feebly as she departed.

CHAPTER TWO

An hour later I was hunched over my desk, deep in thought, when the door to my office burst open. Whoever it was didn't believe in knocking. I glanced up to see a woman standing in the doorway, and it all made sense. Now, this one truly was a damsel. Judging from her jovial expression, not in distress, but a damsel nevertheless. If I were to use clichés to describe her, I would say she had beautiful almond-shaped eyes, lustrous hair — the kind you see in shampoo commercials — and a smile that could light up a room. It was Kavita — my closest friend — someone I had known since I was four. She was gorgeous, yes, but her intellect surpassed her beauty, and my heart went aflutter as it always did in her presence. I loved her, I was sure of it, but when I would muster enough courage to tell her that was anybody's guess.

Kavita still worked in the tech industry. She enjoyed her work and excelled at it. Already a director at one of the prominent firms, she was a shoo-in for a promotion to VP anytime soon. She flashed her killer smile as she approached and almost sat in the chair opposite me before thinking better of it and sitting on the desk instead. Perhaps she remembered the creak too.

"Kit," she said.

"I wish you wouldn't call me that."

"What else should I call the most eligible bachelor in San Jose?"

I rolled my eyes. "It makes me sound like the disembodied voice in *Knight Rider.*"

"Or a character in *Tinker Bell.*"

"Eww."

"Sheesh. Lighten up. Got any lunch plans?"

"None. Why?"

"Dine with me." Her eyes implored me to say yes.

"Don't you have to work?"

"Took the day off. I've been overdoing it lately."

"I got a new case."

Kavita's eyes lit up. "Well, congratulations! Do tell."

"I have to interview a suspect. Want to join me? I'll fill you in on the way. We can eat after that."

"Ooh, sounds exciting. Let's go."

Amber Boyd was a student at San Jose State University and lived in the student housing across the street from the university campus. I shared the case details with Kavita as we walked over to the apartment, knowing I could trust her to keep her lips zipped. I knocked when we got there. The door was opened by a brunette who could only be described as a stunner. For a moment I understood how Jared could have strayed. Still, I found it disgusting that the man had cheated on his wife, and that too with a girl young enough to be his daughter. She let us in once I had introduced Kavita and myself and told her why we were there.

It was a tiny studio, and other than the bed, the only other seating was a set of three beanbags. A man with a scruffy beard stood in the kitchen, stirring something in a mug. He revealed a hint of a smile as he said, "Don't mind me — I'm just the boyfriend."

Another boyfriend? Was Amber stringing Jared along? For money, perhaps? Or maybe that was their arrangement — nothing serious, just a physical relationship. She certainly had a type, for this guy looked much older, too — nowhere near as old as Jared, but he had at least ten years on her.

Amber directed us to sit as she sank into one of the beanbags.

"So that's what she told you?" she said with a smirk when I mentioned the affair.

"Yes. Isn't it true?"

"Do I look like someone who would be involved with an older guy? That's sick."

I glanced at Scruffy.

"He's not *that* old," she said with an amused smile, catching my train of thought.

I shrugged. "So you weren't having an affair?"

"No fucking way." She shook her head vigorously before stopping and locking her eyes on me. "Jared's my father."

For the second time in hours, my jaw dropped. "What?"

"Yes. You heard that right. Before he married Irene, he was with someone else. I'm a product of that relationship."

"Then why did Irene say ..."

"Because she doesn't know. Jared couldn't bring himself to tell her."

"I see. But you go by Boyd?"

"My mom's last name."

"Ah. When did you talk to Jared last?"

"The night before he left."

"Anything out of the ordinary? Anything that might provide some clue as to his whereabouts?"

"Your guess is as good as mine. I just hope he's okay."

"Do you know of anyone who might want to harm him?"

"No." Amber stole a glance at her boyfriend before returning her gaze to me.

"Did he visit often?"

"Yes. He tries to drop by every week or two."

"So you're close?"

"I would say so. We're still getting to know each other, you know?"

"What do you mean?"

"Until a year ago he didn't know I existed. And I didn't know he existed."

"Oh."

"Yeah. Jared and my mom had already broken up by the time she found out she was pregnant with me. She raised me on her own. As I grew older I was more curious about my father. I kept nagging her about it until she caved and told me."

"Wow, that must have been hard."

"It was. But it felt great to finally have a dad."

With nothing more to ask, I stood up and handed Amber my card.

"Call me if you think of something."

"Sure."

❧ ❧

"Now that was interesting," Kavita said once we were back on the street.

"It was. She didn't seem too torn up about his disappearance."

"You think she had something to do with it? Why would she? I mean, she finally has a father in her life. Sure, she might have some resentment about him not being in her life earlier, but not enough to harm him."

"That's exactly why I expected her to be a lot more concerned," I said. "If I had grown up without a father and then found him, I would be very worried about losing him again."

"I see your point. You think the wife had something to do with it? If she thought he was cheating on her, she could have killed him in a jealous rage."

"You think he's dead?"

"Well, people don't just disappear into thin air."

"True. Not ruling out Irene yet."

"What next, Mr. Detective?"

"I have plenty to think about, but how about we tackle lunch first?"

"Excellent idea. I'm starving. What are you in the mood for?"

"Sushi?"

❧ ❧

A five-minute walk later we were seated in Ozu enjoying some sake as we waited for our order. I utilized the time to search for Jared's social media profiles.

"I only see a Facebook account for Jared. Locked, unfortunately, so I can't see any details," I said.

"Irene seems more adventurous. She's on Facebook, Twitter, and Instagram, but not very active," Kavita replied, clearly having the same idea as me.

"Anything interesting?"

"No. Unless you're into random pictures of food."

"Nah, I prefer the real thing," I said as I greedily eyed the plates of sushi that were being placed before us.

"Well, let's get started, then."

CHAPTER THREE

Kavita departed after lunch, and I drove over to the Foley residence in Los Altos. I had been there once before, when Jared and I were still colleagues. He had invited the team over for drinks and dinner to celebrate a software release. Irene had been absent, and he had explained that she was visiting her parents in Burlington.

My knock was answered by Irene. She looked better, and her pleasant smile added to her charm. She led me to the living room. There were a bunch of family pictures all over the place — on the walls, on the mantel, on the tables next to the couches. I remembered seeing some of these on my previous visit, and I realized this was why she seemed familiar back at the office.

"The cops called," she said once we were seated. "They haven't found his car yet. Still working on getting his phone records. I'm beginning to think he never got to Yosemite. I mean, if he had reached it, they should have found his car somewhere in the park by now, right?"

"Yes. I would think so." Or if he was a victim of foul play, the attacker could have moved it to mislead investigators. I kept this thought to myself, not wanting to alarm my client.

"Have you discovered anything?"

"I spoke to Amber."

"And?"

"She doesn't know where he is."

"Of course that's what she would say, right?"

"Did you tell the cops about her?"

"No. The affair is a private family matter. It will blow up if the cops get involved."

"That's understandable. Why do you suspect she has something to do with his disappearance? What would she stand to gain?"

"I don't know. It was just a thought."

"I see. Can I search through Jared's things? Maybe there will be some clues."

"Sure. Whatever helps get him back. His office is right through there." Irene pointed to a closed door near the entrance to the house.

I marched over and entered. It was a sizable room and well-appointed. A desk dominated, with a fully stocked bookshelf taking up an entire wall. It amused me to see some mystery thrillers among the autobiographies and the textbooks on data structures, algorithms and the like. I wondered whether someday someone would write stories about ace sleuth Ankit Pal.

On the desk was a laptop hooked up to a monitor. It was locked, just as I expected.

"Sorry, I don't have the password," Irene said from the doorway.

I gave a start, for I hadn't heard her coming. Next, I tried the drawers and reviewed the documents. Bills, insurance papers, and the usual mundane stuff you would find in any household. Along with some property agreements — second and third homes, rental properties — the kind of luxuries you would expect in such a wealthy household. Nothing to help figure out Jared's disappearance. I tackled the stacks of paper on the desk next, but didn't come across anything interesting.

"Find anything?" Irene asked.

I shook my head. "Do you have your latest cell phone bill?"

"No. But I could login and get it for you."

"Please do. I want to check his call logs. See if there are any clues there. Maybe he called someone, or someone called him — anything unusual."

Irene turned to go, then turned back, her brows furrowed. "I wonder why the cops didn't ask me for it."

"They will get a lot more from the phone company, including location data."

"Ah, I see. I'll be back."

I surveyed the bookshelf closely while I waited, picking up some books at random and flipping through them in case there was any clue — like a note, or photograph. There was nothing.

"I emailed it to you."

I turned with a start. Once again I had not heard her approach.

"Thank you."

"Anything else I can help with?"

"No, that's all for now."

Later that night I was poring over the Foleys' call records. Looking up numbers took time, but I couldn't find any suspicious calls in the days leading up to Jared's disappearance. As expected, there were no outgoing calls after he had gone missing. There were some incoming, but based on the duration, none that had been answered.

The document contained Irene's records too, so I reviewed those as well. For the most part there was nothing suspicious, but I was unable to find the owner for one number. This wasn't surprising, since it was from the BlissVoice network, which meant it was a pay-as-you-go phone. I would have let it go, but there were a few calls to and from that number, all in the last three days. I would have to ask Irene about it the next morning. Feeling exhausted, I jumped into bed.

CHAPTER FOUR

I called Irene first thing in the morning. There was silence for a few seconds once I had asked my question. When she spoke, it wasn't an answer.

"You went through my calls too?"

"Yes. I'm sorry if that makes you uncomfortable, but it's important I scrutinize everything."

"Well, that wasn't nice, but if you want to know, that's my friend Helen's number."

"A new friend?"

"New? No. I've known her for years."

"But I only see calls going back a couple of days."

Irene sighed. "Do you have friends, Ankit?"

"Yes."

"How often do you talk to them?"

"Well ..."

"We hadn't talked in a while. That happens between friends, right? Sometimes you go months without talking, but when you do, you just continue where you left off."

"She only registered this number a week ago."

"So?"

"If you hadn't talked in months, how did you learn about this number?"

Silence again.

"She messaged me on Facebook to tell me about it."

"I see."

"Anything else?"

"No."

I sat in silence after hanging up. Something about the conversation nagged me. Irene was hiding something, of that I was sure. Perhaps my initial hunch was true — she did have something to do with her husband's disappearance. Not surprising if she suspected he was involved with someone else. I would have to keep an eye on her.

I arrived at the Foley residence an hour later. This time I parked a couple of houses away and stayed in my car. I was prepared for the stakeout, lots of snacks and beverages sitting beside me. I had barely opened the bottle of Sprite and taken two sips when the garage door opened and a white Porsche Macan backed out of it. Irene was at the wheel. She took off and I followed. As she drove east and switched freeways, going to I-680 and then I-580, I was confident she was going to Yosemite. But why? Was she joining the search party? My hunch was further confirmed when she switched to I-205 and then to I-5. By this time the Sprite bottle was empty, and I had to pee. Stopping was not an option, so I soldiered on.

Irene surprised me by skipping the CA-120 exit. If not Yosemite, where? I had an answer in another two hours as we entered the South Lake Tahoe area. Five minutes later she stopped in front of a cabin in the woods. There was a covered car parked outside. The street and house number jogged my memory, and I realized this was one of the properties I had seen in Jared's papers. Their vacation home. Perhaps she was here for a quick getaway. But then what was the other car doing there? Was Jared here too?

Irene walked up to the door, unlocked it and disappeared inside. Parking my car a short distance away where it wouldn't be easily spotted, I crept over to the cabin. I went around the structure, trying to get a glimpse inside, but all the blinds were closed. I was rounding the corner to the front when something hard and heavy struck my head, causing me to drop to my knees and collapse to the ground. Then I blacked out.

CHAPTER FIVE

When I came to, my head was throbbing and I felt woozy. There was a chill in the air. My watch told me I had been out for four hours. I was thankful this hadn't happened in winter, for the area would have been blanketed in snow, as it was on my last ski trip. I might not have woken up at all.

The state of my head reminded me of the time when I was ten, enjoying a game of cricket with my friends. We were goofing around during a break when one of the boys swung the bat and it accidentally connected with my head. That had hurt. A lot. This was a hundred times worse. And I didn't have the option to curl up in Ma's comforting lap as I had done back then.

I surveyed my surroundings but didn't see anyone. It was eerily silent. I tried to stand up slowly. Once I had stabilized, I relieved myself in the bushes, thankful I hadn't wet my pants while unconscious. That would have sucked. I walked to the front of the cabin. The Macan was gone. The cabin door was ajar.

I pushed the door open and stepped inside, cautiously scanning for any occupants. The interior appeared inviting until I noticed the broken lamp on the floor. I did a quick survey of the rest of the cabin to assure myself there was no one else in there. There was a suitcase in the bedroom, men's clothing hanging in the closet. A wet towel in the bathroom along with a toothbrush and shaving supplies. There were some dirty dishes and glasses in the kitchen sink. I grabbed some ice from the freezer and placed it on my head. I winced at first, but it helped soothe me. What I would give for a hot cup of *chai*. I filled a clean glass with water and downed it in two gulps. That's when I realized my mistake. I had left a DNA trail everywhere. Something bad had gone down here, and I didn't want to get caught up in it if the cabin was investigated as a crime scene.

I found a pair of latex gloves in the cabinet below the sink. I put them on and went about cleaning all the surfaces I had touched. Next, I washed the glass I had used. Only then did I enter the bedroom and start searching. The first thing I noticed was a cell phone on the dresser. It was a basic feature phone — the kind you would expect to be offered through a pay-as-you-go service. I pressed a key and found that it was locked. On a hunch, I pulled out my phone and dialed the number I had seen in Irene's call log. The phone on the dresser lit up. I couldn't resist a smile. So much for Helen.

I continued my search, and soon I found a wallet. It had a driver's license, two credit cards, and some cash. All the cards had the same name on them — Jared Foley. So he had been here. He hadn't gone to Yosemite after all. He had come to Tahoe. This raised a lot of questions. Had Irene lied about Jared's destination? Or had he changed his mind at the last moment? And why was she at the cabin? Did she know he was here? And the most important question of all — where was Jared now?

The covered car. I had a sickening thought and ran outside, pulling the cover off the car. A blue Mercedes E300. The license plate matched the number Irene had given me. It was Jared's car. The interior was empty. There was a chance he was in the trunk. Thankfully the car was unlocked. I popped the trunk and walked to the rear, my heart thudding away, fearing the worst. But the trunk was empty.

I had suspected Irene. Now my suspicion was strengthened. I was quite sure she had kept Jared captive, or perhaps even murdered him and disposed of his body. She was the one who had knocked me out. I had to confront her.

CHAPTER SIX

I t was dark when I returned to the Foley residence, but it was early enough that I figured Irene would still be up. A thought occurred to me as I got out of my car and walked towards the house. Irene was dangerous, and I was going in to confront her. Not a smart thing to do, but I couldn't resist. I pulled out my phone and typed out a text to Kavita.

Going to talk to Irene. Call the cops if I don't message back in an hour.

That would spook Kavita for sure, but I didn't have time to explain. I slipped the phone back in my pocket and rang the doorbell. There was no response at first, so I rang it again after a few seconds. This time I heard movement inside. Irene opened the door, dressed in a mauve nightgown and sporting an expression that screamed *What the hell are you doing here at this hour?* I decided it was best to get right to the point.

"What did you do to Jared?"

"What do you mean?"

"Don't act all innocent. I saw you at the cabin. You attacked me."

She stared at me as if I had gone crazy. Opening the door wider, she said, "I have no idea what you're talking about, but come inside."

We walked together to the living room. Irene sat down. I remained standing.

"So you've been following me?"

"Yes."

"Then you know the truth."

"Which is?"

She hesitated before replying. "I'm so embarrassed to say this, but he didn't go missing. He faked the whole thing."

"What? That doesn't make any sense. Why would he do that?"

"You know Jared. He was always doing stuff, keeping busy. But after he retired, there was a void. Suddenly he had all this time and nothing to fill it up. There's only so much hiking one can do. And then he heard you had started this new gig and it wasn't going all that well. *He's a smart kid. He deserves better.* That's what he said about you. So he got this wild idea that would kill his boredom and help you out."

I couldn't believe what I was hearing. "You're telling me he faked his disappearance so I would have a case to work on? That's crazy. And it still doesn't make any sense. Surely he realized that the cops would find him first."

Irene smiled. "But they haven't, have they?"

"He thought I would be able to find him?"

"Yes. And you proved him right."

"Not really."

"How's that?"

"I was too late. You got to him first."

The puzzled expression returned to Irene's face. "What do you mean?"

"I don't buy your story at all. You made him disappear. Probably killed him and hid the body. Going to the cops, coming to me for help — that was all an act to show the world you didn't have anything to do with it."

"What are you talking about? You saw him at the cabin, right?"

"He wasn't there. You bonked me on the head and then got rid of him. That's why you were there today, wasn't it?"

"I ... I don't understand. He was there when I left. And I certainly didn't see you there or attack you in any way."

"Then who hit me? And where's Jared?"

"Out for a walk, perhaps?"

"Leaving the door open?"

"No, no. He would never be so careless." She paused for a few seconds before continuing. "So you're saying he has disappeared for real?" Her hand went up to her mouth, and for the first time since I had met her, I saw distress on her face.

"What's going on?" The anxious voice caused us to turn to the source.

Amber stood at the entrance to the living room. I wondered whether all the members of the Foley clan were blessed with the ability to sneak up without a sound.

"What are you doing here?" I asked.

She didn't answer, her eyes searching for a satisfactory response.

"It's okay, honey. He knows," said Irene.

"You two know each other?" I asked.

"I'm sorry we lied to you," said Amber. "Jared did tell her about me."

"Oh. Why did you lie?"

"Just to make this whole caper more interesting."

"Hang on. Let me get this straight. So the three of you hatched this plan to have Jared disappear, and then hire me to find him. You created all this misdirection about him having an affair and all that BS." I glanced from one woman to the other and continued when I did not get any response. "You are one sick, sick family! You realize the cops, the park rangers at Yosemite, volunteers from the public — those poor souls — they're all spending resources trying to find him? What a waste! How selfish are you people?"

"I'm sorry. That's what I told Jared, too, but he was so insistent," replied Irene.

"Something's not adding up. I don't believe you. Either of you. I have a feeling the two of you are in it together. For whatever reason — most likely money — you wanted to get rid of him, and this is what you came up with."

"No, that's not true," said Amber. "And if you don't believe us, why not ask Jared?"

"Because he's nowhere to be found," I replied.

Amber gasped, her hand going up to her mouth as she turned to Irene with concerned eyes.

"Nonsense!" said Irene. "I'll prove it to you." She picked up her phone and placed a call, waiting for thirty seconds before speaking again. "He's not answering." I detected a hint of fear in her voice. For a moment I considered believing her, but it could all have been part of her act. She called again, with the same result.

"You're calling his burner? The number I asked you about and you said it was Helen's?"

"Yes."

"I found it on his dresser at the cabin."

"Oh."

"Irene, is he really gone?" asked Amber.

"I don't know. I don't know. Why would anyone want to do anything to him?"

"Well, if it wasn't either of you two, then someone else was lying in wait. That person knocked me out first, then waited for you to leave before abducting Jared. We should call the cops and tell them everything."

"No!" Amber and Irene said in unison.

"But we have to find him. I'm concerned."

"And so are we. But you can do it. Besides, we'll be in a lot of trouble if we tell them the truth."

"You should have thought of that before creating this mess."

"Please," Irene pleaded. Amber trained her puppy eyes on me.

"Look, I want to help, but I'm still a rookie here. The cops are way better equipped for this."

"No. You've got to find him. Fake or real disappearance, that's what Jared would have wanted."

My phone buzzed. It was Kavita. The hour had flown by. I answered and assured her I was safe before hanging up. Then I turned to the women.

"Irene, please notify the cops. This is not a game anymore. Jared's life hangs in the balance."

"Let's give it one more day. If you still don't have any leads, then I'll talk to them."

I reluctantly agreed.

"Are you sure Jared didn't have enemies? No one who would want to harm him? Think carefully."

Both women shook their heads.

"Okay, then this was probably done for ransom. If my hunch is right, we should expect contact within the next day or two."

"So you think he's still alive and well?" asked Irene.

"I hope he is. Call me as soon as you hear anything. I'll return to the cabin tonight to search for more clues."

I was exhausted by the time I got back to the cabin, and my head was still throbbing, but I didn't have time to lose. The place looked spooky by night. Under different circumstances I would have chickened out and hurried home. I entered the cabin and confirmed that it was undisturbed since the last time I had seen it. I scoured the area, searched through every nook and cranny for any clues as to the identity of the abductor, but I came up empty. Finally, caving in to fatigue, I crashed on the couch.

CHAPTER SEVEN

Kavita was as radiant as ever, rocking the black dress she had on. I wasn't too shabby myself in the navy blue blazer and jeans I was wearing, with a light blue dress shirt underneath. We were seated outdoors at The Grandview Restaurant on Mount Hamilton, the lights across Santa Clara Valley shimmering in the distance. Having wrapped up the scrumptious dinner, we were waiting for dessert. As Kavita turned to admire the view, I figured it was the right moment. My heart was beating hard, and in spite of the cool evening air I was beginning to sweat. I discreetly fished out the box from my pocket and went down on one knee in front of my lady love. Her eyes grew wide in surprise when she saw me, and an excited smile spread across her face. It told me I would get the answer I was hoping for. But before I could open the box and pop the question, my phone started ringing. Kavita's face fell, and with it, my hopes.

I woke up with a start. It took me a few seconds to figure out where I was. The Grandview it wasn't. My head was still aching, and the rest of my body felt worse, for the couch had not been kind to me. Seeing that it was Irene calling, I answered.

"He ... he called," she said, the panic evident in her voice.

"Who called?" I was quite sure she meant the kidnapper, but I was clinging to the slim chance that it was Jared.

"I don't know his name, but he said they have Jared."

"They? So there's more than one kidnapper?"

"I guess."

"Did he give any proof?"

"No."

"Did he say what he wants?"

"One million dollars."

"Whoa! That's ... that's a lot of money."

"Yes, it is. He said we must get him the cash in two days or ... or ..." Irene was sobbing now.

I gave her some time to calm down. "Irene, I know this is difficult, but don't worry — Jared will be fine." *Would he really be fine?* I didn't know, but it sounded like the right thing to say. "Do you have the money?"

"I ... I think so. Not at home, of course. I'll have to withdraw it from our account."

"Did he say where to drop it off?"

"He said he will call in two days to tell me the exact location."

"Okay. Listen, Irene, this is getting serious. I still think we should notify the cops. They'll know how to handle this."

"No!" The response was shrill and immediate. "The kidnapper specifically said not to involve the cops or they will kill Jared. Amber and I are the only ones allowed in on this. I'm already risking things by involving you."

That was pretty standard abduction protocol, and I wasn't surprised. But I was concerned. *What if they took the money but didn't return Jared safe and sound?* If the cops were not an option then I would have to figure out something else.

"Did he really mention Amber?"

"Yes. Not by name, but he said the daughter can help."

"Okay. Irene, what number did he call from?"

"Hang on a second." There was a pause before she read out the number. I noted it down.

There was another thought that had been nagging me. This was the right time to follow that hunch. "Irene, are you alone?"

"Yes. Why?"

"Do you trust Amber?"

"What ... what do you mean? She's Jared's daughter. She's a good kid. Of course I trust her."

"But you've only known her what — a year?"

"Right, and I think it's enough to know. Besides, Jared adores her."

"Is he sure she's his?"

"What do you mean?"

"Did they do a DNA test? Isn't it strange that he comes into all this money and this daughter suddenly appears out of nowhere?"

"You think she's an impostor?"

"It's possible."

"No. I don't think there was any test. She was so convincing. She had all these pictures and documents showing us she was Sheila's — that's the woman Jared was with — that she was Sheila's daughter."

"Does he have a will?"

"We have a living trust."

"Who's the beneficiary?"

"It's me currently, but we're working on adding her. It's only fair."

"Does she know this?"

"Not yet. We were going to surprise her on her birthday." Another pause. "Do you truly think she has something to do with his disappearance?"

"I don't know for sure. Just a hunch."

"I think you're going down the wrong path here. She could never do such a thing. I know she adores Jared too."

Adores Jared or adores his money? There's a difference. I kept the thought to myself.

"Okay, then. You start arranging the money. I'll try to get some leads on these kidnappers."

Once I had hung up, I ambled over to the kitchen and downed a glass of water. More ideas swirled through my head. Irene was already a suspect, and what she had just told me bolstered that idea. As things stood, she would have the entire fortune to herself if anything were to happen to Jared. But with the update, Amber would get a slice of the pie. If there was ever a time to eliminate Jared, this was it — before Amber was included in the trust. *Had the impending change forced Irene's hand?* And then there was Amber. She had no clue she would be added to the trust soon. *Did she see this as her chance to get her hands on the Foley fortune?*

Stepping out of the kitchen, I searched the cabin and surrounding area again for clues. Everything would be clearer in the light of day, and I wanted to take advantage of that. But I didn't find anything of interest and returned inside. I decided to drive back to San Jose, but as I picked up my things and headed towards the front door I heard a sound outside. It couldn't be Irene — she was at her home. Concerned that the kidnapper was back, I hurried to the bedroom and hid by the door so I could see who it was. I was thankful I had not parked out front but had left the car in the same secluded spot as the previous time, or the kidnapper would know someone was inside the cabin.

Soon the door opened and a familiar figure entered. I was breathing easier now, but I wondered what Amber was doing here. *Was I right in suspecting her earlier?* She stood by the front door and scanned the living room and kitchen before walking towards the bedroom. I moved behind the door and prayed she wouldn't peek there. Once she was inside, she pulled the dresser drawers open one by one until she found the wallet. Opening it, she took out the cash and stuffed it into her jeans pocket. She tossed the wallet back. Then she picked up Jared's watch — a Rolex, I had noted earlier. She pushed it into her other pocket. She closed the drawer and stood there for a few seconds before turning towards the closet. Something on the floor caught her eye and she bent down to pick it up.

I was close enough to notice that it was a matchbook — the kind you would see at bars. Amber flipped it open and frowned before placing it on the dresser. Then she left the room. I didn't move until I heard the front door shut. I hurried out, and from the window I saw her enter her car and drive off. Her visit raised a lot of questions. *Why had she come? Why did she steal the money and the watch?* And the most important question — did she have anything to do with Jared's abduction, or was she just being opportunistic?

I returned to the bedroom and picked up the matchbook. It was from Dave's Bar, a couple of blocks away from my office. I remembered seeing the sign a while back. A new establishment, if I recalled correctly. Flipping it open, I saw a sketch of a woman drawn with a blue pen on the top flap. It resembled Amber.

CHAPTER EIGHT

On returning to San Jose, I went home first for a quick shower, then lingered over a cup of *chai*, enjoying it with a couple of Good Day cookies. These had been my favorite ever since I was a kid, and thankfully the Indian grocery stores in the area stocked them. I didn't dunk them like Ma, for that got them soggy. I preferred my cookies crisp and crunchy. Besides, I was always worried the cookie would dive into the cup and ruin the *chai*. Feeling refreshed, I headed out.

Once back in the office, I tried to look up the number Irene had given me. It took me a while, but I finally traced it to the BlissVoice network. BlissVoice again. *Was it a coincidence or were they really that popular?* As expected, I couldn't find who the number was registered to. I could go to the cops and have them pursue it further, but I didn't want to cross Irene on that. Leaning back in the chair, I closed my eyes.

A minute passed, and a thought struck me. *Didn't I know someone who worked at BlissVoice?* Yes, buried somewhere in my memory was a piece of information that could help me out. It was the girl — Bharathi. Bharathi Jayaraman. We had first met over a year ago, and I recalled her mentioning she worked at BlissVoice. Hopefully she still did.

I searched my contacts and found her number. I hesitated before calling, considering how things had ended between us, if ended was the right word for it. We had connected through *shaadi.com*, which touted itself as the premier Indian matrimonial site. Not that either of us had been actively looking. As is often the case with Indian families, our mothers had opened accounts and were matchmaking on our behalf. I had been reluctant at first when Ma announced she had a match for me. But one glance at Bharathi's profile pic changed my mind, as I expect it would for most guys. That and the fact that Ma had broken out of her rigid constraints of finding me a "nice Punjabi girl" and had picked someone outside the community. It was a change I could support. *Or was she that desperate to see me settle down?* Either way it didn't matter.

Long story short, I had accepted. Bharathi and I exchanged some messages, and soon enough we were out for coffee at Starbucks. She was as attractive in person as her photograph suggested, and she was engaging too, but I didn't feel the chemistry. I sensed that it was the same for her. Neither of us had the heart to tell the other, and we found ourselves on a dinner date the next weekend. By the time that wrapped up, I was sure it wasn't going anywhere, but I never mustered the courage to tell her that. Instead, I ghosted her, and she didn't contact me either. Reflecting on it, I felt like a class A jerk, though I knew this was common practice, having been at the receiving end of such behavior myself. I put my concerns aside and placed the call. Jared's life was more important. She answered at the second ring.

"Hello," she said, her voice devoid of any emotion.

"Hi Bharathi. This is Ankit. Ankit Pal. I don't know if you remember." Awkward — that was the thought racing through my head. *And why was I trembling?*

"Of course I remember. What do you want?" Sharp, and to the point.

"Why ..."

"Why do I think you want something? Well, why else would you contact me after what — a year? It's either that or you've been turned down by every other woman on the planet and now you're thinking — *you know, that Bharathi, she wasn't so bad after all. I can settle for her.*"

"I ... I'm sorry. I ... I ..."

"It's okay. I get it. You weren't into me and didn't know how to break it to me. The feeling was mutual. Now, what do you need?"

"You work at BlissVoice, right?"

"Yes."

"I need your help."

"Don't tell me you want a free line." Her tone was light now, almost mirthful. "Wouldn't be the first time someone asked me for one, you know."

"No, no, not at all. This is for a case I'm working on."

"A case? You mean you actually went ahead with that private detective plan? I remember you told me something about it."

"Yep. It's been a year now."

"Wow. Honestly, I thought it was just idle talk. I didn't think you would actually do it. Most techies keep talking about how they have a dream — like opening a restaurant or becoming a writer — but that's all it is, talk. They never go through with it. This is something." A pause. "So, what do you need from me?"

"My client — her husband has been abducted. She received a ransom call earlier today from a BlissVoice number. I can't tell who it's registered to. Can you help with that? And perhaps get the location data as well?"

"Don't you need a warrant or something for that?"

"A subpoena. But only the cops can request one."

"Then have them do it."

"The kidnappers specifically warned my client not to get the cops involved. Besides, that will delay everything. We don't have that much time."

"It's not right, you know. Violating someone's privacy like this."

"This is a criminal we're talking about. I understand everyone has rights, but some things are more important."

"Oh boy, you're going to get me into a lot of trouble, aren't you?"

"It's all for a good cause."

"I'll try, but this could take a while."

"She has to pay in two days."

"I'll call you when I have the information."

"Thanks, Bharathi. I genuinely appreciate this."

A wave of relief passed through me once I hung up. That had gone well. Hopefully she would be able to get me the information I needed. Reflecting on the time we had spent together, I realized she was the last date I had been on. One advantage of switching from a tech job to sleuthing was that none of the *shaadi.com* crowd was interested in me. They were looking for doctors and lawyers, techies and financial wizards — guys who were in respectable professions and making gobs of money, not someone goofing around as a detective and drawing a meager income.

CHAPTER NINE

I couldn't sleep that night. I tossed and turned, worried about Jared's fate. Would I be able to save him? At least there was a backup plan — pay the ransom. But it would mean I had failed. And what if the kidnappers absconded with the money without returning Jared? What then?

When my mind got off those concerns, I thought about Bharathi. Would she help me? Or had she agreed just to get me off the phone, and would she wreak revenge on me by not doing anything? She sounded sincere enough, but then, hadn't I sounded sincere on that second date when I had told her I would call her later that week?

It was just after 6 a.m. when I crawled out of bed and started getting ready for the day. My brain was foggy, but between the hot cup of *chai* and the steaming shower that followed, clarity was restored. I got to work trying to figure out who had abducted Jared Foley. But every path I took, I hit a brick wall. The fact was, I had no clues. Only hunches. What could I do with that? I couldn't just walk up to the suspects and ask them if they had done the deed. During some weaker moments I considered going to the cops, but I held back to honor my client's wishes. The self-doubt built up. *Was I cut out for this line of work?* I couldn't tell whether I was unfit, or if this was a phase every rookie detective went through. Surely even Sherlock Holmes must have started somewhere? He didn't just turn up as an ace sleuth on his first case, did he? Doyle probably didn't bother documenting those early stumbles.

Around 3 p.m. Irene called to tell me she had the cash ready in a duffel bag. It had taken visits to three different banks to get it all together. Now all that was left was to wait for the call the next day. Disappointed and exhausted, I crashed into bed at 7 p.m. This time sleep came, though I felt like I was carrying the weight of the world on my shoulders.

My ringtone blared, waking me up. The clock by my bedside showed 7:01 a.m. I felt refreshed after that long stretch of sleep but was still annoyed. Like most people, I wanted to be in control of when I woke up, and such an interruption was unwelcome. I sat up straight and answered when I saw who it was.

"He called." Irene's voice was breathy, projecting her nervousness. "Five minutes ago."

The nervousness passed on to me. "What did he say?"

"He wants me to drop off the money in Tahoe at eleven."

"Eleven a.m.? Today?"

"Yes."

"Then we don't have much time, do we?"

"Right. I'm already in the car. On my way."

"I'll get going too."

It was an ideal location for a drop off — by the side of U.S. Route 50. Irene was to slow down and move to the side of the road at the exact coordinates that had been given to her, leave the bag there, and continue on her merry way. I figured the kidnapper would be waiting at the nearest exit and would drive up, pick up the money, and flee. Any backup Irene had would find it difficult to monitor the spot undetected, since any vehicle by the side of the highway would stick out. Now, someone could stand watch by the side of the road, but that person wouldn't be able to follow the kidnappers.

At 10:55 a.m. I parked my car on a side street adjacent to the spot. Then I hid behind a tree and waited. It wasn't long before Irene's Macan stopped and she did as instructed. A minute later a black Honda Civic halted at the spot. The front bumper was scraped. The passenger door opened and an arm reached out and picked up the bag. I couldn't see either occupant's face. To make matters worse, the license plate was covered. They were already gone by the time I started sprinting back to my car.

CHAPTER TEN

At 11:30 a.m. I sat with Irene in the living room of her cabin. She was quiet, clenching and unclenching her hands, periodically wiping them on her jeans.

"So he didn't say where he would drop off Jared?" I asked.

"I ... I forgot to ask. I was just so nervous about the whole thing."

"Maybe he will call with a location."

"I sure do hope so. He got what he wanted. There's no reason to keep Jared now."

I, too, hoped that was the case. It occurred to me that throughout this entire saga, we had never received any evidence that these kidnappers had Jared. *What if they never had him?* They might have learned about his disappearance in the news and decided to make the most of it by bluffing their way through. Or worse — they did have him at some point, but they had no intention of returning him and had already killed him.

Another hour went by before a phone rang, and both of us jumped at the sound. Irene glanced at her phone, disappointed. I peeked at mine. *Bharathi!* My heart leapt with joy. Surely she had some positive news for me? I answered immediately.

"So I have some good news and some bad news," she said without any greeting.

"Oh."

"Bad news first — I don't know who purchased the phone."

That wasn't too bad, I thought. I had quite expected this. "And the good?"

"I have the location data. So this guy's been in Tahoe the whole time. Well, he bought the phone in San Jose, but he didn't turn it on until he got to Tahoe."

"Where in Tahoe?"

"There's an address on Olive Court. That's where he spent most of his time."

"And he's there now?"

"No. The last location is as of this morning, just after eleven — on Highway 50."

I wasn't very hopeful, but I got the address and the coordinates for the phone from Bharathi, blurted out a hasty "thank you" and was out the door, with Irene following me, her face a mask of confusion. I explained everything to her on the way. When we reached the spot on the highway, there was no car there. Or person. There was only a smashed budget phone.

The disappointment lasted a few seconds before I remembered the address on Olive Court. I sped towards it, hoping Jared was there, alive and well. As I turned onto the street, I noted that the houses were all ranch-style and built around forty to fifty years ago. Most were well tended, but there was one house at the end of the cul-de-sac which reeked of neglect. The small front yard was full of brown grass and weeds. The house itself had a couple of broken windows and needed a lot of maintenance work. As it happened, this was the address we were looking for.

I parked the car and approached the front door with trepidation, Irene close behind me. The door was not fully closed. I motioned for her to wait outside and pushed the door open slowly. One glance inside reminded me of the abandoned houses from horror movies. There were layers of dust everywhere, with cobwebs hugging the ceiling corners. But there were signs of recent activity. There were patches on the floor that were devoid of dust. I stepped inside, staying alert for any movement. My footsteps echoed in the silence, my thudding heart doing the same at a faster tempo.

It was when I turned into the kitchen that I saw the body on the floor. Blindfolded and gagged, with hands and legs bound with rope. Even with those coverings on the face, I was certain it was my former mentor. Relief flooded my body as I noted that he was moving.

"Jared," I said. In the background I heard someone hurrying. I whirled around to see Irene approach with eager eyes.

"Jared!" she said. "Oh my God, Jared! What have they done to you?"

She seemed genuinely concerned. I felt guilty about ever suspecting she had anything to do with his abduction. I knelt down to untie him while she removed the blindfold and the gag. Jared blinked a few times, taking in his surroundings and adjusting to the light. A relieved smile flashed across his face when he realized he was safe.

"Irene!" he said as they hugged. "I thought I would never see you again." They stayed like that for a couple of minutes while I explored the rest of the area for clues.

"You did it, Ankit. You found me," Jared said once I returned. "I knew you could do it."

"I'm happy we found you, but frankly, you've disappointed me, Jared."

He frowned. "How so?"

"Staging your own disappearance — really? That was so irresponsible."

"Do we have to go into this now?" Irene said. "Look at him — he needs some rest."

"And water. And a big, juicy burger," Jared said. "I'm starving."

"They didn't feed you?"

He shook his head. "Only some water."

CHAPTER ELEVEN

An hour later we were in the cabin after a quick stopover at In-N-Out. We had lucked out, for the usual long lines were absent. Jared had polished off a Double-Double, French fries and a strawberry shake, and swore he could still eat a horse.

"We should notify the cops," I said. A look of alarm spread across the Foleys' faces. "They still consider you missing. It's bad enough what you put them through, but now that you're back, it's got to stop."

"I'm with you on that," Jared replied. "But no talk about the fake disappearance, right?"

"Well ..."

"Hey, I know what I did was inappropriate, but I've already suffered plenty for it. I think what I endured was appropriate punishment."

What the Foleys had done was wrong and a criminal offense. My first thought was that I should let the law take its course. But what purpose would it serve? It was not a serious crime, and California had a prison-overcrowding problem on its hands — a problem so bad that they were letting out people who had done a lot worse. There were better options to deal with this.

"I'm not entirely convinced, but okay, I'll buy that. You can put in some hours of community service to make up for it."

"Good idea. How does ten hours sound?"

"Too low."

"Okay, I'll do twenty then."

"Hundred hours sounds more like it."

"Whoa, whoa, whoa. That's too much."

"You have all the time in the world, Jared. This way your mind will be occupied and you'll remain out of further trouble."

"Alright," he replied with a sullen face, like a child who had been told Xbox time was up.

"At least now you won't be moping around the house going 'I'm bored'," said Irene.

"You'll be doing a hundred hours too, Irene," I said, almost bursting out laughing at her alarmed expression.

"Me? Why me?"

"You are equally guilty."

"But ..."

"No buts. And the same goes for Amber."

"She's not going to like that one bit."

"Should have thought about that before getting involved in this. Now that that's settled, what are we going to tell the cops?" I turned to Jared. "That you were abducted seven days ago?"

"Yes. We will tell them exactly what happened, where it happened — only the date will be different."

"They'll want to know why you were in Tahoe instead of Yosemite."

"I'll tell them I changed my mind on the way."

"Okay. There's one thing you need to consider about the date, assuming they do find the kidnappers. The kidnappers will have a different story to tell."

"Sure, but who are the cops going to believe? Those crooks or an upright citizen like me?"

I smiled. "Alright. Now, tell me everything. Every little detail. We must catch those bastards."

"So, I was enjoying my day, especially after the visit from Irene. I took a shower after she left. Got dressed. Was walking out of the room when this guy grabbed me and put a cloth over my face. I passed out — I'm guessing it was chloroform. By the time I came to, I was blindfolded and had something stuffed in my mouth. My hands were already bound, and he was tying my legs. I struggled to get free, but it was useless."

"How do you know it was a guy?"

"He was strong. And just from my time together with them, I know they were guys."

"How many were there?"

"I would say, two."

"Did you see either of them at any time?"

"No. They never took off my blindfold. Later they also put headphones on me so I couldn't hear them."

"So you have no idea what they sound like?"

"Well, kinda. They did take off the headphones a few times to give me instructions — like drink this water, or time to pee — that kind of thing. But I could tell they were faking the voice."

"Okay, so what happened after they tied your legs?"

"They picked me up and put me in a car. Again, I don't know what kind. They drove a short while and stopped. Then they carried me here and put me down."

"And you never left this place until we found you?"

"Right."

"That's not much to go on."

"I'm sorry I'm no help."

"Don't worry about it. I'll see what I can do. If not me, then at least the cops will be able to nab these guys."

"Yeah, about that ..."

"What?"

"Can you wait another day before you tell the cops? I need some time to recover before the circus starts."

"You realize this would give your kidnappers a chance to get away?"

"Yes, but I'm in no frame of mind to talk to the cops or deal with any of the media."

Why were the Foleys so reluctant to get the cops involved? Some of their reasoning made sense, but a part of me wondered whether they were still stringing me along. As if the prank was not over yet, and this "real" kidnapping wasn't so real after all — that it was all part of their plan. I decided to play along.

"Alright. One day."

"Thanks, Ankit."

"I'm heading back to San Jose now."

"We'll stay the night and drive back tomorrow."

I drove over to the house on Olive Court before heading home. While the house itself had not revealed any clues, I figured a chat with some of the neighbors might be fruitful. No one answered at the place on the left, but I fared better with the unit on the right. The door was opened by an elderly man, probably in his eighties. He was skeptical at first, but he eventually let me in. His wife — he introduced her as Kathy — was seated at one end of the couch, knitting a sweater. The man, Dennis, joined her on the couch. I settled into the chair opposite.

"Would you like some tea, dear?" asked Kathy.

I politely declined. It was nice of her to offer, but all I could think of was the hot cup of *chai* I was craving.

"I have some questions about the house next door," I said, pointing to the abandoned house.

Dennis shook his head. "Awful what happened there. Lovely family. Bank foreclosed on them during the last recession. It's been sitting like that since. Real eyesore now. Somebody's gotta do something about it."

"But wasn't someone in there recently?" I asked.

"Boors," said Kathy.

"Boors?"

"A couple of guys came late the other night and went in there. With two women. They were so loud. Drunk, I guess."

This sounded promising. "Only one night?"

"Yes."

"I seen them during the day as well," added Dennis.

"The guys? Or the women as well?"

"Only the guys."

"What did they look like?"

"Not sure I can tell you much. I don't see too good that far. All I can say is one was kinda tall, the other one was shorter. They were wearing hoodies so I couldn't get much of their faces anyway."

"Do you know what car they drove up in?"

"Don't know what kind. But it was black. I can tell you that."

It all added up. Two kidnappers, both male. And the black car — quite likely it was the Civic. *But who were the two women? Irene and Amber?* It was unfortunate that I didn't have much of a description to go on. Thanking the couple, I departed, happy to be returning to San Jose.

CHAPTER TWELVE

I drove straight to Kavita's home. She had been delighted to learn that Jared had been found, and she had invited me over for an impromptu celebration. I wasn't in the mood to celebrate, at least not until the kidnappers were nabbed, but I wasn't one to miss an opportunity to spend time with her. The plan was to have hot *chai* and *pakoras*. She put the tea on once I got there. The vegetables were already chopped and smothered in chickpea batter, ready for frying.

"Damn burner," she said as she tried to turn on the burner to heat the oil. "Can you pass me the matchbox?"

I found it and was handing it to her when a thought struck me. "Give me a minute," I said as I stepped out of the kitchen and placed a call to Amber. She answered right away.

"Amber, what were you doing in the Tahoe cabin the other day?" There was silence for a few seconds. "Amber?"

"The cabin? I've only been there once, and that was, like, a couple of months ago."

"Don't lie — I saw you. Were you there for the cash?"

More silence. "You ... you were there?"

"Yes. You took cash from Jared's wallet. And his Rolex. How much did you get for it?"

Amber sighed. "Enough to cover tuition this semester. The cash was good for some of my rent."

"Isn't Jared helping you with expenses?"

"He's covering some of it. Gosh, I feel so guilty now. Stealing from him."

"Why were you there? Surely you didn't drive all the way to Tahoe for that."

"Well, it was worth it for sure. But yeah, I couldn't believe he had been taken. I had to see it for myself. Besides, I'd learned that Connor was in Tahoe. I was hoping I would run into him somewhere."

"Who's Connor?"

"My boyfriend. You met him when you came over."

"Ah, right. He didn't tell you where he was?"

"Nope. That's why we had a big fight before he left. We had plans to spend time together, but out of the blue he told me he was going away for a few days."

"I see. Did you find him in Tahoe?"

"I didn't bother looking after I got the money. I drove straight back to San Jose."

"Want to tell me about the matchbook?"

"What matchbook?"

"The one you found in the bedroom."

"Oh, that. I'm not sure what it was doing there. Connor had sketched me on it recently."

"So he's an artist then?"

Amber snorted. "He's talented, yes. But too lazy to make it work."

"Is it possible he gave it to Jared?"

"I doubt they've ever met."

"So how did it end up in the cabin?"

There was a long pause before she spoke. "Oh. You think Connor got Jared? He dropped the matchbook when he was there?"

"Yes."

"I doubt he would do such a thing."

"How long have you known him?"

"A few months. He's a decent guy."

"I sure hope so. What car does he drive?"

"A Civic. Black."

"Any dings?"

"Yes. There's a scrape on the front bumper. Right side."

I couldn't help smiling. This was too much of a coincidence.

"Well, Amber, I hate to break it to you, but he's the one."

"Are you ... are you sure?"

"Almost a hundred percent, but there's only one way to find out."

I considered calling the cops and telling them everything. They would nab Connor and his accomplice with the evidence and wrap things up. But what if I was wrong? That would be embarrassing. I needed to confirm my theory first. Just showing up at Connor's door wasn't an option, since he would recognize me. Amber could do some recon and report back, but could I trust her? What if she was involved and was just playing dumb? In the end, I figured it was worth the risk.

CHAPTER THIRTEEN

An hour later I parked my car across the street from the apartment complex on 18th Street. Amber stepped out and trotted over to Connor's door. I donned my USC hat and followed. The hat would help shield my face somewhat in case Connor happened to peek outside his window. The apartment was on the first floor, and Amber was already inside by the time I got there. I scanned the parking spaces opposite the building until I spotted a black Civic. It didn't take long to confirm it was Connor's, what with the telltale scrape. The license plates were visible this time, and I took a picture. My phone buzzed as I was turning back. A text from Amber. I read it eagerly. She had located the bag of money.

Detective Higgins was in charge of the investigation. I was about to call him and explain everything when the door to the apartment burst open and Connor appeared in the doorway with Amber, grinning pure evil. He had a duffel bag in one hand and a knife in the other. The knife was at her throat.

"One move and I'll slit her throat," he snarled as he shifted towards the Civic.

My heart sank. I had put Amber's life in danger. This was all my fault. How would I ever forgive myself if something happened to her?

Connor threw the bag in the back seat of his car and directed Amber into the driver's seat. Then he slid into the rear, the blade back at her neck. They were off within seconds. I didn't waste any time in dashing to my car. The chase was on, though I wasn't sure how I would stop them and rescue Amber.

Connor got onto 280-N. I dialed Higgins. Thankfully, he responded right away. It took me a while to explain everything. He sounded skeptical, but I was able to convince him. He assured me he would dispatch a crew immediately. I kept my eyes on the Civic, which was racing ahead, going well over the speed limit. I was comforted by the thought that Amber would be safe as long as she was driving, and she wouldn't come to any harm if I could lead Higgins and his team to her.

They continued up the freeway, with me following close behind. Traffic was still light. I wondered where he was headed. Did he have a place in San Francisco? Or was he unsure about his destination, since this escape was not part of the plan? And then a horrific thought hit me. What if Amber wasn't in any danger at all? What if this *was* part of their plan? I recalled how calm she was when Connor guided her out of the apartment. She had a knife to her throat, but not a hint of terror on her face. Maybe they were in this together, and they realized that the only way they would be able to flee was to pretend that he would hurt her if I didn't obey.

I pushed the thought out of my head and focused on the task at hand. All of a sudden the Civic veered across two lanes and raced through the exit. I followed, knowing I must have elicited a few glares and more from the cars I cut off as I did so. Amber turned left, and I expected her to speed up to try to lose me. Instead, she turned into a gas station. This was an interesting development. I wondered whether this was a stroke of luck or a ploy to get rid of me for good.

I waited across the street to ascertain what they were up to. They got out of the car, with Connor staying close to Amber. He had the knife up against her body. *Did this mean she was truly in trouble? Or was it all a show they were putting on for my benefit?* He seemed jumpy, constantly looking around to ensure no one was approaching. Amber started pumping gas. I realized I hadn't updated Higgins on my new location, but it was important that I take advantage of this opportunity. I worked out four days a week and was in decent shape. I figured I could take out Connor. The question now was, how to approach him without being spotted.

I found a hooded sweatshirt in the back seat. I took off my hat and put on the hoodie. At least this would be a different appearance from how Amber and Connor had last seen me. Stepping out of the car, I changed my gait as I ambled over towards them. Amber replaced the handle and shut the gas tank. Connor walked her back to the driver seat. By now I was only a few feet away. He had spotted me but had turned away, apparently not recognizing me and not considering me to be much of a threat either.

He was entering the car when I sprinted over and tried to slam the door on his leg, but he was too quick for me. He pushed the door out and kicked me in the belly. I staggered backwards as he retreated into the car. For a second I was worried he would retaliate and hurt Amber, but I was relieved to see that she had taken the opportunity to exit the car. I stayed alert to her movements, still unsure whose side she was on. I expected Connor to emerge at any moment to attack, but he seemed content to stay inside.

"Amber, call Detective Higgins and give him our location." I rattled off Higgins' number.

She keyed in the digits. Connor sprang out of the car, no doubt spurred into action on realizing that the cops would be there soon. He came at me with the knife, but I dodged it and took the opportunity to land a right hook on his jaw. *Crack!* It was probably not that loud, but that's what it sounded like to me as I winced in pain. My hands could type seventy words a minute. They could churn out code that powered the best software around, but they were not trained for this kind of combat. In that split second I regretted dropping out of karate class.

But I was pleased to see that my punch had shaken Connor, though it wasn't enough, for he was coming at me again. I planted a kick between his legs, and it got him good. He groaned and bent over, but not for long. As I advanced towards him, his knife arm flailed out and barely missed me. I grabbed his wrist and kneed him in the groin, then pushed him towards the car. The weapon fell from his hand when he slammed into it. I landed a few punches in his belly with my left hand, my right hand still in agony. He doubled over. I forced him to the ground and sat on him, ensuring his arms were secure under me. Only then did I notice that we had collected an audience. Amber quickly explained the situation to them.

"The cops are on their way," she told me with a smile.

Relief spread through me. She was on my side all along.

CHAPTER FOURTEEN

The day after all the excitement, I sat in a cold, stark interrogation room, nervous about what was to come. My mind was a mess. On the one hand, I still couldn't believe I had solved the case. That success boosted my confidence tremendously. On the other hand, all the action and the fact that I had come so close to bodily harm had me shaken. I took some deep breaths to calm myself and focus my thoughts, for it was imperative that I was at my best for what was to come.

Detective Higgins sat across the table, a scowl on his face as he studied me. When I saw him for the first time yesterday, it was as if Orson Welles had stepped out of one of his movies. For my money, I preferred *The Third Man* over *Citizen Kane*, but I half-expected Higgins to utter the word "Rosebud" at any moment. He didn't, and when he spoke, his voice pulled me back to reality, for he didn't sound anything like the movie star. I had filled him in on the basics, and he had requested me as well as the Foleys to show up for detailed questioning today. So here I was, ready to field my first question of the day.

"Jared Foley disappeared on the twentieth. And Irene Foley hired you on the twenty-third?"

"Yes."

Higgins shook his head, as if disappointed. "I don't understand what was the hurry. We were all looking for him anyway."

I had resolved to stick to the truth as far as possible. Not only was it the right thing to do, it also made it easier to manage the lies, especially considering that the Foleys had to stick to the same story. I couldn't tell Higgins the real reason why Irene hired me, but I figured I owed him an explanation to assure him he wasn't incompetent.

"She just felt an extra pair of eyes would help in the search."

"Still ..." He paused. "Now, this Connor guy stated his demands on the twenty-fifth. Why did he wait so long?"

"Maybe he wasn't sure how much to ask for? Or he needed time to plan?"

"Maybe." Another pause. "You should have notified us about the ransom call."

"He made it very clear Jared would be in danger if we involved the cops."

"That's what kidnappers always say, but it's always better to involve someone who knows what they're doing."

"I'll keep that in mind next time."

I waited for the next query, but Higgins took his time. It was probably all part of his strategy to break down interviewees and get them to spill the truth.

"You know, Connor said something interesting." He gazed at me, his eyes making me uncomfortable. I had to remain cautious, for he was clearly fishing for something.

"What's that?"

"He said they picked up Jared on the twenty-fourth."

"Must have got his dates mixed up."

"He seemed pretty confident."

"Probably just messing with you."

"Probably. But he had another fascinating story."

"What story?"

"He said Jared didn't really disappear on the twentieth. Foley faked it, and his family helped him. Know anything about that?"

Beads of sweat appeared all over my body out of nowhere. Of course, I had anticipated that Connor would gum the works, but it was still unnerving now that this was happening for real. I tried to act casual, even amused. A smile escaped my lips.

"The things criminals will say to get out of trouble, right?"

"Yeah, I don't see why a guy like Jared Foley would fake his own disappearance."

"Exactly!" I hoped this was the last of it, but Higgins was still lost in thought.

"Now, there's one more thing." He was observing me keenly now. Moving in for the kill, I guessed.

"What's that?"

"He said you were at the cabin when he kidnapped Jared."

I could deny this outright, but Higgins could easily confirm it by reviewing my cell phone location data.

"I was at the cabin on the twenty-fourth. That's true. But only because I had followed Irene there."

My reply sparked his interest, and he leaned forward. "You were following Irene Foley? Why?"

"I suspected she might have something to do with Jared's disappearance."

He chuckled. It was the first time I had seen any positive expression on his face. "You have a good nose. Especially for someone who's new to investigative work. Why did you suspect her?"

"The usual. He was wealthy, and she would get everything once he was gone."

"I see. And do you still suspect her?"

"Not anymore."

"Okay. So you got to the cabin, and then Connor knocked you out?"

This was embarrassing, but I had nothing to lose by admitting it. "Yes."

"That doesn't make any sense either."

"What do you mean?"

"First — what was he doing there if he had already abducted Jared four days earlier? Second — why bother hitting you?"

I shrugged. "I don't know."

"His presence, and his need to hit you, only makes sense if he was there to get Jared."

"Or maybe he was there for Irene and he panicked when he saw me."

"Possible. But what business would he have with Irene?"

I realized I had erred. I should have kept Irene out of it. Any other motive for his presence, like wanting to steal something from the cabin, would have been better.

After all, Jared did have the Rolex and the cash in there until Amber showed up. But I still had an opportunity to fix things.

"I don't know. Maybe he was just there to steal stuff."

Higgins didn't look convinced. "He's getting a million dollars in ransom, and he's there to snag some trinkets?"

"Crooks like that want it all."

"I guess."

I relaxed a bit, for it seemed I had made it home safely. But Higgins had other plans.

"Now, once the ransom was delivered, how did you know where to find Jared?"

"Connor gave the location."

"He denies it."

"I don't understand why."

"How did he share the location? Did he call Irene?"

This would have been the easiest response, but it was dicey. Higgins wouldn't find any such call if he checked the phone records. So I went with the next best option.

"He dropped a note when he picked up the money."

He looked skeptical. "Dropped a note?"

"Yes. A sheet of paper crumpled into a ball. I picked it up and it had the Olive Court address."

"Do you have the paper?"

"No. I trashed it."

He looked disappointed. I suppressed a smile.

"Okay. So you find Jared. Now, how did you figure out Connor was behind it all?"

If only this guy would give up!

"I was filling in Amber on all the details, and I described the kidnappers' car. She said it sounded so much like Connor's car."

"She suspected her boyfriend because of a black Honda Civic? You realize how many of those are out on the roads?"

"Yes, of course. But how many of those black Civics are damaged in that same spot?"

"Fair enough. But you shouldn't have gone there by yourself. You should have called me and let us handle it. In fact, you should have called me the moment you found Jared."

Truce time. "I agree. We — I made a mistake there. I realized that in hindsight."

Higgins relaxed his shoulders and leaned back in his chair. Those were tense moments, for I feared what else that brain of his was cooking up. *Was I out of the woods yet?* Soon I had my answer.

"Well, that's all I got for you. Good work solving this one."

He smiled. I finally relaxed. But my relief didn't last long, for as soon as I stepped out of the building I started worrying about the interviews Higgins would be conducting with the Foleys.

CHAPTER FIFTEEN

My office was packed. I had never seen so many people in there at once — five of them, including me. It was a wonder there was any room to breathe. The Foleys — Jared, Irene, and Amber — had brought a decadent chocolate cake to celebrate and were standing to the side of the desk towards the entrance. I stood by my chair, a delighted Kavita next to me. There was a lot to be elated about. It was my first genuine success as a private eye. I had even gotten some positive press. I hoped this would bring me better business. In addition to the five thousand dollars I had received from Irene, Jared had handed me a check for twenty grand as final payment. That would keep me going for a few months.

Another cause for celebration — the Foleys had got their ransom money back. It hadn't been easy. Higgins had grilled them about every detail. At one point I was sure someone would slip up and reveal the truth about Jared's initial disappearance, but those fears were unfounded.

Connor had learned about Jared's plan to disappear from Amber. It had sparked the kidnap idea in his head. He had roped in his buddy Liam for help. Unfortunate for Liam, for Connor had sliced his throat before fleeing with Amber. Along with Liam's lifeless body, Higgins had found all the plans meticulously laid out on paper in the apartment. Apparently Connor preferred to write out everything, and he had forgotten to destroy the evidence. Quite the sloppy criminal, in my opinion, for he even had the bag full of ransom money sitting in the living room when Amber arrived, leaving no doubt in her mind about his involvement in the whole affair. As for the two women that Kathy had seen with Connor and Liam, neither of them was Irene or Amber. The guys had picked them up in a bar and invited them over to celebrate.

I watched the Foleys. They looked like one happy family, though I still had doubts about Amber. *Was she really Jared's daughter?* If I were him I would have confirmed it with a DNA test. Then again, did it matter? As long as they loved each other it wasn't relevant. She did seem like a decent kid. All she needed was some guidance with judging character and not getting involved with the wrong people. I was particularly impressed by how cool she had remained under pressure. It was a quality that would stand her in good stead over the years.

Laughter and lively banter enveloped the room, an atmosphere more aligned with a party hall rather than a PI's office. I cut the cake and passed around slices. There was silence as everyone dug into the treat. The Foleys left after a while, and Kavita settled into the chair opposite, the creak resonating, reminding me of the pending item on my to-do list. I was about to get up and tackle the task, when she winked and said, "Ankit Pal, you are a genius." I smiled, leaned back, and relaxed. I had earned it.

AUTHOR'S NOTE

This one's close to my heart, for I've wanted to write a story with an Indian MC for the longest time. I'm delighted with the way it turned out. Ankit Pal and I share some similarities — he's from Mumbai and lives in San Jose, just like me. We're both techies, and we both love mysteries, especially with detectives Poirot, Holmes, and Karamchand. I don't like *chai*, though. And I doubt I'd ever be brave enough to become a PI. Even if I did, I'm pretty sure one bonk on my head would have me running for cover. I really hope this is the first of many Ankit Pal mysteries. Would you like to read more about him?

DIGGING FOR GOLD

A FLASH FICTION STORY

The woman was digging — *digging for gold*, as Amanda's primary school teacher would say. The finger went left, then right, plumbing the depths — *or heights?* — of the nose. Every now and then the finger returned from the cavernous expedition, and the woman, who Amanda knew to be Dorothy Manfield, inspected it for treasures. Disgusted, Amanda looked away. She didn't need to see nose picking, not when she was eating, anyway. Not that she was hungry, but she had a croissant and a cup of coffee before her to blend in with the ravenous crowd at the café.

What was taking so long? thought Amanda. She reluctantly took another bite of the croissant and a sip of her coffee, her patience wearing thin. It would suck if her first solo mission ended in failure.

A glance back at Dorothy, who swigged her coffee, the exploration complete. The triumphant finger landed on the burger along with its buddies. *Eww!* The only thing worse than seeing the finger in Dorothy's nose was seeing it touch something else. Food, handshakes, door handles, and more. Spreading the wealth everywhere. Though this was a minor infraction compared to the crimes Dorothy had committed in her lifetime.

Amanda turned to look at the girl at the counter. Delicate gloved hands handling the food. Cleaner. Safer. But did those dainty fingers ever traverse forbidden places when no one was looking? A wheezing sound hit Amanda's ears before she could ponder over that question. She turned to Dorothy again, taking in the dazed expression and the hand on the chest. Another sound, this time louder, as Dorothy started foaming at the mouth. A murmur spread across the café as people stood up, some with fear in their eyes, others frozen, not knowing whether to help her or to flee to safety. Someone screamed.

Dorothy collapsed, her face resting on her half-eaten burger. Amanda's face remained stoic, but she was smiling inside. *Success at last!* Now that justice had been delivered, her appetite returned and she popped the last piece of croissant in her mouth. Her gaze turned to the display counter, eyeing the blueberry muffins. Perhaps she would get one after all.

AUTHOR'S NOTE

*A*re you digging for gold? That's what my primary school teacher would ask when she found one of us with a finger up our nose in class (I assure you, it was never me). I found it amusing then, and I still do. I'm at an age where such older memories spring up often, and they never fail to bring a smile to my lips. Ah, those carefree childhood days. When this memory popped up recently, my author brain quickly wove a story around it. This time I was smart enough to write it down before it flew away, as happens with most of my ideas. This was a delightful foray into flash fiction, and I hope you enjoyed it too. Now the question is, do you want to learn more about Amanda? A longer story, perhaps, as she navigates this new phase in her life?

THANK YOU FOR READING!

If you enjoyed *Devious Minds*, please leave a review. Reviews help more readers find me and my work, so a positive review can be very helpful and is appreciated.

To learn more about me and my work, visit https://www.vineetvermaauthor.com. You can also sign up for my newsletter there to receive the latest updates about my writing, get book recommendations, and follow links to cool book promos.

If you prefer social media, you can follow me here:

Facebook: @VineetVermaAuthor

Instagram: @vineetvermaauthor

Twitter: @VineetvAuthor

OTHER TITLES BY VINEET VERMA

"Barefoot in the Parking Lot is a suspenseful mystery with a cast of characters readers will love to hate."

When the hotshot CEO of a famed AI company and tech powerhouse is found dead, detectives Angela White and Paul Conley are called in to investigate. The deeper they wade into the evidence, the longer the suspect list grows. They soon come face-to-face with the dark and sordid world that lies just under Silicon Valley's polished and pristine exterior. From jealous ex-lovers to rival tech giants, Jay has created powerful enemies, all of whom would be happy to see him dead — and all of whom have solid alibis. White and Conley hit dead end after dead end. And when blackmail schemes and copycat murders come into play, finding the killer becomes increasingly more urgent. Can they catch a break, or will a murderer go free in Silicon Valley?

books2read.com/u/3JXAWA

About the Author

Vineet is a tech professional by day and has been a lifelong fan of mysteries, be it in books or on screen. He enjoys writing and creating a world of suspense that leaves his readers guessing until the end. With his debut novel, Barefoot in the Parking Lot, and the follow up short story, The Stick, he has fulfilled his dream of becoming a published author. He lives in San Jose, California with his wife and twin boys and hopes to keep writing for years to come.

www.ingramcontent.com/pod-product-compliance
Lightning Source LLC
Chambersburg PA
CBHW051137190726
48290CB00006B/1879